NAALUKETTU

'Rarely does a novel published fifty years ago still hold the reader's attention. M.T. Vasudevan Nair's *Naalukettu* is such a unique literary phenomenon, with 23 re-prints and translation into 14 languages.'
—M.K. CHANDRA BOSE, *Deccan Herald*

'Gita Krishnankutty now brings us this affecting work in a skilful English translation. ... [*Naalukettu*] is a novel about growing up in poverty, about sitting in school with an empty stomach and never having enough money to pay the fees. It is also about many other things, things of beauty and feeling—motherhood, young love, school friendship and the old-time teacher who will give all he can to encourage a bright student. Finally, it is a novel about the endless possibility for redemption.'
—UMA MAHADEVAN-DASGUPTA, *Indian Express*

NAALUKETTU
the house around the courtyard

M.T. Vasudevan Nair

*Translated from Malayalam and
with an Introduction by* Gita Krishnankutty

OXFORD
UNIVERSITY PRESS

OXFORD
UNIVERSITY PRESS

YMCA Library Building, Jai Singh Road, New Delhi 110 001

Oxford University Press is a department of the University of Oxford.
It furthers the University's objective of excellence in research, scholarship,
and education by publishing worldwide in

Oxford   New York
Auckland   Cape Town   Dar es Salaam   Hong Kong   Karachi
Kuala Lumpur   Madrid   Melbourne   Mexico City   Nairobi
New Delhi   Shanghai   Taipei   Toronto

With offices in
Argentina   Austria   Brazil   Chile   Czech Republic   France   Greece
Guatemala   Hungary   Italy   Japan   Poland   Portugal   Singapore
South Korea   Switzerland   Thailand   Turkey   Ukraine   Vietnam

Oxford is a registered trade mark of Oxford University Press
in the UK and in certain other countries.

Published in India by Oxford University Press, New Delhi

© Oxford University Press 2008

The moral rights of the authors have been asserted
Database right Oxford University Press (maker)

First published 2008
Fifth impression 2009

MR. Omayal Achi MR. Arunachalam Trust was set up in 1976 to further education
and health care particularly in rural areas. The MR. AR. Educational Society was later
established by the Trust. One of the Society's activities is to sponsor Indian literature.
This translation is entirely funded by the MR. AR. Educational Society as part of its aims.

Kalam illustration (p. 50) by Basanth Peringode

ISBN-13: 978-0-19-568596-1
ISBN-10: 0-19-568596-2

Typeset in Perpetua 11.5/14
by Eleven Arts, Keshav Puram, Delhi 110 035
Printed in India by De-Unique, New Delhi 110 018
Published by Oxford University Press
YMCA Library Building, Jai Singh Road, New Delhi 110 001

Contents

Acknowledgements

I would like to express my gratitude to Sri M. T. Vasudevan Nair for the time he so generously spared to read the manuscript of this translation and to answer with infinite patience my innumerable queries about the terms used in it and about the rituals and ceremonies described in the story.

My sincere thanks to Mini Krishnan for agreeing to publish this translation and for the unstinting help and encouragement she extended to me during the time I worked on it.

I would also like to thank my friend Meera Krishnankutty, who made time for me ungrudgingly whenever I had to grapple with a problem of language or meaning and turned to her for help in solving it.

Gita Krishnankutty

Author's Note

onths ago, when a group of young men were taking a documentary film on me, I had to stay in my village for a couple of days. The river had dried up completely. Because sand had been illegally mined from it regularly over years, it had turned into an area overgrown with thickets. Since the pathetic state of the river always grieves me deeply, I now seldom visit the village. While I relaxed in the *tharavad* house after dinner with my sister-in-law and children, one of them said: 'There are three or four people here to see you.' The visitors had not known I was there. They had made a slight detour on their way back from the Guruvayoor temple in order to see the village and someone had told them I was in Kudallur. They had read most of my books.

The river and many of the people in the village have often featured in my stories and novels. The village of Kudallur is situated on the boundary of the Palghat district, between Kuttippuram and Thrithala, on the banks of the river known as the Bharathapuzha. It is a village familiar to all my readers.

When the visitors left, my sister-in-law said: 'Every now and then, people turn up like this. What all of them want to know is whether this house is the old *naalukettu* that you wrote about in your novel.' The old naalukettu does not exist anymore. Most parts of the building were demolished and even I have never seen the original building that housed sixty-four people in all, including adults and children. All I know about it is what my mother and grandmother described to me when I was a child.

Old naalukettus were part of the *marumakkathayam* or matrilinear system of inheritance that prevailed in Kerala. A central courtyard flanked by wooden pillars, open to the sky, rooms along its sides, a dining hall beyond, the kitchen, a gatehouse, a building called the *pathayappura* that had a granary downstairs to store the harvested grain, and rooms upstairs, a *kayyalappura*, or outer building to dry the grain during the rains—a naalukettu belonging to an ordinary family consisted of all these. Wealthy families had naalukettus with two central courtyards, sometimes even four. In these naalukettus, each courtyard was flanked by four pillars; there were eight- or sixteen-pillared structures, also known as *ettukettu* and *pathinarukettu*, respectively. There are two or three of these eight and sixteen-pillared naalukettus still left in old Malabar. Our present tharavad house is a disappointment to readers who turn up to see the village and the naalukettu of the novel.

I wrote *Naalukettu* in 1957. Before that, I had written stories that featured some of the older members of my family, stories pieced together from what my mother and grandmother had told me. One of them, an uncle whom we called Porayamman, a very hard-hearted man, never gave his nephews enough paddy, or coconuts for the household. Porayamman stayed upstairs in the gatehouse. The women of the household had to take his food up to him three times a day, elaborate meals with numerous dishes. His young nephews eventually concocted a plot to get rid of him and forced the women to agree to execute it. Poison was mixed into the chicken curry taken up to him one night. Caught in the throes of death, he was consumed by thirst and began to scream for water, but the nephews lay quietly behind the closed doors of the naalukettu. The story goes that the old man's ghost haunted the garden at night. Another uncle, Thashamman, a terrible miser, changed all the money he had made from the sale of the areca nuts and coconuts he cultivated, into gold coins and stored them in a copper vessel which he buried in the compound. Towards the end of his life, this uncle became insane. Having forgotten where exactly he had buried the gold coins, he began to run around with a spade, digging up the earth at various spots. My grandmother had heard Thashamman's ghost digging in the compound.

We children grew up hearing innumerable stories like these. Kondunni Uncle, the *pagida* player in *Naalukettu*, lived next door to us, in his wife's house. I used to see him very often when I was an elementary school student. A rumour that his business partner gave him poison and killed him spread through the village. I still have a clear image of him in my mind: when we came home from school, we children used to have a bath in the bathing tank in the house next-door, on the northern side. Kondunni Uncle would be seated on the verandah, having dinner. He would call out to each of us by name and make us sit down near him. He had a rule, that every one of us should eat at least a handful of rice. So about ten of us, children would gather around him.

Many people have asked me during interviews whether Appunni, the protagonist of *Naalukettu*, is myself. No, he is not. All I have done is to use the village and the ambience of the old naalukettu in the novel. I published three short story collections before I wrote *Naalukettu*. Many members of our old joint family featured in them. Around the time I started to write short stories, I wrote a short novel. I dealt with the unhappy lot of the *cheruma* folk who worked as agricultural labourers in our area and with the rebellion they organized against the landowners. It was inspired by the well-known novel, *Randidangazhi*, that Thakazhi wrote about the revolt of the agricultural labourers in Kuttanad. When I reread what I had written, I felt that it was not satisfactory at all, so I abandoned it. Later, in 1955, while making a living taking classes in a tutorial college in Palghat, I wrote another novel for a magazine they published there. This work, published in twelve instalments and entitled *Paathiraavum Pakalvelichavum* had a Hindu–Muslim theme. The readers of the magazine liked it. But I was dissatisfied. I thought I would write a novel set against the background of the old matrilinear tharavad that I had heard my mother and others talk about. I mulled over this idea for many months, until the novel took a shape that satisfied me. Then I decided to call it *Naalukettu*. Readers still enjoy this novel. What is being marketed now is the eighteenth impression. Between 1970 and 1990, another publisher took over and published five textbook editions. My present publisher tells me that the copies of the novel sold so far should number about five lakh. *Naalukettu* was written and published after I had been singled out from among the younger short story writers. I was anxious about how the novel would be received. A few months after the book appeared, I was invited as a delegate to a huge conference held by the Kerala Sahitya Parishad at Madras. Two illustrious writers who are no longer with us took part in this important conference: Joseph Mundasserry and Thakazhi Shivashankara Pillai. While discussing the contemporary scene in Malayalam literature and its future, Thakazhi praised *Naalukettu* in particular. I was seated in the audience, my head bowed. It was only years later that I actually came to know Thakazhi. But I treasured the words he said that day in my heart as proof of the generous acceptance he had extended to me, a new writer. The novel was selected for the Kerala Sahitya Akademi award in 1958.

I was a trainee in the editorial section of the *Mathrubhumi* at Kozhikode while writing *Naalukettu*. Sunday was my only free day. I used to get back from the press only after eight at night. So I would have a few hours every night and then all of Sunday. Using this time, I finished the novel in three weeks. I took me a month to make a fair copy. I thought at first of giving it to someone to read, then gave up the idea. I had never shown my work to anyone even earlier. I went straight to Thrissur with the handwritten manuscript. I had a friend, M.J. Thomas, a new publisher. I handed over the manuscript to him and went back, knowing that Thomas was neither a discriminating reader nor a critic. He called me after three or four days to say that the book was being elegantly printed and would be released in a hardcover edition. This was not common practice in Malayalam. Moreover, it was going to be priced at five rupees! Which was expensive at that time. Thomas, however, was extremely confident.

Once our tharavad was partitioned, the main naalukettu went to my eldest brother as his share and the granary building, the pathayappura, was the share given to the brother immediately elder to me. When the old house was demolished and rebuilt, my brother gave the contractors strict instructions to retain the door and walls of the sacred room that was believed to be the dwelling-place of the goddess Bhagavathi exactly as they were. While the pathayappura was being demolished, the younger of my older brothers said in jest: 'What, if we come upon the treasure that Thashamman buried while digging up the earth in this area? Let's look …' Since they too had heard this story, the workmen kept listening as they dug, for the sound of the spade hitting against the pot of treasure!

Some of the villagers still enjoy relating these old tales enthusiastically to occasional visitors. The topography of my stories is very familiar to them.

The team working on the documentary film left. I thought I would sleep that night in the upstairs room of the old house. In the old days, the river used to be visible from there. There is no river now. There is only its outline.

The pathayappura was taken over by new owners. They demolished and rebuilt it. There used to be two rooms upstairs in the old building and it was in one of them that I made my first attempts to write poems and stories when I was a child. Beyond the curtain of time, I saw that little boy rereading what he had written, weaving dreams with the material he wanted to write about. He did not have the slightest idea then that literature would become his profession. Nor did he know that writing would bring him remuneration. He kept writing reams in pages torn from old bound books, and tearing them up because he was not satisfied. He tried his luck with certain pieces which he thought were not too bad, but nothing appeared in print, ever. Despite this, he kept trying, over and over again. His mind was filled with unwritten stories and he was always trying to give them shape. And then one day, below a title in a magazine that came in the post, he saw his name in print!

I sat in the verandah at night, gazing out into the garden, thinking of those days. The thickets in which darkness used to hide had all disappeared. And because of that, our old uncles could no longer indulge in their nocturnal wanderings.

However, even now the children of the new generation do not forget to light the little oil lamp that throws its pale gleam in our Bhagavathi's shrine-room.

M. T. Vasudevan Nair

Introduction

Situated in the Ponnani taluk of Malabar, Kerala, the village of Kudallur remains, even in the twenty-first century, astonishingly untouched by time and the relentless march of modernization. A handful of small buildings on either side of the narrow main street, a river, a Shiva temple on a hill, a Bhagavathi temple. No gaudy jewellery or textile stores, so dear to Kerala hearts; no multi-storeyed or multicoloured structures that vociferously proclaim imported wealth; no bar-cum-restaurants with glittering lights. All of which makes it possible to believe that M.T. Vasudevan Nair (M.T. to everyone in Kerala and now, increasingly, to those who know him and his work all over India) can still find, when he visits this village to which he belongs, the landscape that safeguards the memories of his childhood. True, he laments that the river he loved, the gracious Bharathapuzha that was one of Kerala's richest and longest waterways, has dwindled to a narrow channel; that the *kannanthali* flowers that once bloomed in profusion on the hillside have disappeared; that many a colourful festival he watched enthusiastically as a child are celebrated no more; that the customs and rituals that were observed with such fervour in the forties and fifties do not live even in the awareness of the children now growing up in the village. But the Nila river, which is another name the Bharathapuzha is known by, still flows generously when the rains are plentiful, the ancient game of *pagida* is still being played in Kudallur and its vicinity, and there are still, among the players, those who remember the legendary Kondunni Nair whose presence is a guiding spirit in M.T.'s first novel, *Naalukettu*.

Meanwhile, for readers of M.T.'s short stories and novels, Kudallur continues to evoke the landscape they are set in, and is peopled with the characters whose tales they tell. Do these characters seem real because they are drawn from M.T.'s life experiences or because his fiction has gifted them flesh and blood and tears that are untainted by the flaw of mortality? M.T. himself speaks of the debt he owes his village in the preface to the first edition of his short stories:

My small world of Kudallur draws me to it in an irresistible way. You can ask: do I insist that I will not go beyond its borders? I do not. I have often wandered out in search of other and different worlds. But again and again, I come back to Kudallur. Possibly, this is a limitation. But I love the Nila river I know more than the mighty oceans that hold unknown wonders in their depths.[1]

Many of the characters in his short stories and novels once lived or still live in his village, and the stories he narrates range from his personal experiences to tales that he heard or pieced together, or was told as a child. He says repeatedly in articles and interviews that the material Kudallur offers him is inexhaustible, that there are still innumerable stories left to tell.

Born in 1933, M.T. was the youngest of four brothers. Even as a child, he was fascinated by words, by the way poets and writers of fiction used them. He read the poems his older brothers brought home, wandered over the hillside in the village reciting aloud those he had committed to memory, and devoured all the short stories and novels he could lay hands on. Then he started to experiment with words himself:

A magazine called *Chitrakeralam* was started from Madras by T.V. Parameswara Iyer. Its standards were high: good paper, good printing, lots of pictures. The brother just older than me contributed poems to it, another brother sent pictures he had drawn. I did not let this opportunity go by. When the first

[1]M.T. Vasudevan Nair, preface to *Thiranjedutha Kathakal* (Selected Stories), Thrissur: Current Books, 1996, p. 6.

issue came out, it contained a poem by Kudallur Vasudevan Nair, an article by V.N. Thekkeppat and a story by M.T. Vasudevan Nair. All three were myself.[2]

M.T. was fourteen years old at this time.

In 1953, a short story that he wrote, 'Valarthumrigangal' (Circus Animals) won a prize in a competition organized by the *Mathrubhumi*. He went on to write more and more short stories, then novels, screenplays, and articles. Together with Uroob (P.C. Kuttikrishnan) and S.K. Pottekkat, M.T. is considered one of the finest exponents of the poetic rhythms of Malayalam prose. M.T. himself acknowledges a deep debt to the poet Changampuzha, whose love-poems shaped the ethos of his generation. Over and over again, in articles and memoirs, right up to 1996, when he made his speech of acceptance on the occasion of receiving the Jnanpith Award, he describes an incident that obviously made an indelible impression on him:

I remember being sent to a neighbouring village to borrow a hand-written copy of *Ramanan*, a poem by one of the most well-known poets of the time, Changampuzha. The copy was handed over to me on the condition that it would be returned the next day. I watched my older brothers and my sister-in-law stay up all night to copy it out. Astonished, I asked myself: so much passion and hard work to make a book of poetry their own? And then I too began to read poetry ...[3]

First, he consumed the works of the great triad: Vallathol, Kumaran Asan, and Ulloor. Then he went on to Balamani Amma, G. Sankara Kurup, Changampuzha, Idasserry, Vylopilli. He realized that they used words that were familiar to him, but arranged them in new, thought-provoking ways. Later, he avidly read every writer he could find in the world of the short story: Basheer, Thakazhi, S.K. Pottekkat, Ponkunnam Varkey, Karoor Nilakanta Pillai, Keshava Dev, Lalithambika Antarjanam, P.C. Kuttikrishnan, Vettoor Raman Nair.

---

[2]Basheer, M.M., ed.: *MT: Kathayum Porulum*, Thrissur: Current Books, 1996, p. 149.

[3]M.T. Vasudevan Nair, in the acceptance speech on the occasion of the Jnanpith Award, *Kathayum Porulum*, p. 509.

The short story has always remained the literary form M.T. likes the most.

Yes, I have a particular partiality towards the short story. Like poetry, it is a literary form that can attain completeness, or be worked upon with completeness as a goal. In a short story, a sentence, sometimes even a word, can become redundant.

He laments the fact: 'It becomes necessary to include in a novel, for the sake of documentation, many sections that lack poetic beauty.'[4] He was one of the earliest Malayalam writers to use the short story not just to tell a tale but to explore the complicated processes of the human mind, the ways in which it moves through hopes, desires, hidden longings, and fantasies. It has been said of M.T.'s stories that they do not simply narrate events or describe characters, that they allow the reader to experience these events, the emotions of these characters. He has eighteen short story collections to his credit, many of which have been reprinted several times. A number of his stories have been made into films. Over the years, he has experimented tirelessly with this literary form and some of his finest stories, like 'Sherlock' and 'Insight' were written and published in the nineties. However, he did not restrict himself to the medium of the short story. He has written eight novels, all of which have been widely read and appreciated in Kerala, a play, and several successful screenplays.

The novel emerged as a literary genre in Malayalam by the last quarter of the nineteenth century. The first novel in Malayalam, *Indulekha* (1889), was written by O. Chandu Menon (1847–1900), with the intention of writing in Malayalam a narrative that would be like an English novel. The social reality he depicted, showing the decline of the Namboodiri Brahmin society and the rise of a Nair society that believed in the value of education, made this a truly remarkable novel that continues to merit study and discussion even today. C.V. Raman Pillai (1858–1922) followed with lively historical novels in the tradition

---

[4]M.T.Vasudevan Nair, in *Samskarikavikaram*, Book 1, vol.1, December 2001, p. 190.

of Walter Scott about the Travancore dynasty, like *Marthanda Varma* (1891) and *Dharma Raja* (1911). The early twentieth century saw the publication of many Malayalam translations of classics of world literature, which were to influence the young writers who read them, but no really notable novels came out for a while. In the forties, progressive writers like Keshava Dev, Thakazhi Shivasankara Pillai, and Vaikom Mohammed Basheer began to write fiction that depicted the struggles and suffering of the working classes in Kerala. The writers who followed these realistic novelists, S.K. Pottekkat, Uroob (P.C. Kuttikrishnan), and Ponjikkara Raphi were more concerned with the inner world of the mind.

M.T., who had already started writing short stories by this time, spoke in a new and different voice, remarkable from the start for its introspective nature. He was one of the first writers in Kerala to concern himself with the inward-turned vision. Throughout the fifty-odd years that he has been writing, this vision has been consistent and is now acknowledged as the distinctive feature of his craft. He situates much of his fiction against the social backdrop of the matrilinear Nair *tharavad* at the point of time when it was slowly disintegrating, largely to emphasize the power, the frustration, or the helplessness that characters who move against this background have to deal with. The protagonists of his early novels, *Naalukettu, Asuravithu*, and *Kaalam* are alienated individuals, painfully aware of being isolated from uncaring and unkind members of society or their own families.

Naalukettu, his first novel, written in 1958, has currently gone into twenty-three reprints and been translated into fourteen Indian languages. Its continued success has been something of a literary phenomenon in Kerala. The novel deals with many of M.T.'s familiar themes: the break-up of the matrilinear joint family system, patterns of revenge, the mother–son relationship. But it is the way the mindsets of the characters develop and change during the course of the novel that make it remarkable. M.T. says of Appunni, the protagonist:

There is very little of the autobiographical element in him. Experiences that any child could have gone through ... Appunni could have been a child in my own family. And there is a happening in the novel culled from the stories in my village. One of my uncles started a business with Syedalikutty. One day, after he ate in Syedalikutty's house, my uncle threw up and died. The rumour that he had been poisoned spread through the village. I was told that the police investigated the case. But everyone said that nothing was proved.[5]

He goes on to speak of the background of the novel:

I witnessed the last stages of the crumbling of the matrilinear system of inheritance. However, the background of *Naalukettu* is not solely that of my own family. There are characters from my neighbourhood in it as well. Some personal experiences, the experiences of other people I knew: I put them all into it.[6]

Kondunni Nair, the pagida player, was a distant uncle whom M.T. had seen in childhood and it was true that he died of poisoning at the hands of a man named Syedalikutty, who lived in Kudallur.

The novel opens with the child Appunni reiterating his desire to kill Syedalikutty, the man who had deliberately poisoned his father, and readers and critics in Kerala have been continually intrigued by the fact that Appunni did not kill him. In fact, Syedalikutty, who first makes his appearance as Appunni's feared and hated arch enemy, is gradually transformed into a friend who turns up at every critical juncture in his young life. Speaking about the people of his village, M.T. says:

Thanks to the complexities of the human condition, a person whose destiny it has always been to be called unmitigatedly cruel can suddenly astonish us by revealing a gentle heart.[7]

Perhaps, it is this facet of human behaviour that Syedalikutty demonstrates, for there is no logical explanation for why he befriends Appunni. When he finds Appunni his first job, the boy suddenly thinks of him as a god. Finally, the roles are entirely reversed: Appunni becomes

[5]Ibid., p. 28.
[6]Kakkattil, Akbar: 'M.T. Vasudevan Nair', in *Sargasameeksha,* D.C. Books, 1991, p. 288.
[7]M.T. Vasudevan Nair in the acceptance speech on the occasion of the Jnanpith Award in *Kathayum Porulum*, p. 511.

financially secure and takes on the responsibility of looking after Syedalikutty's family when he falls ill.

Appunni's uncle, his mother's elder brother whom he calls Valia Ammaaman is another enemy. He exploits his position as the *karanavar*, the head of the matrilinear family ruthlessly, steadily siphoning the income from the joint properties into his wife's estate until his family can bear the situation no longer. He is a fairly typical example of some of the karanavars of the time: imperious, callous, and completely unconcerned about his sisters and their families. He remains dominating and inimical until he is transformed by circumstances into a helpless old man, crippled by debts, forced to agree to whatever Appunni, the boy he once drove out of his house, decides is best for everyone.

Appunni's father, Kondunni Nair the pagida player, is already dead when the novel begins, but he is a powerful presence in the novel. His wife, Appunni's mother, recalls his heroic exploits, including the most daring of them, when he carried her away from her home just as she was about to get married. The old woman who lives in a hut next to Appunni's house, and whom he calls, Muthaachi, grandmother, describes to Appunni the miracles his father wrought with the pagida dice. To Appunni himself, his father is a constant source of inspiration, a man to admire and emulate.

What about Appunni himself, the protagonist of the novel? We see him grow up from a small boy, full of fears and secret longings into a confident young man. As he grows up, he encounters numerous obstacles that appear insurmountable and each time he comes up against one of them, it is Syedalikutty, the man who poisoned and killed his father, Kondunni Nair, who helps him overcome them. Appunni manages to make enough money to buy back the *naalukettu* that had been his mother's home until she was turned out of it. However, his sense of victory is soured when he learns that his uncle's daughter, Ammini, had died in childbirth. Ammini had not only treated him with affection, she had been the first girl to arouse his sexual feelings. The ritual of the serpent *thullal* is woven into Appunni's delicate relationship with Ammini. Witnessing the ritual not only makes a deep impression on the child Appunni during his first visit to his mother's house, it also awakens in him the first stirrings of sexual desire. Later, when Appunni starts to live in his mother's old home, the Vadakkeppat naalukettu, the memories of the beautiful serpent-princess who executed the ritual are fused with disturbing images of his cousin, Ammini.

The ritual of the serpent thullal marks Appunni's introduction to the Vadakkeppat naalukettu. He is fascinated by the beautiful girl Ammini, who is one of the participants in the ritual. It is a cruel blow to him when he finds out that she is the daughter of the uncle who hates him and his mother. Over and over again in the novel, Appunni struggles with this kind of contradictory emotion. Syedalikutty, who had taken root in his mind as an opponent, a wicked and unforgivable enemy, gradually proves that he is a caring friend, but for a long time, Appunni cannot help recalling at their every encounter that he had planned to kill the man. When Ammini makes overtures of friendship, he resents her for being her father's daughter. In spite of this, he is drawn to her, irresistibly. Although his other cousin, the plain, dark-skinned Malu, reveals her concern for him from the start, he despises her—and then feels sorry for having done so, overcome with pity for her. He abandons his mother because he resents the man who came into her life as a protector, but in the end, he realizes that, if he were to go back to his mother, he would have to accept the truth: that there is nothing wrong in her relationship with this man. Appunni is never comfortable with himself or with other people—a welter of troubled feelings, memories, emotions, stand between him and the world, denying him happiness or serenity. In this, he is very like the protagonists of M.T.'s other novels and short stories: Sethu of *Kaalam*, Govindankutty of *Asuravithu,* and several characters in his short stories who are lonely and anxious, longing to break away from their surroundings into a world they are unable to define, a world of unclear dreams and hopes.

The Kerala naalukettu (naalu: four; kettu: building or structure) is a residential building consisting of four wings built around a central sunken courtyard with a stone floor. This courtyard, which is open to the sky, is flanked by thick wooden pillars. Ordinarily, there are four pillars in a naalukettu. However, larger, wealthier residences have courtyards flanked by eight pillars (*ettukettu*: ettu meaning eight) or sometimes sixteen pillars (*pathinarukettu*, pathinaru meaning sixteen). Prosperous Nair families generally lived in naalukettus. The central room with the courtyard flanked by pillars is the actual naalukettu. But the entire structure, comprising the central hall and the four wings around it is also commonly known as a naalukettu. Often, there is a small room called a *machu* that opens just off the central hall of the naalukettu on its western side. The household deity resides in this room and a lamp is lit there at dusk.

Nairs lived in large joint families, tharavads, until the break-up of the matrilineal joint-family system, a process which started in the twenties and continued into the late forties. Properties, in the matrilinear system of inheritance, passed down through the women. However, the lands and the income from them were administered by the eldest male member of the matrilinear joint family, the karanavar. Ideally, the karanavar was selfless, devoted to the welfare of the family. But in reality, he could be greedy and self-seeking, more interested in amassing wealth for himself than in looking after his sisters and their children. Since he wielded considerable authority, he could impose his will on the younger members of the household—as happens in the Vadakkeppat tharavad in *Naalukettu*.

Nair marriages, known as *sambandams*, were contracted between the families. The man negotiated with the karanavar of the woman's family and presented her with a length of cloth. He could then visit her at her house. He had no rights over the woman or the children he had by her, but was expected to give her small gifts from time to time and pay all expenses when she had a child. The sambandham could be terminated with no formality whenever the man or the woman wished to.[8]

The dissolution of the Nair tharavads, which is the theme around which the novel *Naalukettu* is woven, had actually started to take place in the period when the young M.T. was growing up. The first Nair Act became law in 1912 in the State of Travancore, but it did not achieve very much since it allowed only *thavazhis* or branches of each tharavad

[8]Jeffrey, Robin, *The Decline of Nair Dominance*, New Delhi: Manohar, 1994, p. 15.

the right to acquire family property. It was followed by the second Nair Act in 1925, which entitled individual members of each tharavad to a share of the properties and made polygamy illegal. The Cochin Nair Regulation of 1919–20 imposed curbs on the seniormost member of the tharavad, the karanavar, and entitled a wife to maintenance for herself and her children from her husband. The Cochin Nair Act of 1937–8 which followed, ruled that a man's wife and children were his legal heirs and therefore entitled to inherit his properties. Every member of a tharavad could claim a share of the tharavad properties. In Malabar, which was directly under the British, unlike the princely states of Travancore and Cochin, these changes took place later and much more slowly. The Malabar Marriage Bill became law in 1896 and under its provisions, those who followed the *marumakkathayam* or matrilineal system of inheritance could register their sambandhams (contractual relationships) with the government, thereby legalizing them and entitling a man who had entered into a sambandham to make over his self-acquired property to his wife and children. But this Act applied only to those who registered and not many people did.[9] It was the Madras Marumakkathayam Act of 1933 that provided for the individual partition of tharavad property in Malabar.[10] In the period that immediately succeeded these Acts, innumerable lawsuits were filed by individual members or smaller branches of joint families who claimed their shares—and in Malabar, this would have been in the thirties and forties, when M.T. was still young. It is this period, when the old system was crumbling and a new one being forged, that is the background of *Naalukettu*. The karanavars who managed the affairs of the tharavad were beginning to lose their authority, while the legal disputes initiated by younger members who claimed their own shares of the joint properties started to drain the financial resources of the family. The latter part of *Naalukettu* depicts a karanavar of this kind fighting a losing battle with the younger members of the family who stake their individual claims

[9]Ibid., p. 169.

[10]Sreedhara Menon, A.: *A Survey of Kerala History*, Kottayam: National Book Stall, 1967, p. 389.

to the property. In the end, Appunni is able to buy the old family house, the naalukettu that once housed the entire joint family, from this karanavar, in addition to the piece of land he acquired as his own share, since the older man, who had once wielded incredible power and authority over his household, had become helpless, impoverished on the one hand by the vast sums of money he had spent on the legal proceedings connected with the partition of the property, and on the other by the fact that his income from the lands had shrunk to almost nothing.

The success of the novel lies in the way M.T. handles this material, never letting it dominate the narrative, never interrupting its flow with mundane descriptions. Appunni, the protagonist, remains the pivot of the novel: the social background, the progress of events, the shifting positions each character takes, are all seen through his eyes, through the workings of his mind. Except for the short fifth chapter which describes the floods, he is present throughout the novel, and even in that chapter, he completely fills his mother's thoughts.

There are serpent-shrines in the compounds of most old Namboodiri and Nair homes in Kerala. Serpents were worshipped from ancient times as guardian deities of the household as well as to achieve specific objectives—to remedy infertility, to cure skin diseases which were often attributed to their curses, or to avert calamities that threatened the family. In addition, serpent-shrines have an ecological aspect: they help to conserve small forest areas within the compounds of the houses where they have been installed. The area surrounding a serpent-shrine is allowed to grow wild so that the serpents who have made a home there are not disturbed. These shrines, therefore, give the inhabitants of the house the opportunity to nurture a miniature forest within their own property.

Those who have serpent-shrines in their homes make regular offerings to the *nagas*, the serpents, to propitiate them and to ward off evil. An annual serpent-puja is conducted every year in the month of Kanni (September–October), on the day when the Aayilyam (Ashlesha) star is in the ascendant. Besides this annual puja, special offerings are made to the serpents if misfortunes or calamities occur in the family. A *prashnam* ritual is first performed, during which an astrologer identifies the precise nature of the evil that has befallen or threatens to befall the household. The astrologer throws a handful of cowries on the ground and rituals of propitiation are suggested on the basis of the formations the cowries fall into. One of these rituals is a serpent thullal, a long and elaborate ritual which is conducted by the household and which may last for three or four days. *Kanyaka*s or young virgins are the main participants in the ritual and, while it is being performed, they become possessed by the serpents that have been invoked. The girls fall into a trance and finally consecrate the snake-spirit that has entered them in a stone called a *chitrakoota* stone lying inside the compound of the house. Men and women of the Pulluva caste are part of the ritual and sing the songs that accompany it. An entire day is set apart for the ritual for each naga and there are as many chitrakoota stones in the compound as there are nagas.

Before the ritual begins, an enclosure or *mantapam* is made by driving four stakes cut from an areca-nut tree into the ground and stretching a canopy of silk over them. This enclosure is festooned on all sides with streamers made from palm leaves and a *kalam* or sacred drawing is made on its floor. The kalam is drawn with different powders made of rice, paddy husk, turmeric, and green leaves. Powdered paddy husk, which is black in colour, is first sprinkled on the ground and the Pulluvan sketches the snakes on this background with his fingers. The outlines are then picked out in colour. Coconut shells are filled with the various powders and they are sprinkled on the design through small perforations made in the shells. The bodies of the serpents are drawn first, then the eyes and the hoods. The design in the kalam shows intertwined snakes.

Once the kalam has been completed, the pooja begins. It is initiated by a male member of the household, known as the *kalathil kammal*, who has fasted and observed ritual purity for three days before the thullal. He has a bath, wears a *mundu* in ritual fashion, drawing up the ends between his knees and tucking them into his waist at the back. He enters the sacred enclosure carrying a bell-metal vessel with a spout (a *kindi*) filled with water. Brass oil lamps are lit on all four sides of the kalam. Paddy, rice, coconuts, tender coconuts, beaten rice, milk, bananas, and lime paste are also placed on all the four sides. The kalathil kammal places lighted wicks on a banana leaf lying in a new winnowing tray heaped with paddy and circumambulates the mantapam three times.

A group of people then circumambulate the kalam drawing three times, go to the serpent-shrine in the compound of the house, and worship it. They are: the Pulluvan playing his *veena* in the lead, a member of the household carrying a kindi with a cluster of coconut flowers placed in it, women carrying lighted oil lamps, young girls holding brass platters with burning wicks in them, the kammal, and important members of the family.

The group of people go back to the kalam and sits down. The kammal then washes the feet of two young girls who carry platters with lighted wicks in them, puts flowers in their hair, and seats them in the kalam. The girls are dressed in narrowly pleated lengths of white cloth whose ends are drawn up between their thighs and tucked in at their waist at the back. In their hands, they hold mirrors of polished brass (*vaalkannaadi*) and clusters of areca nut flowers. The girls fix their eyes on the serpents' hoods in the kalam. The Pulluvan, who has only been drumming on his earthen pot until then, begins to sing. The songs tell the legends of the serpents. One Pulluvan sings a line and the others repeat it. There are at least two Pulluvans and two Pulluvathis (Pulluva women). As the singing increases in volume, the girls begin to toss their heads and move, erasing the kalam with the flower clusters they hold in their hands. At this stage, spectators can ask them questions, which they answer. At the end of the ritual, the girls run out of the mantapam into the compound and consecrate the flowers at the chitrakoota stone.

The outdoor game of pagida, played with metal dice, is very popular in Kudallur and the neighbouring villages. A diagram is drawn on the ground and counters are moved along it according to the numbers shown on the dice. The unique quality of this game is that it can continue over three or four days, sometimes even a week, without a break. The participants may leave to eat, or sleep, or rest. Each one who leaves is immediately replaced by a fresh player from his team. It is said that the rival teams spend enormous sums of money on the offerings they make to the local temples to ensure that they win each round—more than is spent on any other boons that devotees ask of the gods! The dice can be made of very heavy metal (Kondunni Nair is presented in the novel with a pair of bell-metal dice that weigh four pounds). They are crafted so cleverly that, however heavy they may be, when thrown by expert players, they spin over the ground before they fall face upward. Pagida is still played in and around Kudallur and Kondunni Nair is proudly remembered in the region as a great champion.

What imparts a magical quality to M.T.'s fiction is his capacity not only to create characters like those that appear in *Naalukettu* but also to persuade us to experience their emotions. It is rare for the first novel of a writer who is so prolific to retain the interest it held for readers at the time when it was published—but this is exactly what *Naalukettu*, which came out fifty years ago, has achieved for readers in Kerala.

Gita Krishnankutty

Kinship Terms and Malayalam Months

Kinship terms used in the novel:

Achamma: grandmother, father's mother
Achan: father
Amma: mother
Ammaaman: uncle, mother's brother
Ammamma: grandmother, mother's mother
Ammayi: aunt, uncle's wife
Cheriamma: aunt, mother's younger sister
Edathi: elder sister
Ettan: elder brother
Valia Ammaaman: mother's elder brother
Valiamma: aunt, mother's elder sister

Malayalam months:

Chingam: August–September
Kanni: September–October
Thulam: October–November
Vrischikam: November–December
Dhanu: December–January
Makaram: January–February

Kumbham:	February–March
Meenam:	March–April
Medam:	April–May
Edavam:	May–June
Mithunam:	June–July
Karkatakam:	July–August

1

He would grow up. Grow up and become a big man. His hands would become very strong. He would not have to fear anyone. He would be able to stand up and hold his head high. If someone asked, 'Who's that there?' he would say unhesitatingly in a firm voice, 'It's me, Kondunni Nair's son, Appunni.'

And then, the day would come—he would certainly meet Syedalikutty. He would have his revenge then. Twisting Syedalikutty's neck between his hands, he would say, 'It's you, isn't it, it's you who ...'

Whenever he thought of it, Appunni's eyes would fill with tears.

The scene in which he confronted Syedalikutty was one he often imagined when he lay with his eyes closed, or sat by himself in the afternoons in the shade of the *kumkumam* tree at the gate of the Kundungal family house.

Who was Syedalikutty? Appunni had never seen him. He used to pray that he would not come upon him now, that he would see him very much later, after he grew up and became big and strong. He would go and find him then.

When he started out for the shop that day at dusk, he had neither thought of Syedalikutty nor expected to meet him.

He had come home late from school, having wandered around the temple with his friends, thrown stones at the cashew trees in Sharody's grove, and brought down the fruits. There was no way they could pluck fruit from Parangodan's or Achutha Kurup's cashew groves. They were terrible people. If they caught the children plucking fruit, they would hurl insults at their parents. But Sharody always allowed them to take the fruits if they asked his permission. All the old man wanted were the seeds. It was said that he had a certain affection for children because he had none of his own.

They had gone up the hill afterwards, stamped on wet clumps of grass to shape slippery channels to play in and lost track of time.

On the days when he came home directly from school, Amma would not have come back from the *illam*, the Namboodiri household where she worked. He would swallow the *kanji* in the covered bowl hanging in the rope *uri* in the kitchen in one long gulp. By the time he went to old Muthaachi's hut and sat down to exchange a bit of gossip with her, Amma would be back.

When he got back that day, Amma was throwing paddy husk into the fireplace over which dinner was cooking, to get the fire going.

'Why're you so late?'

'Nothing, Amme.'

'How many times I've told you, Appunni, that you've got to be home by dusk.'

He said nothing in reply. He knew that was as much as Amma would say in rebuke.

He drank his kanji standing. Then Amma said,

'Go down to Yusuf's shop, son, and get me coconut oil for two *annas*.'

He looked out. The sun had set completely. Darkness had not quite fallen, but the sky was black. Once it was dark, he was afraid to go down the lane where screwpine bushes grew thick on both sides. Eroman the sorcerer had been cremated by that lane. Appunni was reluctant to go that way.

'We'll get some tomorrow, Amme.'

'There's not even a drop to touch to my hair. Just make a quick dash.'

He hesitated. If he said he was afraid, Amma would tell him not to go. But that was shameful, wasn't it? He was not such a small child, after all. He was in the eighth now. It was him that Master had made the monitor of the class.

'Get going, Appunni. If you bring it back quickly, I'll give you rice mixed with fried onions.'

He did not hesitate any longer.

'Give me money and the bottle.'

Rice with fried onions was no small treat. He had tasted it only twice or thrice. Oil was poured into a frying pan over finely chopped onions; as the onions started to brown, Amma would toss rice in with a ladle. Ah, the fragrance that rose from it when it was served on a plate and set before him!

Hai, just to think of it brought a potful of water to his mouth.

He thrust the coins into the pocket of his red shorts, picked up the bottle, and ran out.

When he came to the lane that ran through the thicket of screwpine, he hesitated for a moment. No, it wasn't all that dark yet. But there were dense screwpine bushes on both sides. He had heard that hooded cobras lived in the pits between the bushes. They liked the scent of screwpine flowers. Sweet scents, good music, and beautiful women: these were what cobras liked. Were these good things meant only for cobras?

He knew every step, stone, and pothole in the lane. Surely there was danger only if he walked slowly? He broke into a quick run. He did not stop until he reached the edge of the paddy field beyond the lane.

He had to cross one more field to get to the bazaar. It was right on the bank of the river. All the shops had thatched roofs, except one which had a tiled roof. No business was conducted in it. Someone lived on the first floor.

Lamps had been lit in the shops. Most were flickering hurricane lamps. Only Yusuf's shop had a petromax lamp. It was the biggest shop in the village, the only one which displayed firecrackers for sale when Vishu, the Malayalam New Year, drew near. A tailor had come from Pattambi recently: Kudallur's first tailor. He kept his sewing machine in Yusuf's shop and did his tailoring there.

Appunni liked going to Yusuf's shop. He could watch the tailor at work as well. The sight of the needle going rapidly up and down making a 'kada-kada' noise while curls of coloured cloth billowed out was well worth seeing.

He had been thinking for many days now that he must tell Amma not to buy him shirts from Ravuthar. All his three shirts had been bought when Ravuthar came around hawking his wares. Two were too loose and one, too tight. They could buy cloth and give it to the tailor. His measurements would then be taken while everyone in the shop looked on. If the measurements were taken with a tape, the fit was sure to be correct. He would be able to watch the shirts being cut and sewn with a certain authoritative air.

Yusuf's shop was crowded when Appunni entered. It was the time of day when the *cherumis* returning from work with their daily wages were buying provisions.

'Kerosene for two quarter annas.'

'A *nazhi* of salt'.

'Betel leaves and tobacco for a quarter anna.'

'Hurry up, Musaliyar, I have to go.'

All Yusuf did was sit in front of the box. It was Musaliyar, with the long white beard that came down to his neck like a billy goat's who handed out things. There was quite a crowd. The cherumis talked to one another about happenings at home or exchanged news about the houses they worked in while they hurried through their purchases. A young cherumi scolded Musaliyar for letting a drop from the half-anna's worth of coconut oil that he poured on her head fall on the ground.

The tailor had moved his machine into the shop and left.

Appunni stood quietly on the veranda. Oh God, he thought, it's getting late.

It was at dusk that poisonous snakes crept into the screwpine bushes.

Eroman the sorcerer had been cremated on the roadside.

'Coconut oil for two annas.' In the commotion made by the cherumis, Musaliyar did not hear him.

Appunni made an attempt to push his way through them. It wouldn't matter if he touched the cherumi women and was polluted. He would have a bath anyway as soon as he got home. But when he drew closer to their dark bodies, the odour of mingled sweat and oil and dirt nauseated him. He drew back and stood for a while watching the moths flitting around the petromax lamp.

It was then that two people entered. A short, stout man in a white shirt with a small moustache flecked with grey. The other was Padmanabhan Nair who had run a teashop by the ferry for a long time and then gone out of business. Appunni knew him, two of his children were in his class.

Appunni moved closer to the wall and leaned against the shutters stacked there.

'So business is excellent, Moyalali!' called out the short, stout, white-shirted man. The cherumis turned when they heard his voice. Yusuf, who was seated near the table counting out change did not see him.

'Who is it?'

Musaliyar, busy packing coriander seeds in a teak leaf, smiled, baring teeth stained red with betel juice and said,

'My God, who is this? You're not dead yet?'

'I'm ready. Maybe Israyel doesn't want me, Moyaliyar.'

Yusuf got up. When he caught sight of the white-shirted man he too said, 'My God, who's this now?'

Musaliyar asked, 'When did you come?'

'By the five-thirty train.'

Musaliyar said as he tied up a packet, 'The rascal's put on some weight, hasn't he, Pappanavan Nair?'

Padmanabhan Nair, who was watching the cherumi women while he sat on the stone platform smoking a beedi, said, 'It's all that food in strange places.'

Musaliyar caught sight of Appunni as he turned to spit into the courtyard.

'What do you want?'

For no reason, Appunni suddenly felt sad. He was afraid he would cry in a while. He said without looking at Musaliyar's face,

'I came to buy coconut oil.'

The cherumis muttered something to one another.

'Who is this child?' the white-shirted man asked Padmanabhan Nair.

'Our Kondunni Nair's son. Vadakkeppattu ...'

Appunni did not raise his head.

The cherumis suddenly fell silent. Two of them who stood near Appunni whispered something to each other. Those in front moved aside a little. Appunni could go up in front now without elbowing anyone. Musaliyar took the bottle from him, placed a funnel in it, dipped a small ladle in the tin, and poured out two ladlefuls, then an extra drop as well.

Appunni paid and twisted a dry leaf into the bottle to close it. As he was about to go out, the white-shirted man asked,

'You're going alone?'

Appunni did not realize at first that the man was speaking to him.

'It's dark outside, child.'

Appunni muttered something that no one could hear. Kochi, the old cherumi who worked at the *adhikari*'s place, called out:

'Wait, Cheriambra, don't go alone. I'm going that way.'

Kochi tucked the screwpine leaf bag that held her money and betel leaves and all the things she had bought into her ample waist and followed him out. She lit her palm-leaf torch at the oil lamp in the shop next door and said, 'Go on, Cheriambra.'

Appunni was no longer afraid. He thought there was a faint fragrance of screwpine flowers in the lane, but at least there was light where he walked.

He asked, 'Who was that, Kochi?'

'Who, Cheriambra?'

'That man in Yusuf's shop.'

'Don't you know? That was Syedalikutty Mapilla.'

'Which Syedalikutty?'

'Of Mundathayam. He's been away for years now.'

Syedalikutty! Goosebumps burst all over him. The thick, short, rough hands, the hairy body, the round, bloodshot eyes—so that was Syedalikutty. The man who ...

He suddenly remembered waking at dawn to a scene in Kathakali in the temple courtyard: Bhiman, seated on Dussasanan's chest, tearing open his stomach and pulling out the entrails. He, Appunni, would sit like that on Syedalikutty's chest and …

But he wasn't strong enough yet, or old enough.

Appunni gasped for breath.

If he were to give Syedalikutty a push while he walked by the edge of the quarry or in the narrow lane under Anappara … or throw a stone at his head …

'You go along now, Cheriambra.'

He realized he had reached home.

'Appunni!' He heard Amma's voice. She was waiting anxiously at the gate.

He ran up to her, gasping.

'Oh my forefathers! My insides were on fire!'

Appunni did not say anything. He thought of the quarry, of blood streaming from a crushed head …

'Why did you take so long, Appunni?'

'There was such a crowd there.'

He wrapped a worn, shabby towel around his waist and went to the well to bathe. Amma drew water and poured it over his head. Even now, it was she who scrubbed him and gave him a bath. He dried his hair himself, but Amma would look at it, say it was still wet and dry it again, rubbing his scalp hard.

Somehow, the rice fried with onions did not seem to have its usual flavour.

Amma closed the front and kitchen doors, washed the vessels, inverted them on the floor, then spread his mattress in the only room they had and her own mat next to it.

When the lamp was extinguished and it was dark, he felt afraid, he was not sure why. In the dark, he kept seeing a head of stubbly hair and bloodshot eyes.

'Are you asleep, Amma?'

'No. Why?'

Should he tell her? 'Um … um …' He closed his eyes tight and prayed he would fall asleep quickly.

'Amme!'

Amma put out her arms, drew him close and asked, 'What is it?'

He hesitated again. Should he tell her?

'I—I saw Syedalikutty.'

Amma didn't ask which Syedalikutty. She drew him even closer to her, pressed her face against his back and said, 'Go to sleep, my little one.'

It was not Amma who had told him the story. He had gleaned most of it, a little at a time, from Muthaachi. Her hut was in their compound, on the southern side. He spent his time there when he had nothing else to do.

Muthaachi did not stay in her hut all the time though. She sometimes wrapped herself up in her yellow woollen shawl (which he heard had been brought from Colombo) and went off, leaning on her stick. She would come back only after three or four days. There were houses she visited regularly—Thendeth Illam, Mankoth Illam, and a couple of Nair *tharavad* houses. She had to be given rice and coconuts in these places without asking for them. Muthaachi would often say, to console herself, 'I don't go around begging, you know.'

There was no one in Kudallur who did not know Muthaachi. She had had three husbands when she was young but had never borne children. The first husband had abandoned her. And she had abandoned the second and third. Seventy-year-old Muthaachi could still take part enthusiastically in Onam and *kaikottikkali* dances with little children. If she visited wealthy houses, she usually stayed a day or two. The women were expected to give her rice when she left and the young men coins. She would then go around praising the generosity and status of all those who gave her money and rice.

When she was young, Muthaachi used to nurse the women in all the houses where there was a childbirth or an illness. She had brought most of the people in the village into the world. And ushered many to their death. But she did not like anyone saying that Kalan, the God of Death, would come for her one day.

'So you're in a hurry, are you, children, to take Muthaachi to the southern yard to be cremated?' she would ask and then console herself: 'My turn won't come as quickly as all that.'

Whenever she came back from a journey, she would stay in her hut for a few days. That was the time Appunni was the happiest. He would go and sit down on her rope cot. All the good things she had collected, juicy mangoes or jackfruit *pappadams* from Thendeth Illam, were for him. What Muthaachi needed was an audience and even a two-year-old child would have done. She had so much to tell.

It was from Muthaachi that he had learnt many things about his father.

'When Kondunni died, Appu, you were just this high.' Muthaachi called every boy Appu. And every girl Ammu.

When his father died, Appunni had been only half the size of Muthaachi's index finger! Appunni was very amused.

It had not been a natural death. Someone had given him poison to drink ...

'There's never been a boy as affectionate as he was in this whole region. So big-built, an elephant could not have wound its trunk around him. Whenever he saw me, he'd give me money to buy betel leaves.' Muthaachi would stop, stroke Appunni's head and say,

'God didn't will happiness for your mother.'

Appunni had only a vague memory of his father. Everyone Appunni met talked about him. The villagers had loved him. They had needed Kondunni Nair for everything. He had been in demand for every sort of occasion: a wedding, a sixteenth day funeral rite, the construction of a house.

But his own family had hated Achan, Appunni's father, from the time he was a young man.

'Good-for-nothing fellow, let him go around throwing dice!' Appunni had heard that that was what his father's mother used to say. Achan had been an only son and when his mother died, he had been left alone in the world.

Kondunni Nair had had an excellent reputation as a *pagida* player.

They still played pagida on the platform under the banyan tree for the Onam, Vishu, and Thiruvathira festivals. There was a competition between the Kudallur and Perumbalam regions. But all the expert dice throwers had died and there were only a few young players left now. The older people complained: 'No one has a passion for the game anymore.'

Whenever he heard the sound of the dice spinning and ululations echoed through the air, Appunni would think of his father and a sense of pride would outweigh his pain.

There had been only one player in the village who could make the dice fall showing the exact numbers he had predicted—and that was his father.

'Listen, all of you, I saw with my own eyes. It was during the last round with the Perumbalam folks. Marar was playing for their side. They were on the point of winning, the dice had to be thrown only one more time. If we were defeated, we'd lose our honour. None of our players had lasted, they had given up one after another. Imagine, the other side had got washerman Choppan to perform sorcery! We learned about it only later. We needed a total of thirty-two points to win. Achumman stood with the dice in his hand, staring at the sky.

'Oh God, it's all over. The truth was, Achumman didn't dare play. If they didn't win this round, they'd lose the game. He looked at me and said softly, "What now, Kutta? It's the honour of the village that's at stake." But Achumman wouldn't give up that easily. He turned and asked loudly, "Any of you boys want to try?"'

'Give me the dice, Uncle.'

Kondunni Nair!

Marar and his companions invoked all the gods of the earth, screaming to them to make their opponents lose. The ululations could be heard miles away.

'Why should I worship that slut of a goddess?' Infuriated, Kondunni Nair beat his breast. 'Against whom? The Bhagavathi! My hair stands on end as I say it.' He closed his eyes, said a prayer and threw the dice. A crystal clear twelve!

'His eyes were bloodshot. He was a sight to make you tremble.

'He threw the dice a second time. Twelve again!

'And again. Twice three. Six.

'There you are,' he said and spinning the dice once more, he walked off. The dice stopped rolling only when he reached the gate. Pagida: another clear twelve! Thirty-six in all!

'There'll never be a man like him again,' said Kudallur's leading current champion, Kuttan Nair. They said Kondunni Nair had gone to Kuttippuram and Valancheri to play when he was just twenty-one and defeated the experts there.

There was a washerman from the south who had never been defeated in a game. He would play only in front of his ancestors' shrine. Everyone who had challenged him had lost. One *Avittam* day, the day after Onam, Achan set out to play with him. Appu Panikker went along with him. Even now, there was not a day when Appu Panikker didn't talk about it. They began to play early morning one day and it was on the third day that Achan won a round. The washerman tried every trick he knew. The dice stopped spinning only on the evening of the fourth day. The crowd watching the game was so dense that if you threw a speck of sand, it would not have reached the ground. When Achan got up, victorious, the washerman joined his palms and said, '*Adiyan* will never play with you again.'

He gifted Achan a pair of bell-metal dice weighing four pounds. The young men of today would never be able to hold or spin them. It was with these dice that Achan defeated the Panikkers of Kanoth.

There were so many stories like this about his father.

Most of the young people in the village used to be Achan's admiring followers. He was popular with everyone. It was only after his marriage that many of them abandoned him. Because, they said, he had insulted Amma's tharavad. Many people detested Achan for having insulted the Vadakkeppat tharavad.

Achan's tharavad was not a greatly respected one, the reason being that three or four generations ago, one of the women had gone astray. To make things worse, Achan kept company with people of all castes. He drank tea in teashops run by *mapillas*. Drinking tea was considered wrong in itself in those days. And Hindus certainly did not drink tea made by mapillas, that was an even bigger wrong. As for playing pagida, the Vadakkeppat people saw it as a crime. To make things worse, Achan always drank toddy before he played. A girl from the Vadakkeppat tharavad could certainly not be married to such a man.

Amma had a brother who had died. If he had lived, Appunni would have called him Madhava Ammaaman—Madhava Uncle. He and Achan had been great friends.

It happened on a day when Valia Ammaaman, the seniormost uncle and Madhava Ammaaman's elder brother, was not at home. No one used the *pathayappura* in those days. At dusk, Madhava Ammaaman and Achan were seated upstairs in the pathayappura, talking. They did not realize how late it was. They were startled to hear Valia Ammaaman's voice in the front veranda.

'Who's that, Madhava?'

It was Achan who answered. 'Kondunni of Thazhathethu.'

'What business do men who do not belong to this tharavad have here after dark?'

Achan said respectfully, 'I was not in the northern wing, in the women's quarters. I came here to talk to one of the men in the family.'

Valia Ammaaman paced up and down furiously. 'You should have sat in the front veranda, finished your business, and left. The men of Thazhathethu have not risen so high that they can enter the Vadakkeppat pathayappura.'

Achan controlled himself. 'I did not come here in secret. If Kondunni wants a girl from here, he knows how to get her.'

Valia Ammaaman lunged forward and made a sign ordering him out, 'Phoo!'

Achan cleared his throat, spat and exclaimed, 'A fine tharavad, indeed!'

It was Muthaachi who had described all this to Appunni.

Someone had been standing behind the wooden bars above the ledge in the *thekkini* watching the scene—Amma.

Amma had been of marriageable age then. She was the younger niece of the Vadakkeppat family's seniormost male member, the *karanavar*. The family had decided to celebrate her wedding on a grand scale. The *sambandam* partner chosen for her lived twelve miles away and belonged to a prestigious tharavad, owning vast lands and fields. The wedding *pandal* that was put up covered the entire courtyard. The

members of every Nair house from Poomanthodu to Kaithakkadu had
been invited. Brahmin cooks had been brought from Kodikunnathu to
prepare the feast.

But the wedding did not take place.

It was only when the bridegroom's people arrived at the gate that
the women of the house discovered that the bride was missing.

'What happened, Muthaachi?' asked Appunni, his heart
throbbing wildly.

'Kondunni stole Parukutty and took her away, that's what happened.'

Appunni had heard the story of how Ravanan had seized Sita and
taken her away in his aircraft, the *pushpaka vimanam*. Ravanan was an
evil man, it was wicked to have stolen Sri Raman's wife.

Then he thought of how Arjunan had stolen Subhadra. Arjunan
was a great warrior. There was no archer who could defeat him.
The story was in his Malayalam textbook. Arjunan had gone to Sri
Krishnan's household in the guise of a *sanyasi* and made off with
Subhadra. Clever fellow! The Yadavas who tried to attack him could
not even touch him!

Whenever they came to the part in the story where Subhadra was
lifted into the chariot, Appunni would remember the way hunchback
Chathu Nair described his father carrying his mother away.

Only Chathu Nair had the right to describe it. 'I saw it happen,
folks. A man like that will never be born again,' he'd say.

'It was the monsoon season and even the water in the fields had
risen chest-high. Leeches lay thick on the ground. When he came to
the water, he lifted her up in his arms as if she were a sliver of broomstick
and walked right across.' Hunchback Chathu Nair had been just behind,
carrying a hurricane lamp. 'What, if they follow you?' he asked.

He turned and looked at Chathu Nair. 'I'm a man, Chathu. Once a
man is born, he can die only once.'

When Muthaachi told him these stories, Appunni would often think
of Thacholi Chandu and Komappan. Of legends he had heard as a child
of how they had fought and won battles ...

'But God did not will her to be happy.' Muthaachi would say at
the end.

They stayed in the Kothalangattethu family's outhouse for a day. Then Achan bought some land that belonged to the illam, at the edge of the fields. It was bare and he built a house on it.

In two or three years he turned it into a garden.

Amma's family performed her funeral rites and tried to forget the incident that had shattered their family prestige.

The story of how Kondunni Nair had stolen his bride and run away had been a topic of conversation in the village for days.

By the time Appunni was three, Kondunni had taken all the land on the banks of the river on lease. Syedalikutty and he became partners and planted tapioca on the land together.

'They planted tapioca all the way from the Nambram mosque to the northern bank of the river,' Muthaachi told him.

'Any fool would have paid a thousand rupees for it, the tapioca was of such fine quality. Traders from Pallippuram bought the entire crop. And gave them an advance against the next year's crop as well.'

That night, Syedalikutty invited Appunni's father to dinner.

Appunni suddenly had a doubt: 'Do we Nairs eat the rice that mapillas cook, Muthaachi?'

'Remember, it was your father!'

They had *pathiris* and mutton curry. The mutton tasted off.

'It's because it's the flesh of an old goat,' Syedalikutty explained. Syedalikutty's house was beyond the Muthalimkunnath mosque. Achan started to walk back home after dinner. But in a little while his stomach began to hurt. He took two steps forward and threw up. He clutched his stomach, feeling weak, took another two steps, collapsed and fell.

——Tears misted Appunni's eyes.

Chandu of Valia Valappu came that way on his way home after having sold vegetables in the Kumbidi market.

'Who's that?'

'Chandu, it's me.'

'Ayyo, what's happened to you?'

'Syedalikutty played me dirty, Chandu.'

——Appunni's eyes overflowed.

Chandu heaved him up and helped him home. Amma was waiting with a lighted lamp. Appunni had fallen asleep.

'He called out "Parutty" just once, then fell down. By the time people gathered—what's the point of talking about all that, child, good fortune was not in her destiny. Not in her destiny.'

—Appunni sobbed loudly.

The villagers spoke of that death in lowered voices. There was talk about the police coming, cutting up the body and examining it. But that did not happen.

'That was because Athunni Moyalali paid money to hush up the case, didn't you know?' said Muthaachi.

Appunni silently added another name to the list of his enemies. Athunni Mudalali's. He learned later though, that he was dead. Good, he thought.

They said his father had been poisoned. The poison had been added to the meat. The *parayas* usually had stocks of poison. Parayas were to be feared. They knew how to use sorcery to kill. And they had stocks of poison as well.

Muthaachi often used to tell him, 'You belong to a great tharavad, child.'

He would repeat this to himself many times. A tharavad that had once harvested ten thousand *paras* of paddy! But that was very long ago. Around the period when Muthaachi's second husband began to visit her, the tharavad property had been divided. At the time, there had been sixty-four members in the extended family.

A household with sixty-four members!

Muthaachi told him that the house had had two naalukettus at that time. More than half the building had been pulled down later. The naalukettu where the Bhagavathi resided still existed. And the pathayappura and outhouse as well. Muthaachi used to visit the place once every two or three months.

'A tharavad that used to radiate prestige! Even now, I tremble when I enter the courtyard.'

Amma left for the illam every day after serving him his morning kanji. If Muthaachi was around when she left, she was sure to say,

'What a terrible fate for a girl who grew up in the Vadakkeppat naalukettu—to have to pound rice for a living! Unless destiny draws a line of good fortune on your forehead ...'

He had heard many, many times of the Vadakkeppat naalukettu where Amma had grown up. Muthaachi spoke of it often, even in Amma's hearing. Amina Umma and Kochi spoke about it as well. Amma would wipe her eyes furtively.

'Kunhikaliyamma's younger daughter she was. Not allowed to sit on the ground lest ants bite her nor allowed to touch anyone's head lest lice get in her hair! That's how they brought her up. A hundred paras of rice were cooked for her coming-of-age feast!'

That's how his mother had grown up. And now ...

She would have had her bath and cooked the kanji by the time he got up in the morning. Before she left for work, she would pull up a low stool for him, serve out his kanji in a bowl and chutney on a piece of banana leaf, leave his evening meal covered in the hanging uri and lay out the shirt and shorts he would wear to school.

Amma did not like him to go with her to the illam. He did accompany her one day, however, when he was about eight. He still remembered the occasion. It was a huge illam. Amma's tasks were to dry and pound the paddy. Kunhathol would call out, the big, shining golden *chittu*s hanging from her earlobes swaying to and fro: 'Paru, fold up that mat.'

Or: 'Bring me some paddy husk from the pounding shed.'

Amma usually went in by the back gate, which opened directly onto the kitchen yard.

The day he went with Amma, Kunhathol asked, 'Paru, is this brat yours?'

He did not like either word. Amma's name was Parukutty, not Paru. And it was him she was referring to as 'brat'. Brat, indeed!

He hovered around the pounding shed. Amma had a lot of work. A Namboodiri boy was playing under the *mandaram* tree in front. He wore a *konakam* made of palm spathe, slender gold bands that tinkled on his ankles, and a gold ring on a thread around his neck. His hair was knotted in a little bun over his head. He was the son of the senior Namboodiri, the one who was always seated on the wooden ledge in the front veranda with his legs spread out, chewing betel leaves and spitting out the juice. Appunni saw his younger brother as well, the one whose lips were twisted to one side all the time. Appunni had thought at first that he was smiling at him, he had realized only later that his lips were shaped like that.

The Namboodiri men had lunch first. Valia Kunhathol, Cheria
Kunhathol, and the children ate after that. Then Kunhathol called
out loudly,

'Eh, you—you girl!'

She was calling his mother.

Two used banana leaves were at the door, one on top of the other.
Amma gathered them up in her hands and took them to the pounding
shed. There were heaps of leftover rice in both. And mango seeds that
had been sucked dry, and vegetables.

He felt nauseous.

'I don't want anything.'

'Aren't you hungry?'

'I don't want this,' he said, holding his tears back. Amma threw
the leaves on the floor, bent down and hugged him tight. 'It's Amma's
fate, child ...'

He felt her hot tears on his head. He never went with her to the
illam again.

Amma would come back in the evening with some rice grains in a
winnowing tray. Her body would be covered with dust and paddy husk.
After it turned dark, she and Appunni would go to the well for a bath.

The big temple tank was just beyond the illam. Its northern end
was full of rock clusters and hollows. He had heard that crocodiles laid
their eggs and nurtured their young in the hollows. There was a new
bathing ghat with steps at the southern end. The words, 'Donated by
Keshavan Namboodiripad' were carved on the stone. Appunni met many
of his classmates when he went to bathe there. They would swim, glide
under the water, immerse themselves in it. Amma did not like to go to
the tank though. Once she left the house, she went straight to the
northern courtyard of the illam, then back home. That was her routine.

At night, Amma always fell asleep quickly. But if he even moved
slightly, she would wake up and ask, 'What is it, Appunni?'

When he was a small child, she used to sing him to sleep, tapping
his waist to the rhythm of the song. There was a song about cloud-black
Krishnan and the gopis grazing their cattle. And another one about Sri
Krishnan eating fine rice and a curry made with *lantha* seeds.

On the days when he could not sleep, he would hear dice whirling through the darkness and see a burly man wading through swirling breast-high water, carrying a girl on his shoulders … and his eyes would close slowly to the sound of spinning dice.

The heavy dice stood upright on the sand and then spun, faster, faster …

Lips stained red with betel juice …

Did dead people come down from heaven at night …?

It was when school closed after the exams that Appunni found it hard to while away his time. Forty-five days. He had to get through the days and nights somehow.

Once Amma left, he was alone. He did not want to go to the illam.

Forty-five days. He gathered forty-five pebbles and put them on a tin plate. The first thing he did every morning was to throw one away.

He hung around the gate of the Kundungal house, under the kumkumam tree. If Kesu came out, they could make a ball out of coconut fibre and play with it.

But Kesu was not to be seen. Playing in the sunlight made him wheeze. His mother had forbidden him to play outside. And warned him not to play with all sorts of children. Appunni knew this, so he did not want to go in and call him.

Kesu was an only child. The Kundungal family had just come into money. One of the uncles used to work as a servant in Valia Veedu in the old days. He had gradually risen to the position of the *karyasthan* of the household. He established a sambandam with a servant woman in Valia Veedu. His paddy fields began to yield good grain. And he began to make money.

Now Kesu's mother's neck was covered with jewels. Her only tasks were to bathe Kesu, dry his hair, and rub medicinal powder into his scalp, to prevent him wheezing. When she was not thus occupied, she grew *kannikoorka*s around the base of the well, since the juice of this root vegetable was considered a good remedy for wheezing.

Was Kesu somewhere outside?

Appunni lingered for a while, gathering fallen kumkumam flowers, sniffing them and tearing them in four.

School would start after forty-five days. He was certain he would pass. He could collect his certificate then and go to the big school in Trithala. It was quite far away. If he had a lunch box with a handle, he could carry lunch to school. When the hawker of bell-metal vessels went that way, Amma had asked him what one cost. Five and a half rupees. She had said no and sent him away. He had not asked why she had not bought it. Where would she find five and a half rupees?

If only Amina Umma's chit fund would mature soon. Twenty people contributed a rupee a month. Biddings had already taken place eight or nine times. Amma kept saying they'd have a respite once it matured.

The bidding took place on the first of every month. All of them gathered at Amina Umma's in the evening. Amma had given her contribution in Appunni's name and he was always the first to arrive. The names were written on scraps of palm leaves, put into a pot and shaken up. Amina Umma's younger son would pick one out. Each time, he thought they would say, 'Appunni, son of Parukutty Amma.' But it would be some other name—Kalathilpadi Kandankali or Veerankutty Veedaru Kunhiruthu Umma. His own name had never been called.

He heard the tap of a bamboo stick in the lane. Was it Muthaachi? Yes, it was. She was dragging herself along with the help of the stick. She moved like a boat pushed by oars. Muthaachi hadn't been in her hut the last three or four days.

'Muthaachi—'

She drifted along like a boat, pretending she had not heard him, stopped without warning near him, aimed the stick at his head, then banged it on the ground. She laughed loudly, baring her solitary worn front tooth.

'I thought you were a calf!' Muthaachi always made this joke.

Appunni felt her bundle and said, 'You seem to have made a big haul, Muthaachi.'

'What haul, Appunni? My legs can't keep up with my eyes. What are you doing standing here in the hot sun?'

He walked along with Muthaachi. She opened the door of her hut, put down her bundle, leaned her stick in a corner and said,

'I'm tired, child. I can't go around the villages anymore like I used to.'

'How old are you, Muthaachi?'

'Very old, child. I wasn't born yesterday, you know. Your Muthaachi's been to Colomboshingapore and all.'

Muthaachi always pronounced Colomboshingapore as one word. She had actually been to Colombo and always mentioned it to everyone she met.

There were only two women in Kudallur who had boarded a ship. One was Ammalu Amma who lived in the new two-storeyed house on the hill. Her husband used to work in Colombo. Muthaachi had gone with Ammalu Amma to help her with the housework. She hadn't been this old at that time.

'I stayed in Colombo, two years. So much food! I used to get so tired of making and eating *dosais*, I'd give them away to the crows. And to Kannamma, the Tamil girl who lived next door.'

Appunni had heard a great deal about this Kannamma. It seemed she had been bought!

Appunni would forget everything else when he sat and listened to Muthaachi describe how she had thrown up on the ship, how she had taught Kannamma Malayalam, how she had fought with a 'Shingalathi', a Sinhala woman ...

Appunni climbed up on the rope cot. 'Where did you go this time, Muthaachi?'

'Nowhere child. I landed up at Vadakkeppat. They had a Bhuvaneshwari pooja there the day before yesterday. And yesterday, they conducted a *kalampattu* ritual at the Vazhavil temple.'

A Bhuvaneshwari pooja one day and a kalampattu song offering the next. What fun it must have been for the children. Bhaskaran, Krishnankutty, Thangam, he knew only the names. He had picked them up from Muthaachi's chatter. He had not seen any of them. Two uncles, Valia Ammaaman and Kutta Ammaaman; two Valiammas, both of them his mother's elder sisters. And his mother's mother, Ammamma. Which of the children were younger to him, which older? He did not know.

'What all do they have for the Bhuvaneshwari pooja, Muthaachi?'

Muthaachi intoned as if it were a song: 'Beaten rice, puffed rice, jaggery, coconuts, sweet *karolappams*, and *tanneeramritus...*'

Appunni's mouth began to water.

'And chicken as well. I've brought you something, Appu.'

She opened her bundle and took out two small sweet *appams*. Amma did not know that Muthaachi sometimes brought him things to eat. She would not approve.

Amma always said: 'Her bundle is full of rancid things.'

Sweet appams with the flavour of ghee. The burnt bits tasted the best.

The Vadakkeppat children must have eaten a lot of them. He suddenly remembered that he was one of them. It was his tharavad.

'Is it very far, Muthaachi?'

'To Colombo?'

'No, to Vadakkeppat.'

Muthaachi described the route. It was easy. He had to take the lane after the illam, go up and down two hills, and he would be at the back gate of Vadakkeppat. But that was not the way Muthaachi usually took. She found it difficult to climb hills. She took the long route across the fields and arrived at the gatehouse at the entrance.

'Is it a big house, Muthaachi?'

'Yes, a naalukettu, four wings built around a central four-pillared quadrangle. It was constructed many years ago. The prestige it had in the days when I was a child! Three outhouses. There was an eight-pillared hall in the house and two sunken courtyards. But those days are gone ...'

Would he never see the house?

'When are you going there next, Muthaachi?'

'Next week. A *thullal* is going to be held there.'

Appunni did not know what a thullal was. Was it Ottam Thullal? He had seen that at school.

'No, you silly boy, a serpent thullal. It's seventeen years since they've conducted one. They have three serpents there, so it will last at least three days.'

So it was a serpent thullal then. They were held only in houses where there were serpent-shrines.

'They've sent messengers out to invite people. It's going to be a grand affair.'

To invite whom? Relatives from far away and family members who had left after the property had been divided. There would be kanji and *puzhukku* for lunch. The feast would be held in the evening, just before it grew dark. They would start the thullal at dusk and it would go on until well past midnight.

'The Maniyoor children will come, so will the children from across the river. Unnichiri and her family have been ready to start ever since they heard about it. It's Kunhiraman who's gone today to invite them.'

They would all come: those who had taken their shares of the property and gone away, relatives, everyone who lived in the neighbourhood.

But his mother would not be invited.

No one would invite him either.

Why did they have to invite him? Only people who belonged to other houses had to be invited. Did he have to be invited to his own house? But Amma had said he could not go there. 'I won't cross that threshold, child, I'd rather starve to death.'

They were having a serpent thullal there. He might never see one again, it was held so rarely. What if he went along?

'Shall I come with you, Muthaachi?'

'Appu, what are you saying?'

Digging her elbow into her knee, Muthaachi heaved herself up. Her faded eyes were fixed on him in astonishment. She thought for a minute, then said,

'Your mother will never allow it, child.'

'I'll speak to Amma.'

'Don't ask for trouble, child, just stay here,' said Muthaachi, as affectionately as ever.

'I'm going to ask Amma.' He opened the door and went out. Muthaachi called out,

'Appu, come here.'

He walked on without turning back. 'It's my house, isn't it? Why can't I go?'

He thought of it constantly, while walking around or having a bath, or eating. But how would he ask Amma? She would never consent, never. Still, he had to try.

'Amme!'

Amma was just falling asleep.

'What is it?'

'Nothing.'

He lay still, his heart thudding. He closed his eyes tight but sleep would not come. He tossed and turned, then crept closer to Amma.

'What is it, Appunni?'

'Are you asleep, Amme?'

'No. Why?'

'Nothing.'

He hesitated again, then plucked up courage and said, 'Amme, it seems they're having a thullal there.'

'Where?'

'There, at our place.'

He sensed that Amma was suddenly wide awake.

'So why must you lose your sleep over that?'

He did not say anything more. He lay quiet, fighting his sobs.

In the morning, he went to Muthaachi again. Muthaachi, you must tell Amma, you must get her to agree. Muthaachi gave him more advice. Don't harbour such foolish ideas. When she saw he was on the verge of tears, Muthaachi gave in and said she'd try.

While Muthaachi spoke to Amma, he wandered around the courtyard as if he knew nothing. He threw a handful of gravel into the bamboo thicket and listened in delight to the sound it made as it fell. He aimed a stone at the crow pheasant hiding in the bushes in Amina Umma's compound.

Once he was sure that Muthaachi would have finished speaking to Amma, he went back. Muthaachi had left. He crept in very quietly. Amma was standing at the kitchen door. He saw tears in her eyes.

She wiped her eyes and said with a catch in her voice, 'Appunni ...'

He crept up to her.

'You mustn't be obstinate like this, little one.'

He felt very sad, not angry.

'You're not destined for things like that. Your father and mother didn't perform the good deeds they should have in their past lives.'

He dabbed at his eyes.

'Why do you want to go there, son?'

He lost all control then and wept loudly.

'Don't cry, Appunni.' Holding him close, Amma gazed out for a long time.

And then, unexpectedly, he heard her say, 'Go if you want, son.'

He suddenly wished he could tell her he did not want to go.

Amma murmured to herself, 'He's a child, after all. Naturally he'll want to go.'

Appunni was still dazed.

'You've got as much right there as the others. So go along.' Her voice was firmer than usual.

He wiped his eyes, extracted himself from Amma's grasp and ran to Muthaachi's hut.

Parukutty had finished her work and was waiting for permission to leave. Kunhathol suddenly found some more work for her to do.

'Paru, split these sticks of firewood.'

Kunhathol threw a big heap of firewood into the yard through the kitchen door. Parukutty fetched the axe from the pounding shed. The firewood was very dry. It flew in all directions when she began to split it.

Kunhathol chose a moment while she was struggling with the wood to ask her about her domestic affairs:

'Who's there to keep you company at night, Paru?'

She wanted to say, God. Instead, she answered,

'There's just adiyan and the boy.'

'Aren't there relatives on Kondu's side?'

'They sold whatever they had here and left the village long ago.'

'Kondu's mother's elder sister had a son.'

'He went off when he was quite young.'

'What about your people?'

She aimed such a forceful blow at a stick of firewood that the axe slipped and fell on the ground.

Kunhathol saw what had happened. 'Ai, ai, you'll damage the blade of the axe now.'

She pressed down the stick of firewood with her left foot in an effort to split it and succeeded. There were four more. Once she finished, she could leave.

It was then that the accident took place. The blade slipped out of the handle and swung out. She felt a sharp stab of pain on her big toe.

'Amme ...!' She slumped on the ground. She glanced down and saw the blood spurting from her big toe, red as hibiscus. She didn't look a second time.

Kunhathol's voice came from the kitchen:

'Did you injure your foot? And at this time of dusk ... what happened, Paru?'

'Oh ... h ... it was nothing ...'

She crept slowly to the parapet of the grinding shed and sat down. She felt very weak. Her eyes kept misting over.

Parukutty heard a rough voice. 'What happened?' She did not raise her head to look. Cold water splashed over her foot. When she opened her eyes, she saw two dark, rough hands holding her foot. The man bandaged it tightly with a piece of cloth and said:

'It's alright, nothing serious.'

'She's always doing things like this—she's so careless!' Kunhathol said from the kitchen. Her tone sounded as if she thought Paru had deliberately hurt her foot with the axe.

Sankaran Nair said: 'It's bound to happen when you're not used to this kind of work ...'

He put the blade back into the handle, struck it against the front steps to fix it firmly and walked away as if nothing had happened.

Parukutty got up. Her tightly bandaged foot hurt when she moved. Doesn't matter, she thought. She had been so frightened when it happened.

She gathered the twigs lying scattered in the yard one by one in her hand and laid them neatly just beyond the kitchen door. Then she gathered the shavings and heaped them up in the pounding shed. She waited for some time, leaning against the low wall where the grinding stone was kept. She was still feeling confused and scared. What, if the axe had hit her at a spot higher than the toe? She would have lost a leg.

She could not bear to think of a situation in which she might be confined to bed, unable to work. Her constant prayer was that this should never happen until Appunni grew up and could look after his own affairs.

'Kunhathol ...' Kunhathol did not seem to have heard her.

It was growing dark outside. Through the areca-nut trees that soared above the bathing shed, a sliver of the western sky could be seen, red as a flowering *alari* tree. In the distance, darkness seemed to be already settling into the thickness of the trees in Meleparambu. It was dark even by day in the illam compound—the banana and areca-nut trees were so thickly clustered there that even the noonday sun could not penetrate them.

'Kunhathol ...'

'Wait, wait, I'm coming.'

She thought, it is my fate to always stand waiting like this on the northern veranda of the illam, outside the kitchen.

In the days when she lived in her tharavad, it had been her duty to have a bath at dusk and bring a lighted oil lamp to the front veranda. And to place lighted wicks in the serpent-shrine, on the stone step in front of the house and at the four corners of the sunken courtyard of the naalukettu. After which she had to light the small brass lamp filled with ghee and reach out and place it right inside the *machu*, the household shrine, without crossing the threshold. With that, her duties were over.

The children would be saying their prayers at that hour. She would sit leaning back against a pillar on the outer veranda, teasing out the knots in her hair and gazing into the western sky.

That time was so distant now. She took great care not to recall the memories of those lost days.

'Paru!' Kunhathol called out.

There were five nazhis of rice in the circular winnowing tray placed on the kitchen doorstep. She picked up a small palm-leaf basket from the pounding shed, transferred the rice to it and said to the closed door:

'Can adiyan leave?'

'Yes.'

She walked away. It was a relief to know that Sankaran Nair was right behind her. He had to go the same way. Which meant that she did not have to be alone for at least part of the way. She walked ahead and he followed. But they did not speak.

She found it difficult to hold her head high before Sankaran Nair. She had known him in the days when she had lived in her tharavad. He used to come to draw water from the well in their yard. Inferior castes like cherumans and *thiyyas* were not allowed to touch that well. A dark-skinned, rough-looking man with a voice as gruff as his appearance. He looked the same now as he had then. It seemed as if age would never affect his looks.

He had been the karyasthan, the manager, of Valia Veedu for many years. After that he had taken over the affairs of the illam. He had no family of his own. She had heard that he used to have a niece, Nani. The villagers had many stories to tell about her. A threat was often held out to young girls: 'Do you want to be burned like Nani?' Nani had grown up to be headstrong and disobedient. Sankaran Nair had tried relentlessly to reform her. In the end, he had tied her to a pillar, heated the vegetable knife, and held it to her thigh.

Some said she had run away from the village with an Assamese coolie. And others that she had gone with a group that Kandan Maistry had sent to the Anamalais to pick tea.

'Does Appunni go to school?' asked Sankaran Nair suddenly.

'He does.'

When they reached the spot where she had to turn off, he asked again:

'Which class is he in?'

'The eighth. He's ...' she started to say.

'What is it?'

'He's been refusing to eat, saying he wants to go to the tharavad tomorrow for the thullal. What can I do if he won't listen to me?'

'Hmm …'

'God knows what will happen. But what can I do if he cries so hard? I don't have anyone to turn to.'

She had not meant to say all that. It was her anxiety about Appunni that had made her speak.

'There's nothing wrong in going. After all, he too has rights in that house.'

'Make sure your foot doesn't get wet for a couple of days,' he said and walked away, his dark figure dissolving into the darkness like a shadow.

Just as Parukutty entered her gate, Cheeru, the servant woman who did all the outdoor work at Kundungal came up. She said:

'Parukutty Amral?'

'Yes, is that you, Cheeru?'

'Who were you talking to, Amral?'

What a nuisance, why did she want to know?

'Oh that—that was Sankaran Nair.'

Parukutty thought to herself as she went in: now Cheeru has a bit of news to talk about. The bitch!

There were two people in the village whose main occupation was to carry all kinds of gossip from the pettiest scandals to really serious ones to every house. One was Cheeru and the other, Vilakathra Ammalu. But Cheeru could never beat Ammalu at the game.

Appunni was crouched in front of a kerosene lamp, reading with great enjoyment the page of the weekly magazine in which the onions and chillies he had bought at the store had been wrapped. The last few days, ever since he had known he was going for the thullal, he had been full of enthusiasm.

By the time they finished eating, a gale broke out, accompanied by a dull drizzle. The rain was not heavy. But the wind seemed to be spinning through the banana trees in the yard. The palm-leaf screen hanging over the wooden bars in front kept thudding against the wall. Parukutty lay down but did not fall asleep as quickly as usual. Her injured toe throbbed painfully.

The drizzle grew heavier. Parukutty listened to the sound of heavy raindrops drumming on the thatched roof.

Appunni was asleep. She caressed him with her eyes as he lay with his face turned to one side and both hands on his chest. She moved the kerosene lamp out of his reach and blew it out.

Her husband had died when Appunni was three.

That evening, he had dug beds for the vegetable plants, come in and changed his *mundu*, joked about something, laughed loudly and gone out. ... What came back later ...

When she first entered this house, she had been seven months pregnant with Appunni. There had been only a light covering of straw over the roof at the time. It was the month of Meenam. He had told her, he would lay grass mats over the roof before the next month, Medam, began. That night there had been thunder and a sudden shower of rain. It had never rained like that in Meenam again. The raindrops had crashed in through the gaps in the roof and the house had flooded.

They had lighted a kerosene lamp, placed it in a corner of the central room where the water would not fall on it and sat down close to each other beside it. He had stared at her face and into her eyes.

'Parutty!'

He had been the only one who called her that.

'Parutty, what are you thinking about?'

'Nothing.'

'Are you feeling sad?'

She had raised her eyes to his face as if to ask why.

'I know you're not cut out to live such a hard life, Parutty.'

'I've never thought that.'

In reality, she had only just begun to realize how hard life could be.

And the name the villagers had given her had reached her ears: slut! Her family had taken the purificatory baths prescribed after the ritual period of mourning—the baths customarily taken after a death in the family. For her parents, a daughter had died and for her uncles, a niece. She wondered whether her elder sisters had had purificatory baths as well. In which case, for them, their younger sister had died too.

She had been seventeen when she reached out, gripped his hand and came away. It astonished her now to think of how she had found the courage to do it.

She was born in a room on the northern side of the old naalukettu house where her mother said sixty-four people had once lived. She had grown up there. Seated in the downstairs room of the pathayappura along with all the other children, the *ezhuthachan*, their teacher, had taught her the alphabets. The expanse of earth she could see if she stood under the mango tree in the upper yard had comprised her world. She had seen nothing beyond.

In summertime, the water of the bathing tank in their compound would dry up, revealing the bed of sand underneath. They were then allowed to go and bathe in the river. She never went alone. Her elder sisters, Cheria Edathi and Valia Edathi, would be with her, or Kunhukutty from Vadakke Veedu. Kunhukutty was just four months older than she was.

They had to go down the front steps quietly, without making a sound. They went through the gate, crossed three fields, and came to the road. The river ran alongside it. The *kuruthiparambu*, the enclosure where sacrificial offerings were made to the Bhagavathi, was directly opposite the gatehouse and there were steps going down from it to the river. When the women of Vadakkeppat went to bathe there, everyone else would leave. Their seniormost uncle, who had been the head of the family, was dead by then, but his prestige had not yet weakened.

They had to come back through the front veranda after their baths. Sometimes Ammaaman, their uncle, would be walking up and down the yard. They had to go in quietly, their eyes lowered and fixed on their feet. Amma used to tell them: you must walk so gently that the floor does not know you are walking over it.

It was when she went for her bath one evening that she first saw him. A man seated on the stone platform at the turning to the sacrificial enclosure, a towel wound around his head with its edge standing up jauntily. Two people stood below, talking to him. She took a quick look without raising her head too high. Lips stained red with betel juice, red-stone earrings in his ears. She was suddenly reminded of the picture of a prince hanging in Valia Edathi's room. When he said something and laughed, the waves of his laughter seemed to echo along the bank of the river. When she and Kunhukutty came up to the stone platform, the men stopped speaking. Were his eyes on her? She wanted to go quickly past him. But her feet would not move. As they were going down to the river, she turned and looked at him without Kunhukutty noticing. He had got up. He stood tall and straight as a coconut palm, his eyes following her ...

While having a bath, she asked in a studiedly casual tone, hiding her curiosity:

'Who is that, Kunhukutty?'

'Who?'

'The man sitting on the platform.'

'Don't you know, that's Kondunni Nair—the pagida player.'

After that, she saw the king seated on the platform many times when she came to bathe in the river.

One day she went that way alone. Her mother had said: 'You don't have anyone for company. Don't go to the river today. Have a bath in the pond.'

'If I wash my clothes in the pond, they'll be covered with dirt,' she answered quickly and set out. When she crossed the field and came up to the stone platform by the wayside, she lowered her eyes automatically. Were her legs trembling? She snatched her eyes away from the ground and took a quick look—there was no one on the platform. She walked hurriedly to the sacrificial enclosure and caught sight of him at once—he was seated on the roots of the banyan tree.

'Alone?' He was speaking to her! She thought she made a sound of assent. But had her voice been audible?

She saw him again the next day and he called out: 'Parutty!'

She went down to him, her face flushed, her heart throbbing. He said to her, smiling: 'I am from this village too. My name is Kondunni.'

She was amused by the self-introduction. And his air of boldness.

'I know.'

'You know? And you're walking past as if you didn't see me!'

'How can one make conversation on the roadside?'

That was how their acquaintance began.

When her grandmother died, he was among those who came to cut down the firewood needed for the pyre and organize the sixteenth-day funeral ceremonies. Standing behind the railings upstairs, she watched him in the yard, supervising the arrangements.

He was there with them when they were lighting the oil lamps for the *kuruthi* ceremony at the Kodikunnath temple. The young girls had to carry the platters with the lighted lamps from the Vazhavil temple and empty them into the sacrificial enclosure. It was quite a distance. It was the first kuruthi ceremony after the one they had performed during the cholera epidemic. Platters filled with the ritual offerings were brought from all the Nair houses. The platter from Kalathil came first and the one from Valia Veedu right behind. The third was from Vadakkeppat.

That year they had expected riots. During the Shivaratri festival at the Muthalimkunnathu temple, when the sacred *poothan* and *thira* went past the mosque to the accompaniment of drumbeats, the mapillas had rushed out and obstructed them. A fight had broken out and many had been injured.

'Will the mapillas make trouble?' asked the elders. Young girls of marriageable age from all the Nair families would be in the procession, carrying platters. If there was a riot during the *talappoli* ceremony …

It was the young men of the region who conducted the kuruthi ritual and Kondunni was their chief. He visited the houses of all the families who were reluctant to send their girls. 'There won't be any trouble. You have nothing to fear as long as Kondunni is alive.'

The day's rituals for the *pooram* festival were over and the fireworks as well. When the *panchavadyam* percussion ended in the sacrificial enclosure, everyone moved to the Vazhavil temple. The young girls carrying the platters lined up in two rows. Although a line of young men stood guard behind them, the girls were filled with fear.

Parukutty had not really wanted to carry a platter. But her mother had insisted that it was an offering to the gods, that it was not proper to abandon any ritual that concerned Bhagavathi, the Goddess. She was their family deity, she resided in their household shrine. As the *velichappadu*, the dancer of the Goddess, lighted the lamps and moved forward, Parukutty glanced behind her. Cheria Oppa, the younger of her elder brothers, had promised to be there, but it was Kondunni Nair's face that she saw. 'I'm here with you,' his eyes seemed to say. As the crowd increased, they brushed against each other and she felt his breath on her hair. She was hardly aware of reaching the sacrificial enclosure.

After that, there were occasions when they met and talked. Did those occasions occur by themselves? It was perhaps more truthful to say that they were made to occur. He sometimes came to their house as her elder brother, Oppa's friend. Valia Ammaaman did not like his coming there. And that was how the trouble started.

Suddenly, she learned she was to be married. To a man from Maniyoor. He came to her house one day with three other men. They spoke to Valia Ammaaman. Leaves were laid for their lunch in the thekkini. There were two or three old men from the village as well. Cheria Edathi, the younger of her elder sisters, pointed out the young man who was going to marry her from among the men seated for lunch. So she saw him before she was sent to the front veranda with a pot of water so that he could see her.

She took a quick look. He was old and there were disgusting stains that looked like slices of raw yam on his lips and palms. She wept all night but said nothing to anyone. There was no one to speak to anyway. Her mother knew how she felt:

'What can I do? Kunhikrishnan made the decision.'

The man owned forests, hills, farmlands, and had a great deal of private wealth. His first wife had died. He had left the second one. But he was a good man: he provided the children of his second wife money for their expenses. That was the drift of the talk that day ...

She waited for an opportunity to meet Kondunni. Finally, she saw him the day before the wedding. She had gone to offer her grandmother's elder sister betel leaves and receive her blessings, and was on her way back. Valli's daughter, Kuttipennu, was with her.

He was standing in the lane with a careless smile on his betel-juice stained lips, holding onto a branch that he had bent down, his raised leg resting on it. She lost control of herself completely when she saw him and began to weep.

'Parutty ...'

'What is it, Parutty?'

She could not find words to tell him. Hardly conscious of what she was saying, she babbled on and on. He listened. Then asked without any preamble:

'Do you trust me, Parutty?

She could not speak, her heart was too full ...

'I do not have a house with a naalukettu or a granary filled with paddy. But I am a man, strong and capable. Come with me if you have the courage to. I will look after you as long as these hands have strength ...'

His words had more force than his physical presence. She closed her eyes and said softly and clearly:

'I will come.'

He kept his word and cared for her as long as he was alive. And cared for her well. After his wedding—was it really a wedding?—people said he changed completely. He never picked up the pagida dice again. Or got himself dead drunk as he used to. He spent all day and all night working hard on the land.

... The rain had stopped. But the wind still blew in, whistling faintly. It would probably rain again. She could see silent flashes of lightning through the gaps in the palm-leaf screen hanging over the window. There was a touch of cold in the air. She took the towel lying over her pillow and covered Appunni with it, then lay down close to him.

2

The house was full of people by afternoon. There were innumerable women in the thekkini, the *vadikkini*, and the corridors around, and small crying children as well. They were all members of the extended family or close relatives. The front of the house and the veranda teemed with older children, and the yard and pandal with men.

A long shed screened by palm leaves had been put up next to the pandal. The *pulluvas*, the musicians who sing for the serpent thullal, were seated in it. It was Malu's responsibility to get them betel leaves to chew and water to drink whenever they needed either. She was the daughter of the nephew of the head of the tharavad. She liked this sort of work.

Raman was the chief of the pulluvas. His woman was a singer as well.

Once people began to flock into the room beyond the naalukettu, Malu found it difficult to attend to those who were in the pandal and the shed. Someone would hold out a crying child to her and say: 'Here, girl, take this child out and get her to stop crying.'

At first she enjoyed getting each child to stop wailing. Her task did not end there, however. As people crowded in, the number of crying children increased. How could she say she couldn't handle them? When she left home with her father, she had been instructed:

'Do whatever they ask you to do. Be obedient.'

They were all part of the family. Malu did not know many of them. She had to ask and find out. Don't you know, that's Kuzhilthodi Pappi Cheriamma's younger daughter?

And that one must be from Ammukutty Edathi's husband's house, right?

She too had been looking forward eagerly to the thullal. She had only heard of a thullal, had never seen one.

There were two serpent-shrines, one below and one above the hill, and three serpents in all of them together. She had learned their names: Karinagam, Maninagam, and Anjanamaninagam. Karinagam was wicked and belonged to a lower caste. Malu assumed he was like Ayyappan or Chathappan, workmen who belonged to inferior castes. It was because he was wicked that Karinagam had to be appeased during the Shivaratri festival by being given the offerings of milk and banana first, before they were offered to the others. If they were offered first to the serpents in the other shrine, he would come out and pollute the offerings.

Malu had never seen these serpents. Their dwellings were below the *chitrakootam* stone in the serpent-shrine. There were many serpents in each dwelling—children, nieces, nephews and servants. Obviously, it was one of them that they had seen on the front steps a few days earlier. Thangedathi had cried out when she went to place a lighted wick there at dusk: 'Amme, a snake! Cheriamme, a snake!'

Thangedathi had run into the house without placing the wick on the steps.

'Why are you screaming at this hour of dusk, girl?' Ettan's mother scolded her daughter as she rushed up. Malu called Thangedathi's mother 'Ettan's mother'. Thangedathi came back to the front veranda.

'There's a snake there, Amme!'

Ettan's mother went into the thekkini and called loudly:

'Kutta, Meenakshi, Bhaskara—a snake, in the front veranda!'

Malu's father was younger than Ettan's mother. So she called him by name, Kuttan. He came out, so did Bhaskarettan and Krishnankutty. Achamma got up from bed and came out slowly as well.

'Where? Where?'

No snake was to be seen. They searched all over—in the yard, under the front steps, and at the spot where new coconuts had been heaped up. No snake.

Bhaskarettan found fault with his younger sister.

'The girl must have caught sight of a palm leaf and screamed.'

Ettan's mother took her daughter's side.

'Go on with you, she's not one to do such things.'

'I really saw it, Amme.'

Achamma began to interrogate Thangedathi.

'Did you see it, Thangakutty?'

'I saw it very clearly, Ammamme.'

And she swore, so that Achamma would believe her: 'By both my eyes, by Kodikunnath Amma, I swear I saw it.'

'Did it have a hood?'

'It was so small, Ammamme, this tiny.'

'What colour?'

'Black. And it glittered.'

'Ah ...'

Achamma was relieved. She straightened herself and said to all of them: 'Listen, children. Don't hit it or kill it. It's not a snake to be played with. It must be from the serpent-shrine ...'

Valia Ammaaman arrived after a while. Everyone went in. Malu's father withdrew to the eastern veranda. Achamma had been waiting to tell Valia Ammaaman about the snake.

When he was told, Valia Ammaaman said:

'We've been giving them offerings of milk and turmeric. Then how come this happened?'

He paced up and down the yard for a while, then said loudly:

'No one observes ritual purity. Those wretches must have polluted everything!'

He called Malu's father.

'Kutta, on your way back tomorrow from the fields, tell the Embrandiri that a purificatory ritual has to be performed here.'

Malu's father listened. Whatever Valia Ammaaman said, he usually never said anything in reply. That was his way. He obeyed Ammaaman implicitly. You had to be careful when you spoke to Valia Ammaaman. Whether you said no or yes, he would roar in a voice like thunder:

'What yes? What no?'

He would just yell. That was his way.

They said the snake was seen again in many places. On the steps behind the cowshed and under the jackfruit tree by the bathing tank.

Appukutta Panikker came and conducted a *prashnam* ritual to find out what was wrong.

'The serpents are thirsty. They are not satisfied with offerings of milk and turmeric. You have to conduct a serpent thullal.'

And that was how Pulluvan Raman came and calculated a date for the thullal.

Malu could see everything taking place in the pandal if she sat with the children in front. But every now and then Thangedathi, or Meenakshi Edathi, or one or other of the visitors who had come would call her.

She went to Achamma's room as soon as she had a moment to spare. Achamma had found two people to talk to—fit companions for her. One was an old woman with hair as white as cotton wool. Stout, with a sleek, well-oiled body. She had a gold thread around her neck. The second person was a slender old woman with earlobes that hung down to her neck. She had gathered her hair into a tight knot that stood up like a horn over her head. It was she who asked in a quavering voice:

'Do—you—know—me—girl?'

'Does she live here now?' asked the woman with the gold thread.

She learned later that they were Achamma's younger sisters. It was fun to listen to the three of them talk as they sat on the floor with their legs stretched out, their mouths full of betel leaves. They told tales from the past, the time when they had been children. They had all lived in this house then. Malu found it hard to believe that they had once been children.

Then they began to discuss the thullal. They didn't sound as if they were all sisters.

'Do you remember, Echmu? The year Unnichiri particpated in the thullal, she finally placed the cluster of flowers in the upper snake-shrine …'

'Of course, it seems just like yesterday. It was a terrible ordeal.'
All three recalled it. Achamma began to describe it in detail, perhaps
because she really enjoyed talking about it. The sides of the gutters that
had been dug to channel the rainwater gave way in the heavy rains of
mid-Edavam and the chitrakootam stone was washed away. A new stone
was cut and put in place at an auspicious time. It happened on the last
day of the thullal the following year. The men lighted palm-leaf torches
and stood ready on the path to the upper snake-shrine. They had to
catch up with the girl as she went into a trance and ran to place the
cluster of flowers in the shrine. But the young girl seated inside the
sacred kalam drawing did not go their way when she went into a trance.
She disappeared suddenly into the darkness. When people armed with
lamps went looking for her, they found her seated with her head inside
the bamboo thicket on the western boundary of the compound. They
peered into the thicket and caught sight of the chitrakootam stone that
everyone had given up for lost lying three-fourths buried in the ground.

'The power of those snakes!'

'Narayana, Narayana!' Achamma used to participate in the thullal.
Ammini Edathi and Thangedathi were going to take part in it today.
Ammini Edathi was Valia Ammaaman's younger daughter. Ammayi, his
wife, and her children had arrived yesterday.

Valia Ammaaman was pacing up and down the front yard in his
wooden clogs, his mundu fastened over his breast. He kept running his
fingers through the forest of hair on his chest. He was talking to the
people assembled in the pandal and the yard about the old days.

'All Achu Mama had to do was sit down here in the pathayappura
and not a crow in the village would dare to caw!'

A handful of old men listened to him respectfully.

'I remember him. He was like a tiger,' said the Kalathil Kammal,
the man who conducted the serpent thullal. Clad in an unbleached
dhoti, with a sandalwood paste mark on his forehead, and *thulasi* flowers
tucked behind his ear, Vadakkumuri Narayanan Nair, the Kalathil Kammal,
stood apart from everyone so that he would not be polluted by touch.

Valia Ammaaman usually indulged in conversation only if the old
men of the village came to visit him. He would talk about old times
then. The time they had an eight-pillared central hall, three outhouses

for storing grain, sixty-four members in the household, and tiger-like Achu Mama. The story of how the tharavad had been partitioned.

'Now there's plenty of money in the village. There are so many Nairs who are wealthier than us. Still, is there a tharavad which can compare with this one?'

An old man nodded and said: 'That's true. All the others are just upstarts!'

'That fellow the cherumans caught stealing paddy from my farmhouse—he's put up a two-storeyed mansion now. Phoo!'

The old man nodded again.

'Are you listening? It's not money I value. As long as I live, I'll observe all the customs our forefathers used to. How much do you think this thullal will cost?'

'It's sure to be a lot. In times like these ...' said the Kalathil Kammal.

'This is not an ordinary household, after all. We have an auspicious Bhagavathi here with us.'

'That's why it is blest. She's the mother who brought us food.'

Malu moved away quietly from behind the wooden bars into the vadikkini.

Thangedathi and Ammini Edathi were seated there, bathed and ritually pure. Thangedathi always had a superior air. Needless to say, it was more pronounced than ever today. Ammini Edathi looked beautiful, freshly-bathed, with a horizontal sandal paste mark on her forehead, and a round dot of *chandu* inside it. Malu looked at Ammini Edathi enviously. Her skin was the colour of a new plantain shoot and the blue veins on her neck were clearly visible. Her hair, pulled forward over her left shoulder, swished over the ground like writhing black snakes.

The only one of Valia Ammaaman's children who had not come was Kalyani Edathi. She had just had a baby. Her eldest son, Balan, had come with Ammayi.

You had to walk four miles to get to Ammayi's house. Malu had heard that you had to cross a river first and then a canal. Ammayi did not live in her own tharavad. She had a new tiled house of her own and a coconut grove. When Valiamma went there a year ago for Ammini Edathi's coming-of-age ceremony, Malu had gone with her.

Ammini Edathi's glittering *kuzhiminni* necklace was beautiful.

Malu's flat *elassu* locket, threaded on a string around her neck, had been her mother's. It had been removed just before Amma was taken away to be cremated and had been on Malu's neck ever since.

After a long time, Ammini Edathi noticed her. 'When did you come, Malu?'

It was Thangedathi who answered.

'Didn't you know the girl has been here since last year?'

It had been a year since Malu came here. After Amma had died she'd had no peace at home. Cheriamma and her children were there, the house was theirs. Malu's mother had had nothing of her own. Nor had her father been able to give them anything. It was Achamma who had asked her to move here.

'Let Malu stay here. She'll be a help to Meenakshi as well.'

There was a bustle to lay the banana leaves for the meal in the front veranda. The children and women would eat first. Leaves were laid for the children in the front veranda and for the women in the thekkini and vadikkini.

Valia Ammaaman called out:

'Hey Kutta, let everyone inside eat quickly—we have to start before dusk.'

Thangedathi saw Malu standing apart by herself and asked: 'Don't you want to eat, girl?'

Then she turned and said to Ammini:

'She must have hogged kanji and puzhukku at lunchtime. No wonder the girl isn't hungry now!'

They were making fun of her. She felt hurt. She wasn't such a glutton.

'Go and sit down, girl,' scolded Valiamma as she passed by.

She was reluctant to sit down to eat with the children. She wanted to be with the women. If she ate quickly, she could find a good spot from where she could watch the thullal. She saw a leaf just below the wooden ledge and sat down behind it. About twenty children were seated there in two rows.

She would find a place in front of the pandal, near the pillar. The kalam drawing would be right below her then and she would be able to see it clearly.

She ate quickly, got up before they served the second sweet, the *prathaman*, and washed her hands. Hurrying along the eastern veranda, she came upon a boy seated against the wall among stacks of cut banana leaves. He wore red shorts and a faded green shirt.

Malu hesitated for a moment, then went up to him.

'Didn't you eat, child?'

He raised his head and looked at her in astonishment.

'I asked, didn't you eat?'

'No.'

'All the children have eaten.'

'Let them,' he said, his tone aloof. Malu suddenly felt embarrassed.

'Don't you want any food?'

'I didn't come here because I'm starving.'

His scornful, grave air almost made her want to go away. But when he lowered his eyes again to the ground, she asked softly:

'Where are you from, child?'

He stared at the yard and the dry, moss-covered wall as if he had not heard.

'What's your name?'

'Appunni.'

'Where are you from?'

His face reddened. He looked at her angrily. 'I belong here. And what's that to you?'

His anger did not annoy her. She found it amusing. A child of this house, indeed! He was obviously joking.

'I know all the children here.'

She was about to say something more when she noticed that his eyes were full of tears.

'I'm Kondunni Nair's son. I and my mother belong here.'

She didn't ask him any more questions. She suddenly remembered a story Thangedathi had secretly told her. About how her father's sister, whom she had never seen, had been stolen away. So this was Appunni Ettan then ...

The servant women were taking away the used leaves to throw them into the waste pit. Cheruman children were competing with one another there for the leftovers.

Malu sat down. 'Why are you crying?'

He did not say anything.

'Did you come alone?'

'Muthaachi from next door came along too.'

'I saw Muthaachi. It was I who took her betel leaves to chew. But she didn't say anything to me.' She added a comment: 'The old woman never talks about anything except betel leaves and *kalan* curry anyway.'

A faint smile crept to his face.

'Shall we find good seats before the other children sit down?'

He thought that was a good idea.

'By the pillar on the western veranda—that will be a good spot.'

She led the way and he followed.

The sound of the *idiyara*, the earthen pot the pulluvars used to beat time, suddenly rose from the shed. Malu looked at him eagerly and said, 'They'll begin now!'

All four sides of the pandal were decorated with long streamers made of tender banana and mango leaves. The sacred kalam drawing was ready. Rice flour, turmeric root, and a red powder made from a mixture of lime and turmeric powder had been used to draw two fierce serpents with their bodies entwined, and their hoods unfurled.

In the centre of the pandal was another smaller pandal. Its posts were made of banana stem and a piece of red silk was stretched over them. Its floor was fully patterned with a kalam drawing.

'Raman did that himself. He uses a coconut shell to draw the kalam.' Malu showed off her knowledge.

'With a coconut shell?'

'Yes.'

Malu told him how Pulluvan Raman filled coconut shells with varied patterns of perforations on them with a powder, then sprinkled it over an area smeared with black charred paddy husk, and shaped the kalam.

'Light the lamp in the *thanakkalu*, the small *mandapam*,' called out pulluvan Raman, standing at the entrance to the shed.

Twilight was deepening outside. Oil lamps suspended on chains were lighted and hung at all four corners of the pandal, next to the banana stems. And three large brass lamps with seven wicks in each of them began to glow inside the pandal.

'Bring all the things for the puja,' Raman's voice rose again.

Beaten and pounded rice flakes, fine white rice, and thulasi flowers were set out on whole triangular banana leaves.

'Kalathil Kammal ...'

'Oy ...'

A man entered dressed in an unbleached mundu gathered between his legs and tucked into his waist at the back. Malu nudged Appunni and said, 'He's the Kalathil Kammal, he's the one who will perform the puja.'

Pulluvan Raman chanted as if it were a song: 'Wash your face and feet, fix your mind on the serpent gods, put out your right foot, circumambulate the thanakkalu mandapam, then sit on the low stool facing east.' The Kalathil Kammal obeyed.

'Place white rice and coconuts beneath the thanakkalu.'

The Kammal started the puja according to the pulluvan's directions. He prostrated himself, covered the spout of the *kindi* tightly with his palm, and circled the kalam, sprinkling water as he walked.

As the Kalathil Kammal moved to one side of the pandal, the idiyaras echoed together, their sound as startling as an unexpected outburst of midnight thunder at the start of the mid-Edavam monsoon.

The pulluva men and women were seated opposite him. Three idiyaras, three ordinary earthen pots, two veenas. Whenever the idiyara was beaten, its sound drowned that of the pots and the *veenas*.

The woman whom Malu had said was Raman's wife, started the song:

'*With the sacred pulluva pot of Sree Mahadeva ...*'

Appunni did not find the song very interesting. He scrutinized the people seated in the pandal. There was a large group on a grass mat below the platform on which he sat. Four or five young men stood leaning against the wall of the pathayappura. Behind them and on the front veranda were innumerable women, all seated on grass mats.

A tall, fair-skinned, stout man wearing wooden clogs was pacing up and down the yard, holding himself very erect. The moment he heard a sound anywhere, he would look in that direction. There was something frightening about that reddish face.

Appunni asked Malu softly: 'Who's that?'

She lowered her voice and murmured, 'Valia Ammaaman.'

Valia Ammaaman! Appunni's insides churned violently. He did not have the guts to look at that flushed face a second time. This was Valia Ammaaman. It was he ...

Someone extended the wick of the big brass lamp placed near the thanakkalu on the north with a banana spathe. A dark-skinned man, thin and bent. Malu pointed to him and said, 'That's my father.'

What was that to him? Appunni paid no attention.

'You call him Kutta Ammaaman, don't you, Appunni Ettan?'

Valia Ammaaman.

Kutta Ammaaman.

There were so many others. Bhaskaran, Krishnankutty, and the rest would be with the children. Valiamma would be with the women. And then ...

Malu would know, he had only to ask her. Ammamma, Ammayi, their children. His mother had an elder sister too. What was her name? What would he call her?

No, he didn't want to know anything. This was not what he had expected. He had thought he would start playing at once with all the children. And run around inside the house, upstairs, in the pathayappura, pandal, and compound. He had been full of excitement when he came.

He had not even entered through the gatehouse. When they came down the hill into the lane, Muthaachi behind him, he had stopped. He could see the tharavad!

Yes, the naalukettu was huge! Thatched with straw, just as he had imagined it. Walls from which the whitewash had crumbled. Worn, ash-coloured windows with thick bars. The pathayappura was next to the house and had a tiled roof. He could see the outhouse and a part of the dilapidated wall.

This was the naalukettu his mother had lived in, the one where the Bhagavathi resided. He had heard that that was why the building could not be tiled. The naalukettu had been built very, very long ago. They said even Amma's grandmother's grandmother had no idea when it had been built. And then, one of the older uncles in the family had decided to lay a tiled roof over it. But as the original walls were not strong enough to support the tiles, they would have had to be demolished and new ones built. The astrologers who did the prashnam ritual had said that the Bhagavathi would not like this and that the household shrine and the walls should not be disturbed.

And this was that naalukettu ...!

When he entered the yard, Muthaachi said: 'Go and sit with the children.'

He was stunned. Huge yards, hay stacked high around tall poles sunk in the ground, a cowshed in which seven or eight cows were tethered in a row.

He turned and saw Muthaachi disappear onto the northern veranda through the back of the naalukettu. He was alone.

There were a lot of people on the front veranda and in the yard. He realized that no one had noticed him. He sat down on the eastern veranda at a spot where there was no one. He could hear the bustle of women and the cries of children from inside. He saw a few children on the veranda. He looked to see if there was anyone he knew. No, there wasn't. He sat quietly.

What, if someone came and said something to him?

He did not know who would come or what they would say. But he was afraid, all the same.

No one said anything. No one even noticed him. It was then that he began to think he should never have come. No, he should never have come ...

This was the Vadakkeppat tharavad. He belonged to it.

His mother belonged to it.

The house he lived in had only two rooms and a kitchen. The walls were not plastered. At night, pieces of broken brick would fall onto his mat. There were rows and rows of windows above the naalukettu here ... did everyone have a room for themselves then? Even the children?

A bamboo basket hanging from the corner tile of the pathayappura swayed to and fro. He saw a temple pigeon fly in and perch on it. Maybe the basket was the bird's nest and there were eggs and baby birds inside. If he climbed onto the roof of the pathayappura and peered in, he would be able to see.

He should never have come ...

He wanted to cry out, 'I belong here!' He found it unbearable to sit there with no one taking any notice of him or talking to him.

—I belong to Vadakkeppat!

My name is V. Appunni. That was how his name was called out for attendance in class. 'V' stood for Vadakkeppat.

While these thoughts went through his mind, he heard someone call out, 'Let all the children sit down.' Leaves had been laid for them, for the feast.

'Appu, Vasu, Prabha, sit down, all of you.'

'Where's my Kuttishankaran?'

'Nanu, let Kunhikuttan sit with you.' He heard them call out many names. No one called him.

He did not want this feast. He had not come here because he was greedy for food. Anger rose in him. Anger against everyone. He didn't care about this feast at all.

—There had been only one pagida player who could make the dice fall showing the exact numbers he had predicted. His father, Kondunni Nair. And I am Kondunni Nair's son. Achan should have been alive ...

When he thought of his father, Syedalikutty came to mind. With his short hair and round, blood-red eyes. It was he who had ...

Bhagavathi, you must make him pay the price!

It was at that moment that Malu arrived.

... She sat next to him, listening to the pulluva women singing in unison. The idiyaras were keeping time very softly now. The sound of the veenas could be heard apart.

'They're singing Karinagam's song now,' said Malu. 'It's Raman's younger brother who's singing.'

Raman's woman took up the song. As she began to sing, Raman got up. He said something to the Kalathil Kammal and the latter came out of the pandal. He called out in a loud voice that could be heard above the singing:

'Let those who are going to take part in the kalam ritual come.'

All eyes went to the front veranda.

Two young girls stepped into the pandal. They were dressed in lengths of white cloth, narrowly pleated, gathered up between their thighs and tucked into their waist at the back. The girls carried glowing platters filled with rice, lighted wicks, and clusters of areca-palm flowers.

'You can stand at the eastern door and worship,' Raman said to them and they joined their palms accordingly.

'Take the water the Kalathil Kammal gives you and wash your eyes and feet with it.'

'Circumambulate the kalam three times and sit down with your legs crossed facing the serpents' heads.'

They circumambulated and sat down by the serpents' tails.

'Sprinkle rice and flowers, fix your minds on the serpent and make an obeisance.'

'Pick up the cluster of flowers in your hand.'

They held the areca-palm flowers in their hands and gazed at the hoods of the entwined serpents.

Appunni stared at the women, his eyes wide with astonishment. The girl on the left was dark-skinned and slender, with a longish face. He could not see her properly because she was hidden by a pillar. The other girl was slim and beautiful. Her body, which was the colour of the areca-palm flowers she held in her hands, was bare above her waist! His first thought was, ayye! have these women no shame? As he gazed at her, it seemed to him that the flames of the lamps around her were dancing on her breasts. Her eyes were half-closed. You had to look carefully to make out that she was not asleep. As he looked at this girl who wore nothing except the fine pleated cloth below her waist, he felt a sense of delight as keen as the one he always experienced when he took out the gleaming honey hidden inside the petals of a banana flower.

'Who's that?' he asked Malu.

'That's Ammini Edathi, Valiamma's youngest daughter. The other one is Thangedathi.'

He didn't care who the other one was.

The rhythm of the song and the beat of the idiyara gradually waxed faster.

The serpents in the snake-shrine must be waking up from their sleep now, opening out their hoods and beginning to sway ...

He heard the children say softly: 'The stork is coming, the stork ...'

A man with a white cloth over his head and a piece of banana stem folded into his mouth to make a beak leaped into the pandal, making funny noises. He was the stork.

'The stork will make all kinds of funny faces and try his best to make the girls in the kalam laugh. If they laugh, the snakes will not come onto them ...' explained Malu. The stork leaped around for a while, then picked up the coconut placed over the white rice near the thanakkalu on the north in its mouth and went back.

Appunni looked in turn at the entwined serpents in the kalam and the young girl who sat with her eyes fixed on them, glowing as brightly as the flames of the brass lamps. The stone-studded necklace that lay close around her neck scintillated ... the flames writhed and twisted on her bare breasts. ... Gradually, the pandal, the yard, and all the people faded from Appunni's vision. He was in a dense forest. A prince sat on the curved branch of a tall tree that brushed the sky. He had a turban of gold cloth on his head and wore a shining silk tunic. The precious stones that had been sewn here and there on it glittered. His horse was grazing below. The prince had been allowed to come out and see his kingdom. But he had lost his way when he got to the forest at the boundary. The young minister who had accompanied him had disappeared ...

The night had to somehow come to an end ...

And then he saw a serpent gliding towards him, hissing loudly, making the forest quake with fear. A young girl was riding it, seated behind its hood. The diamond pendant on her neck glittered. ... A narrowly pleated white cloth with a gold border covered her from the waist down. Her hair flowed behind her like a churning forest stream. Her eyes were half-closed ...

The thudding of the idiyaras suddenly stopped.

Appunni came back to his surroundings with a start.

The bodies of the girls seated in the sacred kalam began to sway slowly. The flower-clusters in their hands trembled.

The little smooth stones hung on the idiyaras and pots suddenly crashed down and resounded in unison for an instant. The rhythm of the song had changed.

'*Dance, dance, snakes ... accept these offerings ...*'

As the rhythm of the drumbeats and the song mounted, the girls swayed faster. Their hair undulated like black serpents over the kalam ... the slender, fair-skinned form swayed like a tender banana leaf swirling in the wind.

'They won't take their clusters of flowers to the shrine today,' said Malu.

He paid no attention to what she said.

'*Dance and come ... from my shrine ...*'

'*Dance and sway ...*'

'*Dance and sway ...*'

'*Dance ...*'

The sound of the idiyaras grew deafening. Goose pimples broke out on Appunni's body. He wished he could sway and dance as well.

Holding the flower clusters tight in their hands, the girls swayed like serpents and moved over the kalam, still seated. The drawing of the entwined serpents was being erased bit by bit. ... As he watched the young girl twist and turn, he felt that she was changing. The figure swaying and tossing its hair in the kalam was a creature with a serpent's body and a woman's head. A serpent with a woman's head was unfurling its hood and swaying ...

Malu said something again. Appunni did not hear what it was. The pandal and the people in it disappeared once more from before his half-closed eyes.

The serpent with the woman's face was fanning its hood out to dance.

No, this was a girl riding a serpent, the reins thrown around its hood.

He saw it all without opening his eyes. He was not Appunni now, he was a prince. A prince who had set out to inspect his kingdom and lost his way ...

... He opened his eyes only when a cool breeze brushed his body. There was no forest, no serpent. No snake-woman. He was not on top of a tree, he was lying on the edge of a veranda. Outside was the sky, dim as a piece of wet cloth. Layers of mist clung to the banana trees in the distance. Below him, people were asleep in the pandal, lying at angles to and across one another.

Someone opened the front door, raised a lighted lamp for everyone to worship and went in again. He heard a voice inside intone: 'Narayana, Narayana ...' It took him a few moments to realize where he was.

There was a cool breeze. His eyelids felt heavy.

From somewhere in the house a soft voice chanted:

'Born on this earth, a human creature ...'

His eyes closed again.

He woke up again when a cool hand stroked his body. He saw an old woman squatting next to him. Her hair was completely grey. Her body looked as if it was entirely covered with scales. A mundu with a red border was wrapped around her. When he looked into her faded grey eyes, they seemed to be smiling gently. For the moment, his fear receded.

When he attempted to speak, she said, 'Don't be afraid. I'm your Ammamma.' Ammamma! His mother's mother.

'Get up and come in.'

He got up and followed her. He had to jump over some people who were asleep on the veranda to get to the door. He went through the carved front door into the thekkini. The courtyard of the naalukettu was to one side of the thekkini and the wicks of a brass oil lamp glowed at its western end.

Women were lying all over the thekkini. He cast a quick glance at them. Was the serpent-girl he had seen at night among them? He liked the look of the gigantic wooden pillars at the corners of the naalukettu.

The vadikkini was beyond. Its windows were closed. It was very dark inside. He thought there were people asleep on the floor.

They went through the corridor. When they came to the open hall, he saw Malu, the girl he had met the previous day, busy with some work.

Ammamma sat down on a low wooden stool near the window. She sat him down beside her and said: 'I didn't know, my child. The old woman didn't tell me. It was Malu who told me just now.'

She stroked his head and murmured: 'What a fate ...'

She thought for a while, then said, 'My fate as well. What else can one say?'

He had nothing to say. All he knew was a feeling of suffocation in his heart.

'Aren't you going to school?'

'Yes.'

'Which class are you in?'

'The eighth.' He continued proudly: 'When we reopen, I'll join school in Trithala.'

'You must do well. She ... she ...'

Ammamma's throat sounded choked. 'You're all she has.'

A woman came to the door, looked at him, and went away. Then a crowd of women's faces gathered at the door. All eyes were directed at him. The women kept whispering to one another and new faces kept appearing at the door.

A grey-haired woman wearing a *rowka* came up to Ammamma and cleared her throat. She spoke in a low but harsh voice:

'You're bringing trouble on yourself, Amme.'

'What trouble?'

'If Ammaaman knows, he won't let you off.'

Ammamma sounded really angry. 'So what, will he kill me, girl?'

'Fighting him won't do any good. Ammaaman ...'

'Let him swallow me up then! Look Kunjukutty, don't talk as if God doesn't exist.'

'I and my children want to live in peace. That's why I'm telling you ...'

'Listen, girl, this child's mother was also born from my womb.'

'You can tell Ammaaman that, Amme. I don't want to listen to any of it.'

Ammamma did not speak again. She dabbed at her eyes with the cloth on her shoulder. The woman who had argued with her walked away clicking her heels.

There were no more women at the door, only a number of children. They were looking at him in astonishment.

He caught sight of Muthaachi, whom he hadn't seen since the previous afternoon. She came from the kitchen and said to him:

'Appu, shouldn't we go now? I have to take you home before I ...'

It was Ammamma who answered her. 'Old woman, he's not coming now.'

The women looked at each other and muttered again. The woman in the rowka went past them again, clicking her heels, and clearing her throat. She gave a child who stood in her way biting his nails a sharp slap.

'Come here, Malu,' said Ammamma. 'Give Appunni Ettan some *umikkari* powder and water to clean his teeth.'

Muthaachi waited, not sure what to do.

'You can go, old woman. I'll send him back later with one of the cheruman boys.'

Muthaachi left and Appunni went to the yard with Malu. He cleaned his teeth and came back to Ammamma. She was seated on the ground, her chin on her knee, silent and deep in thought, her eyes on the floor. Appunni sat down too.

When someone came to call Ammamma, saying that her kanji had been served, she asked them to serve Appunni as well. Murmurs of protest could be heard from the kitchen.

Kanji, roasted pappadams, coconut chutney. He was too hungry to relish the food.

He had just begun to eat when he saw the women retreat hurriedly into the kitchen and the children scamper fearfully away from the door.

A voice like thunder roared: 'Sister!'

Ammamma dropped her jackfruit-leaf spoon into the bowl and started to pray softly.

'Narayana, Narayana ...'

A man's form filled the door, touching the top.

Valia Ammaaman.

'Sister, who is this boy?'

Ammamma did not move.

'I asked you, who is this boy?'

'This is ... Parukutty's ... son.'

'And who is this Parukutty of yours?'

He thought Ammamma would weep. But she said very quietly:

'I gave birth to that one as well.'

'Phoo! My tharavad is not meant for good-for-nothings. Who served this boy kanji?'

Ammamma stood up. Appunni got up too, trembling. He thought his uncle would kill him at once. He was going to die ... Those fingers were pressing the nape of his neck ... Ammaaman pointed to the door leading to the yard and shouted:

'Get out! If I ever see you here again, I'll break your legs. Out ...!'

He was pushed out forcefully. What would Ammaaman do next?

Appunni did not walk, he ran ...

Falling on his knees on the sharp gravel in the yard, he heard Ammamma say: 'You'll pay for this ... you'll pay ...'

Appunni fled as though he was terrified someone was chasing him.

He just about knew the way home. He was still sobbing as he ran through the lane and came to the slope of the hill.

The sobs turned into hiccups. Wiping his eyes with the end of his shirt, he climbed the slope where ridges had been put up to plant sweet potatoes and reached the top of the hill. The sunlight was mildly hot. He trampled on gravel as he walked.

Appunni sat down, exhausted, on a smooth rock by the side of a dense thicket.

He had been driven out. Like a mangy dog.

The tears he had held in check until then streamed out. Amma had told him from the start not to go there. And yet he had gone. When she got to know ...

He had never thought that anything like this would happen.

To be driven out ... like a mangy dog ...

All the women had seen it happen. So had the children. He had been caught by the neck and pushed ... shameful! His father had been a man to reckon with, even though he had not been rich. No one had ever had the guts to confront him openly. He was the son of that bold Kondunni Nair. And yet, he had run away like a dog when he was driven out.

But he could not have done otherwise. He thought of that man whose form had filled the doorway.

He wished he could go and hide in some deep pit where no one could see him. Or board a train and go away somewhere. He hated everything.

Like a mangy dog ...

Dying would not be shameful. No one could drive him away if he was dead. Or scold him. God would lift him up and take him to the celestial world that lay beyond the sky. There would be no ancient naalukettu buildings, no Valia Ammaamans, in heaven ...

He heard a sound behind him. He turned. God! He almost collapsed. Who was it who stood behind him? With bloodshot eyes and stubbly hair.

Syedalikutty himself. He had given Achan poisoned meat and killed him. Was he in search of poison now? How was Syedalikutty going to kill him?

He looked with fear and repulsion at those short, stocky fingers.

'Why are you crying?' The man was not shouting. His voice was gentle.

'Why are you sitting here?'

Appunni didn't answer.

'Don't cry, child.'

It was not the voice of a man who was about to kill. Appunni raised his tear-filled eyes to look at the man's face. Those eyes were not

frightening. He saw in those bloodshot eyes the same sadness he had
seen in Ammamma's.

'Aren't you going home?'

He nodded.

'Come along then. I'm going that way too.'

The man walked ahead and Appunni followed. By the time they
descended the hill, Appunni's sobs had quietened.

'What were you doing on top of the hill so early in the morning?'

'Nothing.'

'Where are you coming from?'

'From there ... Vadakkeppat ...'

'Why were you crying?'

No reply.

'Because you lost your way?'

'No ...'

'Did you fall down on the way?'

'No.'

'Then why were you crying?'

'Valia Ammaaman ... he drove ...' He could not go on.

Syedalikutty did not ask him anything more. The two of them walked
along silently for quite a while. Then Syedalikutty said:

'You have as much right to stay in that house as anyone there.'

Syedalikutty laid his hand on Appunni's shoulder as they walked
along. As they passed by the big pit from which stone had been quarried,
an unpleasant memory surfaced in Appunni's mind.

'The edge might give way. Move this side.' They came to the shed
where areca nuts were stored. There were a handful of shops ahead of it.

'Want some tea, Nair-kutty?'

'No.'

'Drink some. It's a Nair who makes the tea.'

He did not refuse. Syedalikutty stooped down to enter a
teashop and Appunni followed shyly. They sat down side by side on
a bench.

Syedalikutty said to the owner: 'Two teas. What's there to eat, Nair?'

'*Puttu* and *kadala*,' said cross-eyed Nair, blowing at the fire through a copper pipe.

'Give the child some. A tea for me, quite strong.'

Thick, cylinder-shaped pieces of puttu and red kadala curry appeared in front of Appunni in a chipped enamel plate.

He no longer thought of the crushed, blood-stained head lying at the bottom of the quarry pit. Or of the meat in which poison had been mixed.

'Who is this child, Syedalikutty?' asked Nair.

'Don't you know—our Kondunni Nair's son.'

'Ah ...'

Teashop-Nair's squint-eyes spun in amazement. Noticing his confusion, Syedalikutty said:

'The child has hiccups. Make the tea quickly, Nair.'

They had their tea. Syedalikutty opened the purse tucked into the green belt around his waist and paid.

They walked away.

When they came to the gate of Appunni's house, Syedalikutty stopped.

'Go along, Nair-kutty.'

Appunni hurried in. Syedalikutty walked off, stroking his head and muttering something about the Creator.

She didn't have to go to work at the illam the next two days. Kunhathol and all the Namboodiris had gone to an illam some distance away for a wedding. Only the senior amma of the illam had stayed behind. Ikkavamma had accompanied them.

Parukutty got up a bit later than usual that morning. Her first thought was that she needed to speak to Sankaran Nair. How could she see him? If he passed by her lane, it would make things easy. Otherwise she would have to send Appunni to fetch him. And Appunni didn't know where he lived, he would have to ask someone the way. The days Sankaran Nair worked at the illam, he usually went this way at dusk to have a bath in the river. Maybe he was at home today, or maybe he was somewhere outside. She knew he was not the kind of person who wandered aimlessly around the village or spent his time visiting people. So most likely he was at home.

She could have spoken to him when she saw him the previous day. But she had put it off. She had not remembered that she did not have to go to work the next day. In any case, she always found it difficult to hold her head up and look straight at him. Had he not seen her as a young girl in the naalukettu of Vadakkeppat?

Her first days at the illam. It still distressed her to think about them. When she pounded paddy in the pounding shed, or sat on the veranda beside the senior amma and gulped down food from a banana leaf someone had already eaten from; when Kunhathol called out to her; when she encountered the other servant women: she had found it unbearable … It was a terrible feeling, as if her clothes were slipping off.

One day, when she was sitting in the pounding shed after her lunch, Kunhathol had called out to her.

'Paru!'

She came out of the shed. 'Go out in front and measure the paddy.'

A tenant farmer had unloaded two cartloads of paddy in the front yard. He had come to give his dues and get a receipt.

The larger para had been placed in the yard. There were two paras at the illam. The larger one which held sixteen measures was used to measure the paddy that the tenant farmers brought. The smaller one, which held only fourteen, was used when paddy was given as a loan.

'Measure out the paddy, woman,' said the senior Namboodiri. All he wore was a short piece of cloth that barely covered his huge stomach. Even if you stood next to him, he always shouted in a voice the whole village could hear.

Picking up the big winnowing tray so that she could gather up the paddy in it and fill the para, she suddenly paled when she caught sight of the man who stood with his head bowed, holding the two circular handles of the para. Sankaran Nair, who used to come to her tharavad to irrigate the fields and help with the thatching of the roof. She felt as if the skin on her body was being ripped off. She composed herself somehow and started to measure out the rice.

She discovered later that he had been coming to work at the illam the last three months. When she met him again that evening as she was leaving, her eyes filled with tears.

He said in his gruff voice: 'These are all God's games, Paruttyamma.'

She had met him after she left her tharavad. But at that time she had still been able to hold her head high. Sankaran Nair had come now and then to her house in the days when Appunni's father was alive. He had been Appunni's father's companion when he went fishing. Sankaran Nair was very good at casting a net. When the fish swam through the river in thick shoals at the beginning of the mid-Edavam monsoon, Sankaran Nair would arrive with a palm-leaf umbrella-hat on his head and a fishing net over his shoulder to fetch Appunni's father. The fish that filled the river in that season were Appunni's father's greatest joy. He had only a small net, enough to catch smaller fish like *paral* and *kurunthala*. They had to use Sankaran Nair's large net if they wanted to catch the bigger varieties like *eentha* and *vala*.

This man has seen me as a young girl in my tharavad and as a wife in my house, she thought. And now he sees me pounding rice in a shed ...!

It's all fate ...!

Appunni had gone to school to collect a certificate.

Parukutty watered the pumpkins Appunni had planted by the side of the well. The bittergourd plant had grown too long, so she propped it up with a branch. Then she loosened her hair and stood under the banana tree for a while, teasing out the tangles. The broken pieces of a mirror that had fallen from Appunni's hand lay under the tree. He was so careless—what, if he trod on them when he ran out into the compound? She started to pick up the pieces to throw them into the bamboo thicket at the boundary.

She glanced at her face in one of the bigger pieces and pushed back the hair that had strayed onto her forehead. Her face looked sunburnt. Long ago, her grandmother used to compare her to a glowing wick. She had been fifteen then. Fifteen, sixteen years had gone by ...

She seldom had an oil bath now. Her hair, dry and dishevelled, was such a nuisance because it would not stay neat unless she smoothed it down with oil. When she was little, her elder sisters used to complain: 'The girl's hair is so heavy, she can hardly bear its weight.' Even now, if she let it loose, it lay thick over her back.

It was after she had thrown the broken bits of mirror into the thicket that she saw the man coming this way from a distance.

Wasn't it Sankaran Nair? Yes, it was. What a bit of luck that he had thought of walking that way, past her house.

When he was on the other side of the fence, she called out:

'Sankaran Nair!'

He saw her through the *kongini* bush. 'Did you call, Paruttyamma?'

'If you're not too busy, could you step in ... there's something I want to tell you.'

He walked back to the gate and came in. She spread the old grass mat for him on the front veranda and stood at the door. He sat there foolishly, his head bent, staring at the black floor and the withered *amara* creeper.

'It's the first time I've come here since Kondunni Nair died.' He spoke without looking up.

Sadness shadowed Parukutty's face. She gulped down a mouthful of saliva and said:

'No one ever comes here now ...'

The minutes hung heavily.

'The garden looks neglected,' he said, gazing out.

'The fence is broken. Everyone's cattle come straying in. There's not a single banana plant left.'

It was Appunni's father who had planted banana saplings on the empty plot of land. No work had been done on the soil after he died. Most of it had gone waste because the soil had not been turned regularly nor the beds set properly apart. The cattle from Kundungal had come in and destroyed whatever remained.

'You must get a fence built. If you grow some bananas, you can make enough money to buy salt and chillies for the household ...'

Parukutty did not reply.

'Where's Appunni?'

'He's gone to school.'

'So school's reopened?'

'It reopens today. He's passed the eighth and has gone to collect his certificate. It's about him I wanted to talk to you.'

'What about him?'

'He wants to join the Trithala school.'

'Um. Once his studies are done and he starts earning a living, he'll be able to look after himself.'

Parukutty ran her nails over the door. And said sadly:

'It's not that I can afford it. But if that's what he wants ...'

'Let him study. God will show you a way to solve everything, Paruttyamme.'

'He has to pay the fees. Four rupees and thirteen annas a month. And they say there'll be other expenses at the time he joins. I've kept apart eight rupees from the money I got from Amina Umma's chit.'

He was sure Parukutty Amma wanted to borrow money from him. He didn't have any. God, what would he do if she asked him? If only he could get Athunni's money today ...

'If you could go and enrol him in school tomorrow ... there's no one I can send along with him ...' She dabbed at her eyes again.

'I'll go, Paruttyamma. Don't grieve,' he said, wiping his face with his towel. 'I don't have much money, but I would do anything I can to help people like you.'

Parukutty looked at him gratefully as if that was all she wanted. With her bent head, her dishevelled hair, and her sorrowful eyes, the woman reminded him of an old picture of Chandramathi standing in the burning ground.

Neither spoke. She was thinking of old times; he was gathering the bits and pieces lying scattered in his mind and trying to put them together. She said as if the thought had suddenly come to her:

'Appunni went there.'

'I heard.'

'He shouldn't have gone.'

'He did nothing wrong in going. Because he's a child, he came away when he was driven out.' Resentment smouldered in him. 'He has as much right there as all the rest of them. They are ...' He blew his nose noisily. 'There's a God. He'll certainly make them pay for all this ...'

He got up. Standing on the steps, he gripped the bamboo pole on the veranda and spat into the yard, then stood for a while, thinking.

'I'll come in the morning. Tell Appunni to be ready.'

'Yes.'

He went down to the yard. Stroking his eyebrows, he said in his gruff voice: 'If there's anything you want, you've only to tell me, Paruttyamme.'

Flicking the towel on his shoulder, he walked off quickly.

The ferryman Athunni had to return the two rupees he had lent him. He was tired of asking him. The previous day, he had caught hold of Athunni on the road. The shameless fellow had been evading him for a few days. He had sworn by the mambram Thangal that he would return the money today. Sankaran Nair had come out expressly to meet him.

But while going back from Parukutty Amma's house, Sankaran Nair forgot about Athunni's two rupees for the moment. His only thought was for the helpless woman who had no one to support her.

She had grown up in such luxury ... the philosophical thought that this was the human condition crossed his mind.

He walked by way of Kaithathodu ... What would become of the boy if something happened to her? If she were to fall ill, the fire in their hearth would stop burning. He kept thinking—she belonged to a tharavad which used to have an income of ten thousand paras of paddy. Now the mother and son were on their own. A woman whose youth was not yet spent, all alone in an insecure little house.

In spite of everything, she was such a gracious woman. She would never lose that graciousness, not even if she had to beg. You could tell that, looking at her.

He knew all about the other woman who worked at the illam. A slut! She was almost forty and still behaved coquettishly. Whenever she called out, 'Changaran Naire!' to him he wanted to give her a kick. Behaving like a sixteen-year-old! She was always hanging around the front veranda, sweeping and cleaning it. And that oaf of a Namboodiri would sit there staring at her.

Rascal! He was a brahmin after all, wasn't he? One would have expected him to behave better. He would instal himself early morning on the wooden ledge of the front veranda, lips twisted and betel leaf

box open, his eyes on the bodies of the women who were folding up
the mats, or winnowing rice. Sankaran Nair had heard that Kayikkolu,
who used to work at the illam long ago, had a child with twisted lips ...

Who had told him that Parukutty Amma was working at the illam?
It had been five or six years ago. He had felt disgusted with her then.
He had thought: she brought shame to her tharavad, now she'll bring
scandal on those Namboodiri men. Then the Valia Namboodiri had
appointed him to take charge of the agricultural affairs of the illam. Once
he met Parukutty Amma there, his opinion had changed. She came every
morning, did whatever work the senior amma of the illam asked her to
do and left. He had watched Parukutty Amma without her being aware
of it. She was quiet and self-effacing. She never stepped into the front
veranda. If someone was sitting there, she would not go that way. She
found it difficult to even look a man in the face and talk to him. She
should never have had to earn a livelihood this way.

She had an evil destiny, the lines on her head boded no good ...

'I have no one to do anything for me ...'

And yet she had a mother, elder sisters, a brother, an uncle. The
Vadakkeppat tharavad was just two miles away. But it amazed him to
think how great a distance those two miles had created between her
and them. They said she had shamed the tharavad!

Appunni had been insulted and sent away. They would pay for it.
What wrong had he done? They claimed to be members of a tharavad!
They had to be human beings first. Members of a tharavad, indeed!

Sankaran Nair cleared his throat and spat out venomously.

'Who are you so angry with, Kammal?[1]'

It was Unniri, coming from Kuttada's shop after his noon session
there. At noon, he couldn't hold much alcohol inside him. So he could
still talk seriously about things and behave with affection and respect
towards Kammals. Unniri became a different person after dusk. He
would demand of anyone walking towards him: 'Who the hell are you?'

'Where to, Unniri?'

---

[1] In south Malabar, members of the Thiyya caste call Nairs 'Kammal'.

'Home. Been ploughing all day, then I had a dip in the river.'

Sankaran Nair suddenly remembered: 'Do you have thorns for fencing, Unniri?'

'Don't you know all my bamboo was destroyed? Still, there might be a few bits and pieces left. You can have them if you want, Kammal.'

'I need four or five bundles. I'll send Appan who works at the illam tomorrow.'

'Then you haven't finished building your fence, Kammal?'

'I have. This is for someone else. Appan will come before evening tomorrow.'

So that was settled then. He didn't have to pay Unniri for the material. If two cherumans worked on it, it would take just a day. He'd have to pay them a wage of two rupees. Right. It was when he thought of the two rupees that he remembered Athunni.

You could never be sure where to find Athunni. He used to be a boatman but he didn't have a boat anymore. He had nothing of his own. Still, he continued to be known as a boatman.

Sankaran Nair went into Esoop's shop. Two people were arguing over prices with an itinerant tailor who sold garments.

Esoop the owner said: 'Look, Nair, he has splendid clothes for women and children. Go on, buy something.'

Sankaran Nair smiled.

Musaliyar stroked his beard and smiled too. 'Why would he need clothes? For a shroud?'

The tailor said the prices they quoted were too low, did up his bundle and went out.

The shop was a refuge for those who had nothing much to do. Ridiculing people, adding innumerable lies to the morsels of news that someone who had gone to the market or the hospital brought back and handing them out again: this was what those who gathered there indulged in.

Once the tailor left, the talk shifted to Appukuttan Nair who had just arrived from Madras. It was rumoured that he had come back with a lot of money. Musaliyar thought he must have stolen it. The man had a watch and a gold ring. And he smoked cigarettes. Those who had met him said he was the manager of some wealthy Chettiar's estate.

'They say he's in a drama troupe.'

'Are you mad? He's with the Chettiar. Want to hear something? These Chettiars will give you anything if they like you. And if they get angry with you, they'll kill you.'

And so the talk moved to the Chettiar diamond merchants of Tamilnadu. Sankaran Nair, who had no interest in diamonds or Chettiars, asked Esoop:

'Have you seen our boatman Athunni?'

'Saw him walking on the road this morning.'

Musaliyar volunteered: 'He must be in our Enuddin's shop. The sly fellow won't come here because he's afraid I'll ask him for money. He owes me four annas as well.'

Sankaran Nair didn't find Athunni in Enuddin's shop. 'Damn that rascal!' he thought as he made his way to the vegetable patch. He had acquired some land by the river when it was auctioned and planted cucumbers and ash-gourds on it. He had harvested the plot twice. He had not watered the plants after the first rains. He borrowed Chandu's wooden bucket, drew water, poured it into the wide, flat palm-leaf receptacle and filled the upper pit. From there, he directed the water towards the beds.

Every year he planted around fifty *nenthran* banana plants. And a few vegetables. He usually made some money on them. Until three years ago, he had leased out some land that belonged to Valia Veedu and farmed it. They said it had once been very fertile soil. Sand had seeped in during the floods in ninety-nine and made it impossible to cultivate. After that, however hard he worked, he could not make more than fivefold the grain sprout—at least tenfold was necessary for a reasonably good crop. Once he gave the owner his share of the crop, it seemed as if the seeds and labour he had put in had gone to waste. In the end, he gave the land back. Which meant that he had to buy straw now, to thatch his house. He made some money whenever he lent the bulls, Kannappan and Mailan, for ploughing. That was a great help.

Sankaran Nair's house was just above Valia Veedu. A flat area between two hills. There were about forty coconut palms. The people of the Thengumpotta tharavad used to conduct *pana*, an offering of music to the Bhagavathi, in the old days. There were reputed experts in the art at the time in the family. Sankaran Nair's grandmother's uncle, Kittashar, had built an ancestors' shrine in the outer compound of the Mankoth illam and settled down there. The people of the illam believed that if Nairs were not asked to kill fowls and conduct a purificatory ceremony in the ancestors' shrine every year, they were sure to experience bad times. Sankaran Nair had wondered why the Namboodiris had allowed Nairs to actually settle on their land. It was Achumman who had explained the reason to him. When Tippu invaded the area, his soldiers had obstructed the Valia Namboodiri as he was running away from Parakkulam Angadi. Kittashar hacked almost 300 soldiers to pieces, then took the Namboodiri to a safe place. And fell dead.

There were three stones on the western side of the house under the kunkumam tree. One was Karinkutty, the second, Kannachan, and the third was the old man, Kittashar. Lighted wicks were placed there even now. In the days when Sankaran Nair's uncle was alive, a pana used to be conducted in the village from time to time. Even that didn't happen now.

'People don't believe in God any more,' said Sankaran Nair.

After he had watered the field, Sankaran Nair went down to the river and had a bath. When he climbed up to the road he heard a hoot in front of Vappu's shop. A fresh catch of fish had arrived. He had a look. They were small *nethila*. It's fish after all, he thought and bought two annas' worth.

As he was about to leave, he heard Achumman call out to him. If he didn't go, the old man would be upset. And if he went, he'd be trapped.

He was Achumman, Uncle Achu, to everyone in the area. His house was very close by, but he stayed in the room above the shop on the roadside. Reading the Ramayana, arranging marriages, and talking about Vedanta to any listener he could find were the main occupations of his old age.

It was dusk by the time Sankaran Nair got back home. Since the house lay in the shadow of the hill, it always grew dark inside by sunset. He placed a lighted wick on the platform under the kumkumam tree, lit the chimney lamp and began to prepare his dinner. He knew how to cook rice and vegetables. After all, he had lived alone for many years. But he was still scared to drain the rice. Most days, he allowed it to cook dry. As the water began to boil, he would grate half a coconut into it.

It was fourteen or fifteen years since he had been on his own. He had a vivid memory of his uncle and his eldest sister. Both had died of cholera. Only he and his niece Nani had survived.

Nani was of no use at all to him in the house. She had not grown up the right way. She was disobedient. During the day she would roam all over the village. She had been like this even as a little child and did not change when she grew up. When he was not at home, she would go wandering off. As time went by, he began to hear unpleasant stories about her.

He warned Nani. Not once, but two or three times: 'If I go on hearing things about you, I'll finish you off!'

But she did not heed his threats. One day, when he caught her red-handed, he lost all control of himself.

He realized only later that he had gone too far——he had tied her to a pillar and branded her.

He wondered if she was alive now. He had heard that she had married someone on a plantation and had children by him. And also that she had caught malaria and died.

He sat watching the flames blazing in the hearth. The water had begun to boil.

He lived alone. The work at the illam was enough for him to live on. Why work so hard then, people had asked him. They were right. What was the point of making money from cultivating vegetables and nenthran bananas?

People would advise him: 'Why don't you get married?'

And he would say, 'After all, I'm almost forty-five now. Let me see if I can continue to manage without a woman and children.'

But what, if he should collapse and fall down one day—there would be no one to hold him up. What would happen once he reached a stage when he could no longer work? Old Muthaachi would come to mind. Going from one stranger's house to the next ... he couldn't bear to think of it. And even that would last only as long as she could walk. After that ... to die like a dog, in some waste pit.

He shuddered to think of it.

There was a time when he had thought of marriage. A time when a girl's figure had filled his thoughts. His uncle and his sister had been alive then. It was Uncle himself who had planted the thought in his mind. And he had clung to it.

But God had not allowed it to happen.

'Why blame God? My destiny was unfortunate ... unfortunate.'

A body that radiated health. He had seen her even at dusk the previous day. In the morning he had heard she was dead! She had thrown up four times, that was all. She had been the first to fall a prey to cholera in that area. Many loved ones had died after that. He became the only survivor in the family. He spent his days working hard. Life stopped flowing and stagnated around him. Bit by bit, sorrow faded from his mind, almost without his being aware of it.

He watched the red tongues of the hearth lick the sides of the earthen pot. It was only as the rice started to boil over that he came back to his surroundings. The water boiled and the froth settled.

He ate, spread his mat on the front veranda and lay down. And remembered the task he had to do in the morning. He had to go to the school, to enrol Appunni there. If he had got married at the right time, he would have had a son as old as Appunni now. A boy who would not have allowed him to toil alone in the fields and the vegetable garden. Who would have learnt his letters and done well for himself ...

What was the point of grieving over the past?

Appunni would do well. He had always thought so when he saw the boy. There was such brightness in his face.

'Amme, Bhagavathi, protect me!'

He lay awake in the dark, his eyes filled with vague images.

The day he was going to join the high school was like a festival day to Appunni.

Sankaran Nair arrived early. But Appunni was ready even before he came. Amma entrusted the money for his fees to him. When he set out, Amma stood in the lane and watched him until he turned the corner, her eyes full of tears.

It was only five miles to the school. Then why was Amma so sad to see him go?

They had to pass by the gate of Vadakkeppat. When they came to the wide lane that led to the gatehouse, he was tempted to steal a glance that side. But he didn't.

It was a large school. In his former school, only the office building was tiled. Here, there were four huge tiled buildings. The name of the school was written in bold, bright letters on an arch at the entrance.

They entered a garden. There had been a garden in the Manamakkavu school as well. But there had not been a single plant that bore flowers. The children had to cultivate ladies' finger and brinjal plants. The masters would pluck the vegetables when they were ready, wrap them up in paper packets, and take them home. A whole period had been set aside for gardening.

The bell had not rung.

The road, the gate, the veranda were all full of children. Among them were children coming here for the first time. He could see that they were as confused as he was. Each one had a guardian with him. He saw a few children from his school.

They waited outside the office room with the other children and their guardians. They had to put down their names and hand them over to the writer who sat at the window. After that they were called in one by one.

He froze with amazement when he entered the Headmaster's room. A table covered with a bluish cloth, glass-fronted cupboards, pictures on the wall, a bell that rang when you pressed it, pretty glass paperweights. A well built man with folds in his neck sat in a huge chair behind the table. The Headmaster.

He looked at Appunni's certificates.

Appunni's name, age, and marks were there.

The Headmaster asked: 'Your father's name?'

'T. Kondunni Nair.' He added, so that there should be no misunderstanding, 'My father is not alive now.'

'Your guardian's name?'

Sankaran Nair thought for a while. Appunni's guardian? Would a woman's name do? What if they required a man? He said, to make sure there was no problem:

'Thengumpotta Sankaran Nair.' He gave his address as well.

Appunni glanced at him, but he pretended not to see.

They went to the writer's window, paid the fees, and took the receipt. Class would start only the next day. They could go.

They went back, relieved. But a doubt hung in Appunni's mind. How could Sankaran Nair be his guardian?

He soon found new friends. Going to school became fun.

Every morning and evening, he had to pass the gate of Vadakkeppat. He would take a quick look when he passed by. There was a thick grove of areca-nut palms at the edge of the fields. He could not see the naalukettu properly through them. Usually, there was no one in the gatehouse. When he went that way in the evening, Valia Ammaaman would walk down on the path that went through the fields in his wooden clogs, his smooth, hairless head held high. From the way he held his head, you would think he shouldered the sky. Appunni's pace would suddenly grow faster. But Ammaaman never once looked at Appunni. So many children walked that way.

The fields had just been harvested. There was a path that went by the side of the Vadakkeppat garden. If he went that way, he could easily reach the road through the tapioca patch on the south of the field. But he never took it.

Two children from Vadakkeppat came to school. Bhaskaran of Class B and Krishnankutty of the Second Form.

The A and B divisions had drill together. It was during this class that Appunni first saw Bhaskaran. He recognized him only when Kuttisankaran told him. Should he speak to Bhaskaran? But Bhaskaran did not speak to him when they stood next to each other at drill or when they met at the spot where everyone went to drink water. Though Bhaskaran had recognized him. Because it was he who told Kuttisankaran.

This was Bhaskaran's second year in the Fourth Form.

Bhaskaran and Krishnankutty came to school in a bullock-cart. A cart drawn by a white bull that had painted horns with blue tassels hanging from the tips and bells threaded around the leather collar on its neck. There was a grass mat inside to sit on. You could hear the cart from quite a distance. It belonged to a mapilla who was paid a monthly rent for it.

Appunni watched them come and go enviously. In a few days he found out that quite a few children in the class were jealous of them. They were the only two children who did not walk to school.

Bhaskaran was sleek and fat. It was obvious from his stance and speech that he thought a great deal of himself.

The cart would be waiting at the gate at four, when they finished school. The cartman was a short, dark-skinned fellow with a green handkerchief tied around his head. Bhaskaran would go down and fling his books into the cart. Then he would say to Krishnankutty: 'Get in, Unni.'

After Krishnankutty got in, Bhaskaran would climb up and sit down with his legs hanging out. He knew that the envious eyes of the children standing at the gate and on the road were upon him.

Muhammad was Appunni's friend. His house was some way beyond Puthan Parambu. He would take a short cut and wait for Appunni near the Yajneswaram temple. Muhammad talked of nothing except the elegant bullock-cart all the time. He wanted to finish his studies, become a merchant, make money, and buy a stylish cart like that, drawn by one bull.

'It's a splendid bull, Maimunni Modalali's bull won't come anywhere near it.'

Sometimes Muhammad would say, 'Why can't that imbecile drive it himself? If it were I ...'

One day when he was fed up of hearing about the splendour of the cart and the bull, Appunni said: 'D'you know, that boy belongs to my house.'

Muhammad said: 'That's a lie. A whopping lie!'

Appunni was annoyed. 'It's the truth. We belong to the same house.'

'Then how is it you don't you come with them?'

Appunni had no answer to that.

'And why do you stay in Puthan Parambu then?'

'We came away.'

'When the property was divided?'

'No, not because of that.'

'Then?'

'Just like that.'

'And why just like that?'

Appunni was upset. He should have kept quiet and listened to the glowing descriptions of the bull.

'A quarrel?'

'Um ...'

Muhammad's questions stopped for the moment.

But it did not end there. Muhammad told someone: 'Bhaskaran who comes in the bullock cart and our Appunni belong to the same house!'

Many children in the class came to hear of this. But the real trouble started when Bhaskaran heard.

Bhaskaran had a gang of his own—Karunakaran, Ranganathan, and some others. They hung around him in the hope that he would take pity on them from time to time and allow them to get into the cart.

So Karunakaran told Bhaskaran. Bhaskaran laughed contemptuously. 'Ha, belongs to my house, indeed! Ask him what happened when he came last year to watch the serpent thullal.'

What happened? Some of them wanted to know. What happened? When they nagged him, Appunni broke down and wept.

Bhaskaran said: 'He'll never enter my house again. Ammaaman drove him away. He'll never do well.'

Appunni heard silently. Bhaskaran—no, he should call him Bhaskarettan. Call him Ettan, elder brother? Never, not in this birth. The oaf!

He was Appunni's mother's elder sister's son. His father was a Namboodiri. His mother had her own house and compound and a manager to look after it.

Appunni wanted to keep as far away from the others as he could. He was the son of the servant woman who worked at the illam. He did not have a large house. Or money. He had just two sets of clothes which he wore alternately. He did not have all the books he needed. Not even a large bound notebook to do his sums.

Lunch had been arranged for Bhaskaran every day at Marar's hotel.

Appunni would have kanji before he went to school in the morning. After that he ate only when he got back home in the evening.

By the third period, the pangs of hunger would grow stronger and stronger. It was then that the vegetables were seasoned and a fragrance would emanate from the kitchen of Marar's hotel, which was just next door to the school. When they were let off at one, he would go to the back of the hotel to drink water and see the rows of banana leaves laid out in the hall for lunch.

Amma had been about to buy him a lunch box with a handle when she got the money from Amina Umma's *kuri*. But he had felt that what he needed more was a shirt and mundu, and Amma had agreed. One of his two shirts had become badly frayed with repeated washing.

One evening, there was to be a performance of Ottam thullal in the yard of the school. Appunni had read the memo saying that everyone had to bring two annas. He had no money. Amma ran around asking the neighbours but met with no success. If Amina Umma had had any money, she would have given them some.

The class master collected the money during the first period. Four children did not give him their contribution, one of them being Appunni.

'You have to bring it this afternoon,' said Nambisan Master, flaring his nostrils and blinking rapidly. Appunni picked up his books and went out.

One of the boys asked him: 'Why are you taking your books? Are you leaving?'

'Yes.'

'Why?'

'I'm not well. I have a headache.'

He went away without telling even Muhammad. When Nambisan Master asked him for money in the afternoon, he would have to stare

at him blankly. All the children in class would look at him mockingly.
At least he would not have to face that.

The afternoon sun was blazing hot. The sand burned like hot coals
as he walked over the path through the field. If he went down and
walked along the edge of the field, there would be some shade. He got
down. As he walked past the fence of Vadakkeppat, he sensed there was
someone in the garden, but did not raise his head to look.

A voice called out: 'Appunni Etta!'

He stopped. It was Malu. She was plucking betel leaves from the
creeper trailing over the areca palms.

'Did class give over early?'

Trying to be friendly, indeed! He was irritated. He grunted.

'I often see you pass by when I stand near the well. It was when
Bhaskarettan told Ettan's mother that I knew.'

He grunted to that as well.

'Achamma always says she wants to see you when you go this way.'

Hadn't she seen him once? Hadn't they all stood watching while he
was driven out? Don't make me say it, girl …

'Valia Ammaaman and Achan have …' She stopped suddenly.

'Who are you chattering to, Malu?'

A girl came walking through the areca-nut palms.

He had wanted to walk off quickly. But when he saw who it was,
he froze.

Ammini Edathi.

The bare-breasted princess who had ridden a serpent …

He looked at her in astonishment. The image of a girl wearing a
narrowly pleated length of cloth around her legs, naked from the waist
up, her hair flying loose, swaying like a snake with its hood spread wide
surfaced clearly in his mind like an ancient dream. She wore a bluish
silk blouse now and an unbleached mundu with a thin border. There
was a little horizontal mark of sandal paste on her forehead. The *kajal*
that rimmed her half-closed eyes flowed out from the corners in a long
straight line.

'Who's this now? Appunni!'

So she knew his name.

He could never have imagined her in the form in which she stood now before him. The glowing, twisting serpent with the face of a beautiful woman.

Whether she laughed or spoke, her eyes were half-closed.

Seeing his astonished look, Ammini asked:

'Why are you looking at me like that? Don't you know me?'

He suddenly thought, yes I know you. The daughter of Valia Ammaaman, who drove me out like a dog! She was three years older than he was, so he had to call her Ammini Edathi.

Resting a foot on a ridge, Ammini Edathi said without opening her moist, smiling lips too wide, 'Even if you don't know me, Appunni, I know you.'

She bent down to pick up a piece of areca nut which had fallen from her hand. Her hair, caught up at the ends in a knot, streamed over her shoulder.

'Give me a tender betel leaf, Malu, if there are any. Let me chew it.'

'I'm going,' said Appunni and walked off.

Ammini Edathi called out: 'Look, Appunni.'

He walked away without turning back.

Amma was at home. He had thought she would be at the illam. And she was not alone. Sankaran Nair was sitting in the outer veranda. Appunni climbed the front steps noisily and Amma moved back behind the door.

'How come you're back so early, Appunni?

He felt irritated with everyone, for no reason. But all he said was, 'I don't know.'

'What's the matter?'

'Nothing.'

He threw his bundle of books into a corner and asked in a loud voice: 'Is there any kanji?'

His strange mood upset his mother. He had never talked to her angrily before. Parukutty served his kanji. He sat down on the ground before she could bring him the low wooden stool.

'Your mundu will get dirty. Get up, let me put this stool in place.'

Once a mouthful of kanji went into him, his unreasonable anger had cooled.

'I don't need a stool,' he said gently.

Amma went to the front veranda.

He heard Sankaran Nair's voice: 'What's wrong with Appunni?'

'I don't know, I was wondering as well. Maybe he was just hungry.'

'I'll see to the other matter. We'll manage without paying a fine.'

A fine: they were obviously talking about his fees. It was time to pay them. Amma must have asked Sankaran Nair for money.

'That will be a great help, Sankaran Nair.'

'I'll try and do whatever I can to help, Paruttyamme.'

Parukutty went in after he left. Appunni was washing his hands.

'Why did you come away so early, Appunni?'

'Nothing, Amma, they said those who wanted to leave early could go.'

He went to the front veranda. He wanted to ask her whether she had gone to work at the illam. But he didn't. He wanted to forget that illam, the Kunhathol there, the Namboodiri with twisted lips. He wanted to forget that his mother worked in their yard and pounding shed. The son of the servant woman at the illam! He could not bear to think of it. He was Kondunni Nair's son. Kondunni Nair, the pagida player who had challenged the whole district in front of the washerman sorcerer's ancestors' shrine and won! Kondunni Nair who had subdued six men all by himself when a fight broke out at Muthaleemkunnu ...

The door of Muthaachi's hut lay open. He realized it was a long time since he had seen Muthaachi. She was seated at the door picking stones from rice spread in a winnowing tray.

'Who's that?'

'It's me, Muthaachi.'

'Pick these stones for me, Appu. Muthaachi's reached a stage where her eyes are useless.'

He took a handful of rice, spread it on the ground, picked up the small pebbles in it, and threw them away.

He no longer had time now to listen to Muthaachi's stories. He had to go off quite early in the morning. He came back late in the evening.

And on Saturdays and Sundays, when he was free, Muthaachi was often not home.

'Who was at your house now, Appu?'

'That Sankaran Nair.'

'What did he want?'

'I don't know, I've just come back.'

'He's a good man, Thengumpotta Sankaran,' said Muthaachi. But she didn't stop with that. 'Still ...'

'What is it, Muthaachi?'

'Nothing.'

When he had picked out all the stones and was leaving, she said: 'People don't need much of a reason to start saying things ...'

What were people saying?

Bending down, he picked up a stone, flung it forcefully into the bamboo thicket, and walked towards the kumkumam tree at the Kundungal gate.

3

All the work in the Vadakkeppat kitchen was done by Meenakshi. Malu's role was to help Meenakshi Edathi, who was Achamma's second daughter.

Meenakshi Edathi was not like Ettan's mother, she did not make Malu work too hard. Which was why Malu liked her. Meenakshi Edathi had no children and it was said that she would never bear one. Achuthan Nair was Meenakshi Edathi's husband. Malu called him Cheriachan, although he was not her father's younger brother and that was not really how she should have addressed him.

Not many people recognized Meenakshi Edathi as a presence in the house. Every morning she had a bath and entered the kitchen before the day broke and left it to go to sleep only after everyone had had their dinner and she had kept aside the kanji for Neeli, the woman who swept and cleaned, and washed the fireplace and hearth. Valia Ammaaman went out for a walk every evening and came back only after visiting the fields and the garden that lay at some distance from the house. On the days that he came back late, Meenakshi Edathi would go to bed only at midnight. She would cook the rice and vegetables and sit down and wait in the kitchen. No matter how late it was, even the children could eat only after Valia Ammaaman ate. He would first smear oil thickly all over his body and walk up and down the yard, wearing only a short towel around his waist. Two buckets of water would be drawn and kept

near the well. The big flat *chembu* used to make *payasam* would be filled
with hot water and Malu and Meenakshi Edathi would carry it together
to the well. By the time Valia Ammaaman finished his bath, the brass
lamp had to be lighted and placed in front of the machu in the thekkini,
a grass mat spread out, and *vibhuti* kept ready for him. These were
Ammini Edathi's tasks. After praying, he would go to the first floor of
the pathayappura and spend some more time changing his wet clothes
for dry ones. Before he arrived upstairs, a plate of fried fish or eggs
had to be taken from the kitchen to the pathayappura by way of the
courtyard. It was forbidden to walk by the machu carrying fish. Fish
and eggs were fried only for Valia Ammaaman. When he came downstairs
to eat, the children would quickly move into the darkness of the vadikkini.
There would be a strong odour as Valia Ammaaman passed by.

It was said that there were bottles buried inside the paddy heaped
in the granary.

Once Valia Ammaaman had his lunch, Malu's father, Cheriachan and
the boys would eat. The women's turn came next. It was Meenakshi
Edathi who served everyone. By the time she finally sat down to eat, all
the others would be asleep. Malu always felt sorry for her.

'Go and lie down,' Meenakashi Edathi would say to Malu. 'It's almost
midnight. I'm used to this.'

Meenakshi Edathi's voice was seldom audible. The only voice which
could be heard loudly inside the house was Ettan's mother's. She
quarrelled with Meenakshi Edathi a great deal. The latter would never
say a word. If her elder sister went too far, she would lament, 'It's all
my fate ...'

Achamma always sounded sad when she spoke of Meenakshi Edathi.
'Such an unfortunate destiny ...'

However, if any of the kitchen tasks were delayed, Achamma would
lose her temper. 'Listen girl, I used to cook for sixty-four people and
serve them food!' Achamma was not happy unless she reiterated this
from time to time.

Cheriachan had grown old. He no longer spoke to anyone. Most of
the time, he would go to Vadakke Veedu and spend his time talking to

the children there. He would come back only to eat. At night he slept in the room next to the one where Achamma slept. Malu often thought Cheriachan and her own father were alike. They seemed to be afraid even to walk around the house or eat.

Cheriachan was not wealthy. There was a time when he used to be a merchant and owned family property as well. Meenakshi Edathi had led a comfortable life in his house. Then he had made over the title of the house to his nephew. Malu had heard that the nephew had got him dead drunk and made him sign the sale documents. Cheriachan had then come to live here. That was quite some time ago. It was said that the reason Valia Ammaaman detested him was because he had signed away his rights to his family house.

Ettan's mother and her children, on the other hand, had everything they wanted. Her husband, Thangedathi's father, had been the Aphan Namboodiri, the younger brother of the senior Namboodiri, of Parambathu illam. Before he died, he had willed his property to his wife and daughter. Ettan's mother had a house and a compound somewhere far away. Kunhan Nair, the manager, sometimes came to see her. He used to sell the produce the tenant farmers gave them and bring her the money. Malu had heard Achamma say: 'She has loads of money. But what use is it to me that she's my daughter? She wouldn't help me even if I were dying ...'

Achamma and Ettan's mother quarrelled all the time. Whenever they fell out, Ettan's mother repeated the same thing:

'All of you will put me and my children in difficulties.'

There was a terrible row one afternoon. The cow with the broken horn ate up more than half of a mundu that had been spread out to dry on the wall. The creature was like that—if it saw clothes hanging out, it ate them up!

Ettan's mother saw it happen, ran up, pulled the rest of the mundu out of the cow's mouth and scolded it roundly. When the cow wandered off as if it had not heard her, she went into the house and continued to rant and rave.

'Did even a child here notice what happened?'

'Did anyone see the cow eat up the mundu?' asked Achamma.

'No one would have driven the cow away even if they saw it. Is there anyone here who cares if something of mine is ruined? Oh no, all they want is to eat.'

Achamma was annoyed. 'We are all of one family here.'

'Amma, don't you see the property being ruined?'

'Kunhikrishnan will look after it.'

'It upsets me all the same. It's me and my children who will suffer.'

'There are others here as well.'

And so it went on. Finally, Ettan's mother said: 'Amma hates me and my children. Doesn't everyone see how she fondles her son's darling daughter? Does she ever pay attention to my children?'

Achamma began to quietly say her prayers. Ettan's mother had never liked Malu staying in the house and she detested Cheriachan. She would say in a low voice that he'd come there without a paisa of his own, determined to destroy the tharavad.

The three rooms above the thekkini and vadikkini were set apart for Ettan's mother and her children. Malu seldom entered them. There was a cot with a canopy in the first room. Ettan's mother and Thangedathi slept on it. Bhaskarettan and Krishnankutty slept in the middle room and the third one was always kept locked. Malu had been inside it only once. There were two cots in it with mattresses and bolsters piled on them. The canopy had a gold border. The walls were covered with pictures and there was a huge mirror with two clay deerheads next to it. There were crystal and silver bowls underneath the cots and a round table in the middle of the room. Coloured crystal balls hung from the ceiling.

The room was meant for Thangedathi.

'It's a daughter I have. When a young man comes for her, mustn't I have a room ready?' The room had been prepared for the man who would establish a sambandam relationship with Thangedathi.

Thangedathi had attended school until she reached the fifth standard. She was fifteen. Malu would only be twelve next Kumbham.

Malu slept in Achamma's room. There was a room opening out of the thekkini next to the machu. Malu's father slept there. All it contained was a bamboo clothesline and a mat rolled up and placed in one corner.

Achamma slept on a low cot and Malu on a mundu spread on a mat on the floor near it. When the rainy season started, Achamma would say: 'Come up here, Malu.' It was comfortable to sleep under a blanket when it was cold and wet.

Malu's father hardly ever remembered that she was there. He never spoke to her, never bought her anything.

Achamma would say, 'Well, he doesn't have any money, does he?'

Before all the lands were sold they used to have a manager to look after them. Now it was Malu's father who looked after everything. He would get up early morning, go to the verandah on the western side, and hoot loudly. Four or five hoots would be heard in response from the hillside, where the cherumans' huts were. Ayyappan, Chathan, Thami, and Ayyappan's son Kanakrayi would come down from there. They would untie the bulls from the shed, give them water and lead them out, and Malu's father would go with them. He would return only at noon.

There were four pairs of bulls in the shed. Only three pairs were used for ploughing. The other two, Eruthu and Mani, were taken out only for racing. Valia Ammaaman loved the bull race. A race had been held in the Mithunam of the previous year in the racing field. Bulls had been brought from many places. The two bulls used to be taken to Anakkara and Kumaranalloor whenever there was a race. Before he went to bed, Valia Ammaaman always went up to the shed, lantern in hand, to have a look at them. He would make sure that their basket was filled with hay and the ropes around their necks knotted properly. Once a month, sheep's heads from the Trithala market were cooked, pounded, and fed to Eruthu and Mani.

Sesame oil especially extracted for the purpose were filled in tall bamboo nazhi-measures once a week and poured into the animals' mouths. This oil was extracted from the first lot of sesame seeds that were threshed. The rest of the seeds were packed in gunny bags and sent to Ammayi's place. The second-grade seeds were for use in the household. Achamma loved to eat fried and pounded sesame seeds.

A nazhi of sesame oil was set apart for household use. The women had to have oil baths on Tuesdays and Fridays. They would smear a drop on their heads on those days. Ettan's mother and her children took no part in this. Ettan's mother always kept her own stock of oil in a big black earthen jar in the middle room upstairs.

Malu was reluctant to ask her father for anything. When the hook of her chain broke, she wanted to get it mended. She asked Achamma to speak to her father. Kunju the goldsmith would have to be paid four annas.

'I don't know whether he has any money. Call Kunju when he goes this way. I'll get it mended for you,' said Achamma.

Malu knew Achan had no money. And yet Achamma said to him before Onam: 'Kutta, Onam is coming. We have to get two cheap *onnaras*, so that she can start wearing them on Onam day.'

Achan said in a complaining tone: 'I have no money.'

'She'll soon turn thirteen and will come of age. What will people say if she doesn't have proper undergarments?'

Achan did not reply.

'Why don't you say something?'

'What can I say?'

'Who else will get them for her? What a thing!'

Achan remained silent.

'Kutta ...'

'Yes.'

'Have you thought of a way?'

Achan stood up. His dark face turned even darker. He gave his mother a resentful look.

'Listening to you talk, anyone would think I have a hoard of money stashed away.'

'You don't need a hoard for this.'

'Do you know what I get from my tharavad, Amma? Four mundus, two towels, and two *konakams*.'

'I know.'

'What are you talking about then? I don't make anything for myself though I work like a buffalo day and night. I've always said I can't shoulder this burden. A man who can't fend for himself shouldn't start a sambandham. Didn't I tell you I didn't want it?'

'But that burden's gone now, isn't it?'

'Those who pass away don't have to suffer. It's not that I don't want to do anything for her. But where do I have the money?'

Valia Ammaaman had wanted Achan to get married. Malu's mother had been the daughter of one of his uncles. Malu had heard about the marriage at the time when she lived in her own house. Valia Ammaaman had ordered his nephew to marry the girl and he had obeyed. They had sent him to the girl's house with two mundus and a bunch of betel leaves. And four Nair men to accompany him.

'Ask Ammaaman for some money,' suggested Achamma.

'I can't. He's younger to you, it's easier for you to speak to him.'

'Ask him, Kutta. Will he eat you up?'

Achan's voice rose: 'I'll ask him. I've decided I will.'

This sudden change astonished Achamma.

'What do you mean?'

'I know what's happening, Amma, I've just not talked about it. I know what to ask him. He does the roofing there, in his wife's house, repairs their outhouse, whitewashes the walls—he has money for all that ... all that ...'

Malu could not believe it was her father who was speaking. Her father who always sat so quietly, his head bent.

'I wallowed in mud and slush to make that money ...'

Terrified, Achamma placed her hands on her head. 'Keep quiet! Bhagavane, what if Kunhikrishnan hears you?'

'I'll make sure he hears, one of these days. Does he think his nephew's throat is choked with sawdust?' Achan walked out.

Achamma and Valia Ammaaman no longer spoke to each other. In the old days Valia Ammaaman had always called out, 'Elder sister!' if there was anything he wanted done in the house. Achamma was ten years older than he was.

It was the day after the thullal held the previous year that the unpleasantness had begun between them. Appunni Ettan had been scolded and driven out of the house in the morning. In the evening was a quarrel.

Achamma said: 'That boy too has a right in this house.'

Valia Ammaaman stood where he was, placed a hand on his hip, and asked: 'What right? Who is he?'

'He belongs to this house, doesn't he?'

'Shut up, old woman and mind your business.'

The man who had always addressed her as 'Elder sister!' until now had called her 'old woman!'.

'You're a god of death, Kunhikrishnan, a bringer of death to this tharavad.'

'I'll kick you, I'll ...'

Achamma did not say a word after that. She went in, muttering, 'He'll do that too, the good-for-nothing.'

It was Malu who brought Achamma the news that Appunni was going to school in Trithala.

'Is it true?' she asked.

'Yes, Achamma. I saw him.'

'You must have imagined it.'

'I didn't. I even spoke to him.' Achamma had to believe her when she said that.

'May God give that child long life. He's all she has, after all.'

She too had believed once that Parukutty had disgraced the tharavad. When people asked about Parukutty, she would say: 'She came out of my womb, that's all.'

But as the years went by, she longed to know how Parukutty was. Puthan Parambu was only two miles away from the Vadakkeppat tharavad. But she began to realize what a distance those two miles could create between people. No one from the household visited Parukutty. Valia Ammaaman had threatened that if anyone went to see her, they would never be allowed over the threshold of the tharavad again. None of them dared defy that threat.

The news that Parukutty had had a baby had reached the women of the household in secret. One of the cherumi women whispered it to someone on the northern veranda. Achamma had scrambled up excitedly, come out and asked, 'Really, Neeli? Is it a boy or a girl?'

'They said it's a boy.'

'When? Did she have a difficult time? Who's there to help her?'

'The pains started yesterday as she was about to go to bed. And she delivered before the day broke.'

'Was the midwife there to ...' She did not complete the sentence. Her daughter stormed in.

'If you're so concerned, Amma, couldn't you have gone there to be with her?'

Achamma went back quietly to her dark little room and sat down on the bed.

The day she heard that Kondunni Nair died, she sat in that room and wept. Who would look after Parukutty now, she wondered.

She could not speak about Parukutty aloud. If she came upon one of the mapilla or cherumi women in the northern veranda while she was by herself, she would ask for news. She had to take care her elder daughter did not hear. As for Meenakshi, nothing she heard affected her. She never seemed to find occasion to weep, nor did she seem to know how to smile.

Achamma wanted to see Appunni again. She knew he went past the gate twice a day. He was in the same school as Bhaskaran and Krishnankutty.

It was difficult to get anything out of Bhaskaran. If she said to him coaxingly, '*Mone*, Bhaskara, come here, my little one,' he would come to her if he was in the right mood.

'Do you see Appunni at school, son?'

'I don't.'

'But isn't he in your school, Bhaskara?'

'Do you think I keep count of all the children in school?' he would retort.

She could see Appunni if she went up to the fence in the evening. But she found it difficult even to go down to the yard. She could not hold her back straight. She had to go down twelve steps to reach the yard. Even if she managed to descend, it would be a terrible effort to climb up again. And if her brother caught her standing at the fence and talking to Appunni, that would be the end of her.

He had once threatened to kick her. Try how she might, she had never been able to forget that. As a child, when he had eczema all over his body, it was she who used to rub medicinal powder on him and give him a bath. Their mother had never had time for the children. Once she hoisted the little boy on her hip early morning, she would put him down only to rock him to sleep at night. Her little brother Kunhikrishnan, whom she had raised, whom she used to carry around, feed, bathe, put to sleep next to her. Once he became the seniormost member and the head of the family, the karanavar, she had to wait for suitable occasions to speak to him. And in the end, he had said, 'I'll kick you.'

Her eyes filled as she thought of it.

'He'll pay for it, he will …'

'Who are you talking to, Achamme?' asked Malu, peering into the room.

'No one, child. Is it four o'clock?'

'Almost, Achamma.'

'I would have liked to see him, but my legs won't allow me to walk up there.'

'Appunni Ettan goes this way only a little later.' Malu had her own way of calculating. 'He'll be here only a little while after the shadow of the papaya tree falls on the stone on which we scrub the vessels.'

'What's the use, that death-god will be lurking at the gate by that time.'

'Valia Ammaaman is not here.'

Achamma was displeased that Malu had realized whom she meant when she had spoken of a death-god.

'As if you know!'

'I know, Achamma. Ammini Edathi and Valia Ammaaman went away together. They'll come back the day after tomorrow.'

'Who cares whether he goes or comes.'

But she thought to herself, her brother was not around. What, if she met Appunni and asked him how he was?

Her daughter Kunhukutty would not like it. But what did she care what Kunhukutty thought?

Kunhukutty had not been like this at all when she was small. She had been the most affectionate of the three daughters. Once she had established a sambandam relationship with a Namboodiri, everything had changed. She had not wanted the relationship, but had not protested when her mother and uncle insisted. And now she flaunted her arrogance. Well, once they grew up, you couldn't fondle them anymore, she comforted herself.

'Malu!'

Malu came back from the kitchen.

'What is it, Achamme?'

'Where's Ettan's mother?'

'She and Thangedathi are in the bathing tank.'

Achamme got up slowly. 'Come with me, let's go down to the compound.'

She was reluctant to say she wanted to see Appunni.

'Will you be able to go down the steps, Achamma?'

'I can manage all that, girl.'

She climbed down slowly with Malu's help. It was not easy to make her way between the pits in which the saplings had been planted. Her eyesight was not very sharp. They came up to the fence.

Malu's eyes combed the width of the field. No one was visible. After a while, she saw a speck of white on the south, next to the patch of tapioca. When it came nearer, she said, 'There's Appunni Ettan.'

But Appunni did not take the path by the fence, he was striding over the one that went through the middle of the field.

'Call him here,' urged Achamma. 'Tell him his Ammamma is waiting for him.'

What, if he did not hear if she called from here? Malu ran through the gap in the fence into the field.

Appu was walking slowly, drenched in perspiration, his books tucked under one arm and his mundu hitched up over his knees.

Malu ran up to him and said: 'She's calling you, Appunni Ettan.'

He kept walking. 'Who?'

'Achamma, she's at the fence.'

'I'm not coming.'

'Achamma said to call you. There she is ...'

'Didn't I tell you I'm not coming?' He quickened his pace.

Malu went back, disappointed. Achamma called out as she came nearer, 'Where is he?'

'He wouldn't come, Achamma.'

'I'm sure you didn't tell him I sent for him.'

'I did, Achamme. He said he wouldn't come.'

Achamma stood there a while in silence, lost in thought. Then she said with a sigh:

'He won't come. How can he come here?'

4

I t was the day before the Thiruvathira festival. There was an unusual rush in Esoop's shop.

Sankaran Nair needed red chillies. He had set out after his work at the illam to get them. Business was dull in Vappu's shop, so the groceries there were bound to be old. Sankaran Nair usually bought what he wanted from Esoop's.

All the unemployed people who usually frequented the place were seated on the veranda. A handful of children had gathered around the tailor.

The subject of conversation was the Pooram festival at the Mulayan Kavu temple. One of the group had gone for the festival the previous year—Velappan. Ravunni and Assankutty were listening to Velappan describing the delights of the festival. Palathil Kunhu and Ookkan Baputty were calculating the accounts from the sale of banana leaves.

The excitement about the Pooram festival died down when Sankaran Nair entered. Ravunni asked:

'And how are the preparations for Thiruvathira coming on, Sankaran Naire?'

'What Thiruvathira do we have?'

He made his way through the crowd and asked for five rupees' worth of red chillies.

'Why so little, Chankaran Naire?' asked Musaliyar.

'That's all I need.'

Velappan, Ravunni, and Assankutty exchanged meaningful glances. Assankutty lighted a beedi stump, flung the matchbox on Esoop's table and laughed.

'Sankaran Nair has a lot of expenses these days, don't you know?'

'What kind?' asked Esoop.

'Ask him yourself.'

'You're crazy! If he had, Nair would tell me about them.'

'This is no way to celebrate the first Thiruvathira after marriage, Naire.'

Sankaran Nair trembled from head to toe. But he did not say a word. Musaliyar had not wrapped up the chillies.

Ookkan Baputty moved from the accounts of the sale of banana leaves to this new topic. 'Why, does Sankaran Nair have something new going on, Esoop-ka?'

'I don't know. Ask Ravunni, he'll know.'

'Why didn't you tell us about it, Naire?'

Sankaran Nair's patience had started to give way. Baputty said in a low voice:

'Not bad at all, Naire. Ammukutty's a treasure even now.'

Sankaran Nair had been standing with his eyes half-closed, holding on to the pillar and looking like a wet chicken. He suddenly turned toward Baputty who sat there with a sly smile, pursing his lips and puffing on his beedi, lunged forward and slapped his cheek soundly.

The talk and laughter died down suddenly. The slap had been completely unexpected. The atmosphere froze and all those who had come to buy groceries huddled to one side.

Everyone looked at Baputty anxiously. There was fire in his eyes. He was the sort that stopped at nothing. He had been the accused in three criminal cases. He had been in jail only once, but was convinced that the Cannanore jail was meant for real men.

He sprang up. The knife tucked into his waist was now in his hand.

'Don't ruin me, Baputty!', implored Esoop, his hands on his chest. But Sankaran Nair stood absolutely still even though he saw the knife glittering in Baputty's hand.

The hand that held the knife rose but a thick, strong, hairy hand suddenly shot out and gripped it. Syedalikutty's.

'Let go, Syedalikutty-ka!'

'Put the knife back, Baputty.'

'If I don't pull out this Nair's entrails, my father's name is not Aithruman.'

'I said, put the knife away. Or else you'll feel the strength of my hands.'

Baputty withdrew his hand reluctantly, gasping. Syedalikutty took the knife from his hand, tucked it back into his belt and said:

'Baputty, don't do anything foolish.'

Baputty stood still, his face reddening.

'Nair, go away now.'

Sankaran Nair went out as if nothing had happened. As he walked along the road, his thoughts buzzed like a wasps' nest.

'The dogs! They want to ruin my reputation.'

But then, he thought, he was guilty. What he had heard was scandalous. Was he not responsible for it himself? Obviously people had noted that he went there often, talked to her. He shouldn't have …

He had done nothing wrong. He had extended his help to a family that had no one to lean on, that was all. And for that …

His blood began to boil. He hurried on. As he walked past Achumman's shop, someone hailed him from upstairs.

'Sankara!'

'What a nuisance,' he muttered. He would have to go up now.

'Come up here,' said Achumman.

Sankaran went up.

'What is it?'

'Just crush these betel leaves for me.' He moved the small mortar and pestle towards Sankaran Nair. Full of anger against the whole world, Sankaran Nair pounded the betel leaves fiercely.

'Don't break the mortar, *edo!*'

Sankaran pretended he had not heard. He scraped up what he had pounded and gave it to Achumman.

'What's all the news in the village?' asked Achumman, churning the betel leaves around in his toothless mouth.

'Nothing much.'

'How are things at the illam?'

'Not bad.'

'Have you plucked all your vegetables?'

'They're not yet ready.'

'Um.' Achumman stroked his chest, fanned himself with a palm-leaf fan and leaned back in his chair.

'I hear you're looking after affairs at Puthan Parambu now. Is that true, Sankara?'

Sankaran Nair found that he could not move his tongue.

'What about it, edo?'

Sankaran Nair grunted.

Achumman asked with a mocking laugh:

'When did all this start?'

He had to answer Achumman. Keeping his anger in check, he said, 'It's been a few days.'

'Nothing wrong. It's only right that you should. That woman has no one to lean on.' Achumman spat out noisily through the bars of the window and went on: 'But don't get her a bad name. Why don't you call a few people, go to her place, and make it a proper arrangement?'

Sweat broke out on Sankaran Nair's forehead. What did Achumman mean?

'You're forty now. There's nothing wrong in having a sambandam relationship ...'

Sankaran Nair could not bear to stay there any longer.

'I have some watering to do. I'll see you later.' Not waiting for a reply, he hurried away.

He did not sleep that night.

Whenever he saw Parukutty at the illam after that he was reluctant to meet her eyes. Had the things people were saying reached her ears? It needed very little to set them talking. It was true he went there sometimes, that they spoke of many things. It was only with him that Parukutty discussed her problems.

It was he who had taken Appunni to his new school. He who had had the fence repaired and found the money to pay Appunni's fees when she had not had enough. And so he had given people reason to talk.

But when he thought about it he felt like asking them: what had he done that was wrong? She had no one to help her. He had done whatever he could. In the eyes of God, that could not be wrong.

Let them talk, he thought. He couldn't care less. The barking dogs! He was a man, he had lived without assistance from them all these days. He would not allow her reputation to be sullied. If he had to ... he said to himself: 'Thengumpotta Sankaran is a man of character.'

His decision made, he walked to Puthan Parambu. Let everyone see, he thought as he walked in through the gate. The sun had set but it was not yet dark. As he entered the yard, Parukutty Amma was coming to the front veranda with a lighted oil lamp in her hand.

'Deepam, deepam ...'

The glow of the small brass lamp illumined her face. He could not believe that this was the servant woman he usually saw in the pounding shed of the illam. She had just had a bath and her wet hair lay loose on her back. The vibhuti mark on her forehead stood out clearly. Something about her face, over which lay a gentle radiance, hurt him.

A feeling of guilt distressed him as he stepped into the veranda. He mustered his courage and asked for the sake of saying something:

'Is it already time to light the lamp?'

Holding the lamp in her left hand, Parukutty lengthened its wick with the index finger of her right hand and said:

'I thought it was. Are you on your way back from the illam, Sankaran Naire?'

'I came away at noon. I had some watering to do, but couldn't get the watering apparatus for myself.'

He sat down on the ledge. 'Where's Appunni?'

'Gone to have a bath.'

Conversation lagged. Parukutty put the lamp down and stood near the door, leaning against the wall. Words whirled around his mind like a hurricane. He had to speak ... When he came in, his throat had been filled with confident words but they would not come out now. He said with great difficulty, not raising his head:

'Paruttyamme ...'

She looked at him.

'People are saying all kinds of things about my coming here.'

She said very gently:

'Is there anything people will not say?'

That gave him courage:

'I don't want your reputation to suffer in any way because of me.'

Parukutty looked at him, puzzled. 'But you've only been of help to me.'

Sankaran Nair's confidence rose even higher.

'Paruttyamme, you mustn't think ill of me. I came to ask you something.'

'What is it, Sankaran Naire?'

'You have no one to help you. And I ... I have been on my own for a long time now. If you have no objection, Paruttyamme ... a relationship that would ...'

'No, Sankaran Nair,' she said firmly.

He did not have the courage to look at her.

'I have done with all that. That aspect of my destiny is over. I cannot think of it again. Please don't feel bad ...'

He sat still, his mind seething. And heard a footstep. Appunni. The boy went straight in without looking at them.

Sankaran Nair got up.

'Forget what I said, Paruttyamme. It was wrong on my part to ...'

Parukutty Amma's head was bent.

'Don't misunderstand me, Paruttyamme. I'd like to help you in any way I can. Forget what I said.'

Her eyes were full of tears.

He went away.

Appunni began to study by the light of the chimney lamp. Parukutty stared at him as he lay on his stomach, his eyes fixed on the book. He was growing up. Physically, he was more well-built now than a fifteen-year-old. Was he growing away from her as he grew up?

He no longer talked as much as he used to. He answered only when he was spoken to. Once he came home from school, he did not stay in the house much. He would wander around the compound, or the neighbourhood, or go to Muthaaachi's house. It seemed as though his thoughts were not in this world at all. He lost his temper very quickly these days. Was he changing?

Her heart shrank. She could have borne anything. But to feel him growing more and more distant from her as the days passed …

He would read until she called him for dinner. After eating, he would read again. When he felt sleepy, he would blow the lamp out and go to bed.

Had he nothing to say to her?

'What are you thinking about, Appunni?'

'Nothing.'

'Why do you look upset?'

'It's nothing.'

All he had to say was 'nothing.' The more he repeated it, the more anxious she became …

'Bhagavathi, may all good things come to him!'

Ambling along aimlessly, Appunni reached the bank of the river, the spot where it took a turn. The water was deep here even in summer. The rest of the river had dried into a narrow channel. But the waves rippled gently around this spot, known as the Ayyappan pool.

Appunni climbed up to a high ledge and sat down.

The calm of the pool was frightening. Small waves rushed up one by one to the bank and broke against it.

It was a holiday. But he did not want to stay at home. He had no one to play with. So he had decided to take a walk and reached here.

He watched the ripples on the surface of the pool. People who sank into it never came back. He had heard as a child that the god Ayyappan had a palace underneath. Those who crossed the river in a boat during the rains generally threw coins into the pool in order to avert danger. No, there couldn't be a god or a palace underneath, it was just a story …

He thought of what Ramakrishnan Master had said the previous day:

'Wherever a stone is carved, a god comes into being. And the gods are of many kinds. Some want only meat and alcohol. Others want milk and bananas. That's how it is in our country.'

Ramakrishnan Master was new to the school. He was an eloquent speaker. His classes were like orations. Often, it was not about the lesson they were doing that he spoke. But it was enjoyable listening to him.

Appunni felt that holidays were a curse. On schooldays, he could leave home in the morning and needed to come back only in the evening.

He found it difficult to stay at home.

Whenever he saw Amma he would remember what Muthaachi had said. And feel infuriated.

He had gradually come to realize that what Muthaachi had said was true.

When people saw him at the bathing ghat, didn't they whisper to one another? Didn't everyone he met look at him mockingly? He knew they did ...

Why did that man come to the house? Why did he stay there, talking ...?

When he heard what they said, he felt as if his skin was being peeled away from his body. They said he was going to marry his mother!

He had gone to the temple tank above the illam the day before. The men's ghat had been crowded. Next to it was the ghat where the elephants were washed. No one bathed there since there were no steps. He went down to it.

The women's ghat was adjacent to it. He heard someone ask:

'Who's that boy?'

'Parukutty's son.'

His heart thudded fast at what he heard next. He did not want to hear, but he was forced to.

'They say that Thengumpotta Sankaran Nair hangs around there all the time.'

He plunged his head under the water, came out and dried himself, hardly aware of what he was doing. He walked home trembling with anger. And what did he see? That man, seated on the front veranda. That man, Sankaran Nair. Whispering secrets to his mother ...

He wished he could drive him out. It was his house, after all. His father's house. Thazhathethil Kondunni Nair's house. And the man was sitting there, whispering to his mother.

What people were saying was true. The man would continue to
come there. He would become Amma's husband. Achan had laid her
over his shoulder and carried her over the chest-high water in the river.
And yet, when he died, she and Sankaran Nair …

He watched the wavelets breaking on the bank, feeling weak and
tired. He threw a stone into the middle of the rippling pool.

That man would become Amma's husband. And he himself would
become a nobody …

He had no place of his own.

They were all enemies—Sankaran Nair, Bhaskaran, Valia
Ammaaman, everyone. And Amma was on their side.

He should have grown up in the Vadakkeppat tharavad. But when he
went there, they had driven him out. Like a dog … a mangy dog …

Because of his mother, he had lost his tharavad. And now he would
lose his home as well.

He should have had a place just like Bhaskaran had in that ancient
tharavad with its naalukettu and courtyard. But …

He was ashamed to think of it.

He found it impossible to hold his head high in front of his friends.
The son of the woman who pounded rice at the illam!

And his mother was Thengumpotta Sankaran Nair's wife.

He threw another stone into the pool. He scrambled up and walked
along the river bank, his mind seething. Someone called out from behind:

'Isn't that you Appunni?'

He recognized the voice. The man came up beside him. Appunni
looked at Sankaran Nair resentfully.

'What are you doing by the river?'

'Nothing.'

'Just came out for a walk?'

'Um …'

Appunni walked ahead and the man behind, the wooden bucket
used for irrigating the fields balanced on his shoulder. When the path
became wider, he came abreast and their shoulders touched.

Appunni fumed silently.

You are no one to me.

Nor am I anyone to you.

I am Thazhathethil Kondunni Nair's son.

I hate you.

Beads of perspiration broke out on Appunni's forehead. He began to walk faster. The man walked alongside him silently.

Ookkan Baputty, wearing a checked lungi and a round-necked banian, came from the opposite direction with a bundle on his head. He stopped as he came up to them, so did Appunni and Sankaran Nair.

Ookkan Baputty gave Sankaran Nair a look that seemed to say, 'I remember ...'

'Where to, father and son?' He flung the question at them as he passed by.

Appunni froze. When he had composed himself somewhat, he gave Sankaran Nair a vengeful look, as if he would have liked to kill him. Sankaran Nair stood very still, his eyes riveted on the sand below.

Appunni walked away quickly, feeling that he had averted danger for the moment.

When he reached home, he suddenly wanted to weep. He sat down in the inner room, his face pressed to the mattress that was kept folded on the cot. And did not get up when his mother came and called him at dusk.

Parukutty served his food and came again to fetch him. 'Appunni ...'

'Do you have a headache?'

No answer.

'I've served your rice.'

He did not reply.

She bent down and placed her hand on his back. He sprang up and burst out like a madman:

'Don't touch me ... don't ...'

Parukutty was shocked. Her voice trembling, she asked:

'What's happened, son?'

He kept repeating, 'Don't touch me ...'

He did not eat.

Neither did his mother.

They lay next to each other. Neither spoke. Her harsh sobs grated against the cold silence of the night.

He got up very early in the morning before the day broke.

His mother was lying with her eyes closed but she was not asleep. He put on a shirt hurriedly, took his other shirt and the mundu lying on the clothesline and stuffed them into his school bag. His mother opened her eyes as he went out through the door. Sitting up, she asked in a feeble voice,

'Where are you going Appunni, so early in the morning?'

'I'm going away.'

'My son ...' she sobbed. She got up.

'Where are you going, son?'

'Somewhere.'

'Who do I have but you, son?'

'You ... you have Sankaran Nair, don't you, Amma?'

He opened the front door noisily and went out.

'Appunni ...'

He did not turn back.

He walked along, trembling violently. Her cry sounded fainter and fainter behind him.

He was seated on one of the rocks scattered between the *kannanthali* bushes on the slope of Narivalan hill.

He had been sitting there since early morning. If he walked to school, he would encounter his companions on the way and there would be hundreds of questions to answer. He didn't want to see anyone, be asked anything.

The hillside was deserted. At a distance, a goat with crooked horns was grazing on the grass. He could see a herd of cattle beyond, like black spots.

The sun had grown very hot. Perspiration poured down his back and chest and his wet shirt clung to him.

A cheruman carrying a bundle of bamboo on his head came up the footpath. A cheruman he didn't know. He asked:

'Why are you sitting here, Cheria Thamburan?'

'Just like that.'

In the distance, he saw people coming that way, so he got up and walked along the path to the west. It was an area covered with soft, thick grass, and there were herds of cattle and cowherd boys around. He had no idea where he was going. Potter women who were gathering heaps of cowdung stopped their chatter to glance at him. He was very tired by the time he came to a lone *jamoon* tree on the hill. He decided to sit down in its shade.

He did not notice a black cloth umbrella moving towards him on the winding path or bother to look up as it came nearer. What did he care who it was? The man passed by him, then stopped and turned.

'Nair-kutty?'

It was Syedalikutty.

Appunni looked up at him tiredly thinking that the last time too, as he had sat here, on this hillside, after being driven out of his tharavad, this man had come upon him.

'What are you doing here?'

Appunni's heart overflowed with emotion and he tried hard not to cry. But his tears streamed down.

'Why are you crying?'

He didn't say anything.

'What are you doing here?'

'Nothing.'

'You didn't go to school?'

'No ...'

'Why are you sitting here in this deserted spot?'

He did not answer.

Syedalikutty folded up his umbrella, put the packet he had under his arm on the ground and sat down near him.

'Where are you going? Tell me.'

'Some place somewhere ...'

'How can you say that? Come, I'll come with you to the river.'

'I'm not coming.'

Syedalikutty changed his tactics.

'Then tell me where you're going. I'll come with you. Or we'll go to my house.'

To Syedalikutty's house! He felt as if a heavy door that had lain closed was being pushed open. A meal of pathiris and mutton curry. The mutton would taste granular and he'd be told it was an old goat. It would be white poison. White.

'I'm not coming anywhere.'

Syedalikutty did not speak for a while.

'When did you leave home?'

'In the morning.'

'And when will you go back after your wanderings?'

'Never. That's not my house.'

Syedalikutty tried his best to persuade him to go back. Maybe his mother had scolded him, slapped him. All that was normal. Appunni listened silently.

'That poor mother, you're all she's got.'

'Amma won't care if I go away, she's got other people.'

Syedalikutty looked at him in astonishment. Not certain what to say, he sat there, doodling on the ground. Then he got up.

'You're the son of a bold father. Don't let these things get you down. If you quarrel with your mother, does it mean you should sit here on the hillside?'

Appunni's look said: then where should I go?

'Look, why don't you stay somewhere else for a couple of days? Your anger will cool down and then you can go back to your mother.'

Appunni's fury directed itself at Syedalikutty.

'Where can I go?'

'To Vadakkeppat. That's your house, isn't it?'

Vadakkeppat. From where he had been driven out.

'You have as much right there as anyone, don't you? Show some spirit now. If they tell you to get out, say you won't.'

'He said he would break my legs if he saw me in that compound.'

'Let's see if he will. What are the lawyers and courts in this country for then, child? This Syedalikutty has seen a bit of the world.'

Appunni kept quiet.

'You can't keep sitting here. Either go home or go to Vadakkeppat. I won't go away until you decide one way or the other.'

Appunni wiped his reddened face and got up.

'I'm going.'

'Where?'

He said firmly: 'To the tharavad.'

'Go along then.'

They walked on together. When they reached the Vadakkeppat gatehouse, Syedalikutty said:

'Go on in, Nair-kutty. But look, when your anger has cooled, go back to your mother. Don't upset her.'

He did not respond to that. Syedalikutty walked off.

Appunni pushed the door open.

There were steps going up. On either side were moss-covered walls that had crumbled in places. The old naalukettu towered above them. There was a *kuvalam* tree surrounded by a platform in front and the pathayappura on the southern side.

He hesitated for a moment, then climbed the steps. There was no one in the yard.

Probably Valia Ammaaman was watching from the upper veranda of the pathayappura. Let him see—that the Appunni he drove out had come back.

He entered the veranda. He thought he glimpsed a head at the front door, but it disappeared before he saw it properly.

He put his school bag down on the wooden ledge.

'Who is that?'

'It's me.' He whispered to himself, be bold, you're the son of a fearless father.

It was Valiamma who came out. Bhaskaran's mother. She said with an expression of complete indifference:

'Yes?'

He was suddenly at a loss for words. After a while, he said, 'I want to see Ammamma.'

Malu came to the door at that moment, saw him and went back.

'Appunni ...' Ammamma came out from the thekkini. He walked boldly in through the carved door. When he came up to Ammamma, his heart was full to bursting. Stroking his head and shoulders, she said:

'I've been longing to see you for days.'

Appunni went in with her. Thangedathi, who was just entering the vadikkini, gave him a long look. What was she staring at? As if she was looking at some spectacle ...

Valiamma walked past a couple of times, clicking her heels. And then said in a voice meant for everyone to hear:

'Ammaaman will bring the roof down when he gets back today.'

Since no one responded, she turned to Appunni and said in a studiedly polite tone:

'Look, I'm not saying this because I dislike you. But have you forgotten how you were driven out from here?'

'I still remember.'

'Then why have you come here?'

Appunni's face darkened.

'Ammaaman may come back any moment. Go away quickly now.'

'I'm not going.'

'What?'

'I said I'm not going.'

Valiamma tossed her hair back, muttered something and walked off.

Appunni turned to Ammamma. His voice grew soft as he looked at her wrinkled face, her faded eyes and her affectionate expression.

'I'm going to stay here, Ammamma.'

He thought she would batter him with questions, But all she said was:

'Stay.'

He wanted to put his arms around that shrivelled, shrunken figure then and weep.

Valia Ammaaman had gone to his wife's house the previous day. He would come back any moment. Everyone was afraid of what would happen when he got back. Appunni felt that that fear hung heavy over the house.

Malu watched Krishnankutty carefully. He was the one who would tell Ammaaman as soon as he got back. He always had access to

Ammaaman because Ammaaman liked him. Someone had only to pluck a papaya and whisper, 'Don't let Ammaaman know,' and the news would go up to the pathayappura at once.

As time passed, however, Appunni began to feel more confident. He was not going to give up easily. Let Ammaaman come back, send for me and scold me, he thought. If he drives me out, I will not go away.

Why was Valia Ammaaman not coming?

He came at last. In the evening, with Ammini Edathi. It took a few minutes for the news to reach him.

'Woman, who is that inside?' he shouted from the yard.

Everyone rushed to the front door—Ammamma, Valiamma, Meenakshi Edathi, Thangedathi, Malu.

'Which of you bitches has dared disobey me?'

No one answered.

'Where is he?'

Appunni came out slowly. He was trembling all over.

When he caught sight of Appunni, Ammaaman shook off his wooden clogs and sprang into the veranda. 'I told you ...'

Ammamma came between him and Appunni and screamed: 'Kunhikrishna!'

'Move. I'll tear out his entrails and ...'

Valia Ammaaman pushed Ammamma away and lunged towards Appunni. Mustering every ounce of courage he had, Appunni said:

'Don't touch me.'

'And what if I touch you?'

Valia Ammaaman's hand fell on Appunni's cheek. As he raised it again, a roar arose from the kitchen:

'Don't slap the boy.'

Valia Ammaaman turned, his eyes full of anger and amazement. And saw his nephew, Kutta Ammaaman, standing there. Kutta Ammaaman stepped forward.

'Don't touch the boy. It's I who say so.'

Valia Ammaaman lowered his hand.

'And who are you to give me orders?'

'Never mind who I am. It's I who say you cannot beat him up. If you do, there'll be consequences.'

Valia Ammaaman turned his fury towards his nephew.

'Phoo! And since when have you grown so powerful?'

Kutta Ammaaman's tone remained firm.

'I will not consider the fact that you're an old man.'

Valia Ammaaman suddenly looked crushed.

Valiamma, Meenakshi Edathi, and Thangedathi looked at one another. Valia Ammaaman stood there for some time, uncertain what to do. Then he went down to the yard.

Muttering, 'Such a thing has never happened in this tharavad,' he went to his room upstairs in the pathayappura.

At dusk, Appunni went to the eastern veranda. The glow of the big brass lamp placed in front did not reach this far. He thought of all that had happened that day. It seemed to him that a whole year had gone by, not just a day.

A shadowy figure came up in the faint light.

'Appunni—'

He recognized her. Ammini Edathi. She touched his left cheek. It still hurt.

'Did it hurt badly, Appunni?'

He hated her, the daughter who had come to find out how he was.

'Why won't you speak, Appunni?'

Someone called from inside: 'Amminikutty!'

She ran in quickly.

Leaves were laid for dinner for Kutta Ammaaman, Bhaskaran, Krishnankutty, and Cheriachan. Malu came and called Appunni as well.

Four whole banana leaves and a small torn one for him. He was given a mat to sleep on in the little room under the staircase next to the vadikkini.

The naalukettu was plunged in silence. He felt afraid, alone in that small room. Would the ghosts of all his dead ancestors be wandering around? Was that the sound of ankle and waist bells from the machu where the Bhagavathi resided?

When he was exhausted, physically and mentally, his eyes closed.

In the morning Ammamma called him when Bhaskaran and Krishnankutty went for their kanji. He sat down with them on a small wooden stool which had a leg missing.

Appunni started for school early, unconcerned about those who were going in the bullock-cart. He went to Ammamma's room before he left. 'Ammamme, I'm leaving.'

He came out of the gatehouse. If he took a short cut through the nenthran banana grove, it would take him to the front of the Yajneswaram temple. That was the easier route.

When he came home from school in the evening, Valia Ammaaman was walking up and down the yard. He saw Appunni but turned his head the other way, pretending as though he hadn't seen him and stared at the western yard.

As he entered the thekkini, he heard Ammaaman's voice: 'This tharavad will come to ruin. All the pollution rules have been broken. And it's a pure and holy Bhagavathi who resides in the machu.'

Meenakshi Edathi gave him a piece of advice. Come in by the northern entrance when you get back from school. You cannot walk past the machu until you have had a bath.

Bhaskaran and Krishnankutty studied in their room at night and came down only for dinner. Appunni lay stretched out by the brass lamp kept at the door of the thekkini and opened his book. But he could not concentrate. What were they saying about him?

Once a week, the granary was unlocked and the paddy needed for the week was measured out. When the day came around, Meenakshi picked up the basket as usual and went to the pathayappura. Valia Ammaaman said to her: 'There's someone else here now to manage the affairs. Let him measure out the paddy for you.'

Meenakshi waited uncertainly. Valia Ammaaman said firmly:

'I won't give you a single grain of paddy. Let me see whether that will teach you.'

Valiamma began to weep. 'I and my children are going to starve.'

Kutta Ammaaman heard of what had happened when he got back. Malu told him. Kutta Ammaaman was about to go up to the pathayappura but Ammamma would not let him. Kutta Ammaaman said:

'I have stayed quiet all this while. Let me see whether I too have some authority here.'

A quarrel broke out upstairs in the pathayappura.

'I refuse to open the granary. Who are you to order me to?'

Malu, Valiamma, and Thangedathi were listening from the front veranda.

'Who am I, you ask. One of the male members of this tharavad. It's thanks to my blood and sweat that there's paddy here.'

Kutta Ammaaman went on to revile all the people in Valia Ammaaman's wife's household.

Valia Ammaaman did not unlock the granary. Kutta Ammaaman came down. He took out the paddy stored in the downstairs room of the pathayappura for sowing the next year, measured it, and gave it to the women. Meenakshi Edathi was hesitant to take it until he shouted:

'Didn't I tell you to take it and go away?' Meenakshi Edathi gathered the grain in the basket and asked Malu to carry it for her.

It made Ammamma very unhappy to think that they had been brought to a state where they had to eat the grain kept aside for sowing.

Kutta Ammaaman said to Ammamma:

'Either there has to be a settlement or I must be given my share of the property. I'm going to stand firm on that.'

The village buzzed with the news that there had been a quarrel at Vadakkeppat between uncle and nephew, that the nephew had almost slapped the uncle and so on ...

Lawyer Kumaran Nair grew very restless when he heard this. To handle the partition of Vadakkeppat was no trivial matter, he would make a packet on it.

It was Kumaran Nair's guru, Kunhan Nair, who had conducted the partition at the time when they had had a sixteen-pillared courtyard and sixty-four members in the household. He had accompanied his guru as his assistant. Kunhan Nair had taught Kumaran Nair how to draft land deeds. There would never be anyone who could draft land documents as well as Kunhan Nair. Once he drafted a deed, the registrar never had occasion to change a single stroke in it. He was dead now and Kumaran Nair was proud to be the disciple of a man who had been so expert at drafting title deeds.

As far as Vakil Kumaran Nair was concerned, a partition meant a feast. He was a manager for the affairs of the village and could plead cases in the adhikari's village court. That was how he had earned the title of *vakil* or lawyer.

He hung around Vadakkeppat waiting for an opportunity to see Kuttan Nair and find out how far the matter had proceeded. What was more important, he had to make sure that Korukutty Panikker, his competitor, was not involved in this affair at all.

It was while coming back from the registrar's office in Trithala after the registration of a piece of land that had been pledged that he saw Kuttan Nair seated in the field, watching the cherumi women swinging their nets to trap pests.

Kumaran Nair went down to the field. 'Guruvayoorappa! I'm dead tired,' he said.

'What's the matter, vakil?'

'Nothing. I had to go to Trithala. Had to register the pledging of a piece of land.'

'It's done?'

'Yes. The present registrar is a good sort. But walking makes me short of breath. Guruvayoorappa! I'm tired.'

'One can't stay young forever,' said Kuttan Nair indifferently.

'Are there any pests?'

'Not as many as last year.'

Kumaran Nair talked at length of agricultural matters and village affairs. Then he began:

'Look, I know it doesn't concern me, but I heard your uncle had a disagreement with you. Is it true?'

Kuttan Nair said very calmly:

'What's the point of disagreeing? The people in the house have to eat.'

'Still ... I'm only saying this because of what I heard. Ammaaman is old. It's you who must be forgiving, Kuttan Nair.'

The shot found its mark exactly as the vakil had intended it to.

'What do you say I must forgive? It's I who kept quiet till now. I work day and night like a buffalo and not a coin, not a grain of rice, ever comes into my hands.'

'But Vadakkeppat is a prosperous tharavad. The senior members ...'

'The days when we had to count measure after measure filled to the brim—that was long ago, Kumaran Nair. I've done all I could but things are in a bad way.'

Kumaran Nair lowered his voice and whispered as if imparting a secret:

'I know something of what's happening. But how can one speak of it openly? I heard there were debts ...'

'I don't mind working really hard. But I can't wait around respectfully like this all the time, waiting for a chance to speak.'

'How will Ammaaman ever take the right path when it's that Koru Panikker's advice that he heeds?'

'Let him listen to his advice. Let him pawn or sell whatever he wants. I've decided on what I must do.'

Kumaran Nair said in a conciliatory tone:

'We could settle the matter without making trouble.'

'There's nothing to settle. All I want is to get whatever is due to me.'

Vakil Kumaran Nair placed his hand on his head in astonishment. 'Guruvayoorappa! What is this I hear? You mean, divide the property?'

'Yes, why not? Each one to his own. Don't suggest anything else, I'm not going to listen. I'm thirty-eight years old. And I'm a man. Not even the little children in that house respect me ...'

'Look Kuttan Nair, we'll find a way out. We'll get some respectable people to speak to your uncle. But ...'

Kuttan Nair was growing angrier and angrier.

'What's the 'but' about?'

'I think it's shameful to divide the property. Such a prosperous tharavad ... If people come to know you've quarrelled and split up ...'

Kuttan Nair's face darkened with fury. 'I know all of you, Naire. Ammaaman has only to open his mouth to speak and you'll follow him with your tails between your legs.'

Kumaran Nair changed his tactics.

'Kuttan Nair, you're as close to me as my late nephew. What can I do for you?'

Kuttan Nair pondered deeply. Then he said:

'There's something you can do. You must do whatever you can to see that the property is divided. Can you do that?'

'Can I? I organized the partition of the Poruthedathu illam, which had an income of fifteen thousand paras of paddy, down to its minutest detail. All by myself too. Did you know that? I'll attend to this, Kuttan Nair.'

Moving his white cloth umbrella from one shoulder to the other, Vakil Kumaran Nair moved two steps forward and repeated: 'Don't worry. You're like my late nephew to me.'

Kumaran Nair went home amply satisfied.

Kuttan Nair had known that a time would come when this story would end. But he had not expected it to happen so soon.

He had begun to work in the fields when he was fifteen. That was more than twenty years ago. And even now, he did not have decent clothes to wear. He had no money to buy himself a cup of tea if he wanted one. His annual wages were four mundus, two towels, and five paras of paddy. The cherumans who worked for the family received gifts for the Onam, Vishu, and Thiruvathira festivals every year: unbleached mundus, paddy, coconuts, and oil—though this meant that they could not work for another master. It seemed to him that their situation was better than his own.

He spat resentfully into the field.

All he had was the name of a great tharavad. What use was that?

It distressed him to think of Malu. In another two or three years she would be of marriageable age. Her ears and neck were bare of jewels. She was treated like a maid servant in the house. He had watched her carry heavy buckets of water morning and evening. Kunji Oppol did not even like her staying in the house.

Ammaaman's daughter stayed in the house as well. She never came down from the pathayappura. And Kunji Oppol had a spoilt daughter who never lifted a finger to do a thing. After all, there was a Meenakshi Edathi to do the housework and a Malu as well.

He had borne it for a long time. And then, that day, everything had exploded. He had not known of Appunni's arrival. He had neither affection nor dislike for the boy. But when he remembered how he had once been caught by the neck and thrown out, he had felt a twinge of pain. After all, he was a human being and a child, wasn't he? And he too belonged to the Vadakkeppat tharavad. Just because he had no one to speak for him ...

He thought of Malu again. This was the human condition: if he died now, Malu would be in the same plight. She too would be driven out. And she did not even have a right to stay there.

And then he had come upon that scene when he returned home one evening. He had thought it would be the end of the boy. The voice he had suppressed so long had suddenly risen.

Kuttan Nair realized that the trouble was just beginning. Ammaaman had insisted that he would not give them any paddy. He had locked the granary and went around now with the key tucked into his waist. There was a rumour that he was going to sell paddy to the cartmen. Let's wait and see, thought Kuttan Nair, let him sell the paddy that had been dried and pounded for their meals to those cartmen ...

Surely, there was no rule that only one person in the Vadakkeppat tharavad had the sole right to everything there.

5

It had been raining for four or five days now. There was no thunder, no wind, only the incessant rain. No sooner did a cloud appear in the sky than it would start to rain. By the time it stopped, the sky would darken again.

Parukutty watched the bubbles rise and dissolve as raindrops fell into the water-logged courtyard. There was no work at the illam, Kunhathol had said that they would take the paddy out only after the rain stopped.

There were raindrops in the faint breeze that swept over the wet fields.

The path beyond the thickets at the fence was full of slush. As Parukutty's eyes reached out into the endless distance that stretched beyond that path, she thought, Appunni had not come back.

Would he not come? Would he never come back?

The day he walked out, she had thought he would come back when school gave over, his anger cooled. But he did not return even at dusk. She asked several people whether they had seen him but there was no one who had. She wept as she ran around at dusk looking for him. She went quite far, beyond the shed where areca nuts were chopped up, beyond the shops. She knew that Kadiru Mapilla's son was in Appunni's class. He was sure to know where Appunni was. It had grown dark. Normally, she never went out after dark, but that day she ran all the way desperately, gasping for breath. At Kadiru Mapilla's place, his son Muhammad said that he had not seen Appunni in class that day.

She placed her hand on her breast. My little one …

She came back, lighted the lamp, and stayed by the gate, waiting. If Sankaran Nair went past, she could ask him to go and find out what had happened. But Sankaran Nair no longer came this way. He had not come since that day. He would never come again. She had been trying to avoid meeting him face-to-face at the illam.

She had no one to turn to. Muthaachi was not in her hut. She waited up all night with a lighted lamp next to her. Would he not come?

Afterwards, she could not remember how she had made the night go by.

Muthaachi came back the next day. It was Muthaachi who told her that Appunni had gone to the tharavad. Syedalikutty had told Chakkamma and Chakkamma had told Muthaachi.

How could Appunni stay in the tharavad? They had insulted him and sent him away. He would never be able to endure life there.

Parukutty waited. My son will come back, he has to come back.

When she went to the illam, the senior amma asked: 'Has your son come back, Paruttyamma?'

She said: 'He'll be back.' So people knew then? That her son had got angry with her and gone away …

She felt unbearably sad in the evenings, as it grew dark. After the rains had started it had begun to grow dark earlier. The compound was full of water. A fear for which she could find no clear reason would creep into her heart. Muthaachi came to keep her company at night. Muthaachi would feel sleepy the moment she saw her mat spread out. Parukutty could not sleep if she closed the door. She would listen intently if she heard the slightest sound in the front veranda. Appunni was unlikely to come so late at night. Still, she could not help listening every time something moved.

Would he be going to school in this rain? She had heard that the river was full. Amina Umma had told her so. The boat had not been plying for the last three days.

'If it goes on like this for another two days, there might be floods,' said Amina Umma when she came back from the bazaar. The river had risen to the level of the road that ran alongside it. You had to walk carefully along the edge of the road because it was ready to crumble. God, that was the way to school. Would Appunni be careful?

Bhagavathi, protect him ... Parukutty vowed an offering of payasam to the goddess.

There was no rice in the house. She had borrowed some from Amina Umma in the afternoon and there was a handful left. She could manage on that the next day. And after that?

The rain was not going to stop.

Muthaachi had been in Parukutty's house ever since it began to rain. Wrapped in a shawl, she sat there stroking her legs. Every now and then she cursed the rain.

'The astrologer said there would be heavy rain. No wonder it's pouring ...'

A cold wind blew in. Muthaachi cursed as she shivered: 'This terrible rain will ruin us, it's the rain that was predicted for the *kaliyugam*.'

Amina Umma came in through the back of the house, an umbrella hat on her head.

'Did you hear, Paruttyamme?'

Parukutty could hear nothing through the deafening roar of the wind.

'The water has risen to the level of the Pooman canal. Will God desert us?'

Muthacchi invited her in. Umma slanted her head to let the water drain off her umbrella-hat and came up.

'Do you remember the flood in 1924?'

'Of course. All of us moved to Syedali-ka's house. My God, that was the time our old jackfruit tree fell on the house.'

Muthaachi had many things to say about the flood. The water had entered her hut and her calf had been washed away. Muthaachi told them how one of the Vadakkumuri women had managed to wedge herself into the fork of a jackfruit tree and escape from being washed away.

'The Vadakkeppat garden was flooded. The water rushed in as fast as a baby snake. And went away as fast.'

Parukutty had only a memory as faint as a dream about that flood. Many people who had to move out of their houses had sought refuge in the tharavad. Although the house was by the riverside, it had been built at a height and water could not enter it. People stayed in the outhouse and on the verandas for two or three days, cooking their own food. Cheruman families crowded into the cattle sheds. The level of the water started to come down by the evening of the third day.

Muthaachi described to Amina Umma as if she had seen it happen with her own eyes: how an elephant had floated away and a mapilla had managed to throw a rope around its neck, and catch it at a spot near the Karanoor bridge. Umma listened entranced. There were stories of people who had come upon money boxes and cooking vessels when the water level went down; and of people who had come back much later to the houses that had been flooded and found snakes swaying with their hoods unfurled in the fireplaces and around the pillars.

Amina Umma had her own stories to tell.

'Do you want to hear, dear Muthaachi? We came back in the evening to the hut after the water had gone down and heard a hiss in the corner. A huge cobra!'

Amina Umma ended with a prayer: 'May God help us. If the water rises, the village will be destroyed.'

Amina Umma's daughter called out to her from the fence. As she went out, Amina Umma said, 'If we have to move out, we'll go together, Paruttyamme. What else can we do?'

Parukutty grunted. And prayed, Bhagavathi, may this rain stop.

The whole village was in distress. People had taken up positions by the side of the river to see how far it would rise. The river was usually full in the months of Karkatakam and Thulam. But it never rose to this dangerous level. The year before it had looked as if the water would rise to the level of the Pooman canal. But the heavy rain had suddenly stopped and afterwards there had been alternate spells of sunshine and rain.

The fields were filled with the first crop of the year. If the road gave way, they would be completely submerged. Even if the level of the water went down now, the entire crop of paddy harvested in Chingam was sure to be just chaff. Sand was certain to seep into the fields near the river. Only if money was spent to secure the legal rights to the land could it be divided properly into fields.

People walking on the road, people huddled inside the shops, they were all afraid. The rain stopped in the afternoon and the sky grew a little lighter. Everyone was relieved. If the rain stopped and the sun came out for a couple of days, they would be saved.

But deep in the night thunder roared from the sky like a massive explosion of dynamite. A brisk drizzle set in and with it a wind.

Muthaachi said, to comfort herself, 'Good that there's a wind. It will carry the rainclouds away. And then there won't be any rain.'

But that was not what Parukutty was worried about. Where would Appunni be sleeping? God, what if he were sitting on the front veranda while it thundered and blew?

The sky was full of noise again. It sounded now as if wildcats were fighting. Deep growls rolled over the sky followed by dazzling flashes of lightning. And then thunder exploded again.

'Narayana, Narayana ...' Muthaachi began to pray. Parukutty got up, lowered the palm-leaf screen and closed the window.

The wind was growing stronger. The banana plants swayed wildly. The drizzle grew heavier and it seemed as if the wind and the rain were competing with each other. The drumming of the raindrops on the roof became louder and louder.

Only an ocean of darkness was visible outside the window. The growl of thunder in the sky, the roar of the rain, and the shriek of the wind as it tore through the banana stumps that were scattered through the yard combined to make Parukutty tremble with fear. Whenever she peered through the window into the roaring sea of darkness outside, there would be a flash of lightning and the black outlines of the trees would take shape for a second in its glow like sentinels keeping watch over the endless night. Then the darkness would close in again and its roar would sear her eyes.

'It's a cyclone moving in, child. The astrologer predicted a *vayumandalam*[2] this year, that means there'll be a cyclone,' said Muthaachi without opening her eyes.

Parukutty lighted a chimney lamp and placed it at Muthaachi's head, away from the direction of the wind.

Muthaachi lay flat, her eyes closed tight, muttering her prayers rapidly.

They heard the sound of a palm branch crashing down in the garden, then an uprooted papaya tree collapsing with a thud into a clump of banana plants.

Muthaachi opened her eyes. She looked weak and terrified.

'Parutty, will we be caught under the house if it falls down?'

'Don't worry so much, Muthaachi.'

'Narayana, Narayana, Narayana ...'

A sudden gust of wind tore in through the window and blew out the chimney lamp. Muthaachi's prayers grew louder.

Parukutty thought she could hear a sound that was different from the roar of the rain outside. Could she? She listened carfeully. Yes, someone was calling out. She lit the lamp again and said to Muthaachi:

'Someone's calling from outside, Muthaachi.'

Muthaachi opened her eyes but continued to pray, making no attempt to get up. Her prayers frightened Parukutty more than the roar of the gale.

She opened the front door a little way, very hesitantly. Amina Umma was standing on the veranda, completely drenched, an umbrella-hat on her head and a hurricane lamp in her hand.

'Paruttyamma, we're finished.'

'What is it, Umma?'

Water dripped from Amina Umma's clothes. She was gasping for breath and weeping.

'My mapilla's just come back from the bazaar. The road is about to give way. We'll have to move out.'

'Where can we go, Umma?'

---

[2]During Samkranti, if the astrologer predicts a 'vayumandalam', the belief is that there will be a cyclone.

'It doesn't matter where. Maybe to someone's house on the hill. My children are bundling up things. I don't know what to do with the chickens and goats.'

Seeing Parukutty standing absolutely still, Amina Umma urged: 'Come on quickly. Only God knows what it will be like in a little while.'

'I'm not going anywhere, Umma.'

'Are you mad? Come along, quick. The Kundungal folk have moved the women and children already and the men are taking the cattle now.'

Through the rain, in the glow of the moving hurricane lamps, she could see people walking along the other side of the fence carrying bundles.

'What are you waiting for, Paruttyamme?'

'I don't have anywhere to go, Umma. You go along.'

Amina Umma could not believe her ears. 'What are you saying?'

'I'm not coming, Umma. You go along.'

Amina Umma's eldest son came up to the fence to call her. 'Come on, Umma'

'Paruttyamme!'

'Go on, Umma. Let Muthaachi come too.'

Muthaachi had already hobbled out, enveloped in her shawl.

'My betel leaf box is in my hut, Umma.'

Umma lost her temper. 'Shut up, old woman. People are running for their lives and you talk about a betel leaf box!'

Amina Umma's husband called out to her in a voice louder than the shriek of the wind.

'Get going, Umma.'

'But who will keep you company, Amma?'

'God will, Umma. Go on now.'

All Amina Umma could do was exclaim: 'O my Maker!' Muthaachi and she climbed down the front steps, huddled under her umbrella-hat. A shower of raindrops hit the hurricane lamp so hard that its glass broke. The wick inside went out as well, probably because water had splashed in. Amina Umma hesitated again and Parukutty said:

'Don't worry, Umma. If I don't die we'll meet again.'

In the darkness, neither would have seen the other wipe her tears away. Parukutty stood outside watching them until their shadowy figures melted into the darkness. Then she went in and closed the door.

Her pain and fear had disappeared. All that remained was a numb awareness that she no longer cared what happened.

... The whole village was sunk under water. She sat clinging to a log of wood that was floating over the water. If her grip loosened ... her fingers had begun to feel numb. Caught in a whirlpool, the log slipped away and she began to sink into the depths of the water. Ayyo! She woke up, startled, and realized it had been a dream.

She sat up on the mat, trembling with fear.

She got up. When she opened the door and peered out, she felt dizzy. She could see nothing but water around her and its level had risen considerably. It seemed as if she was standing on a small island that was fast dissolving into a vast and limitless ocean. The green fields she had seen the day before were completely submerged. Rushing in through the compounds and nursery beds, the water had reached the level of the steps. Boats moved over the fields that had been almost ready to harvest.

All her neighbours' houses were empty. There was no sound, no smoke. Human beings were visible only as white specks in the small boats that moved over the distant fields now under water.

The rain had not abated. But the wind that had roared all night was now exhausted and asleep. All the banana trees in the yard had fallen down. The bamboo poles that had made the fence lay bent and slanted in all directions. Branches of mango trees that the wind had blown in from other compounds lay scattered in the slush in her yard. Only two or three palm leaves were left on the roof of Muthaachi's hut.

And the water could still go on rising ...

If she were to scream, no one would hear her. She experienced no fear, only a quiet pain. Perhaps this would be the end.

A handful of rice left over from the day before lay in a basket inside the house. But she did not feel like lighting the fire or making kanji. She held on to the wet, crumbling edge of the veranda and stared at the limitless expanse of water.

The water had risen to the level of Amina Umma's yard. If the frame of the gate broke, it would flood the place.

She heard the pathetic bleat of a goat somewhere in the distance. The animal must have realized its impending death.

The small boats moved on ...

A kid bleated faintly ...

Was it the bleat of a kid? Or a baby crying, 'Amma!'

By noon, even the boats were no longer visible. Nothing moved. Neither the goat nor its kid bleated. This was not the silence of a house of death. It was the numbness in a room where one awaited death.

She could hear the fence giving way. The gate broke. Streams of reddish, muddied water slithered like starved snakes into the yard through all the crevices. As she watched, the entire compound was submerged and the water came up to the edge of the steps.

She was convinced that her end had come.

She went back into the house. She did not dare look out. The water must be rising, there would be only a few minutes left now ...

Towards dusk, she heard something crashing down on the southern side. She took a quick look through the gap in the window: Muthaachi's hut had collapsed.

The rain stopped as darkness fell and so did the sound of the wind. All around her it was wet and dark. Now and then she could hear the water drumming on the outer walls.

Her heart had become as dark and numb as the night.

The thudding of the rain against the walls grew louder and sounded like footsteps. Footsteps that came nearer and nearer.

She wished she did not have to think. In spite of trying not to, her mind kept slipping back along the paths she had trod. Figures and images kept surfacing and disappearing. A naalukettu, a sunken courtyard guarded by massive wooden pillars. A platform with a jasmine plant at the centre. A broad-chested man with lips stained red by betel juice. A young girl lying exhausted over the shoulders of a man who walked rapidly, perspiring, under a sky overcast with clouds. Wavy hair and a forehead on which the veins stood out. The face kept slipping farther and farther away ...

Her dead body would float away the next day. As the water drained away, it would be caught on the thorns of a fence, or wedged in a screwpine bush. Maybe no one would recognize it. Maybe no one would come to claim it.

If only she could see Appunni once ... She had never given up, even at the moments when she had endured agony ... May he never experience agony, she thought. ... He should never have been born as the son of the servant woman who worked in the pounding shed of the illam.

Let Appunni be happy, she prayed again. Bhagavathi, may all good things come to him.

If only she could fall asleep, lying prone on the mat, her face pressed into the pillow, she would know nothing. She must somehow fall asleep, she thought, before the water came and touched her with its cold fingers. Maybe she would be asleep when the walls crumbled and fell down. It would all be over in a few minutes after that.

As a child, whenever she found it difficult to sleep, her mother used to tell her to chant Shiva's name: 'Namah Shivaaya'.

She lay with her eyes closed, praying.

'Namah Shivaaya, Namah Shivaaya.'

The walls were drenched. The cold hands crept nearer ...

'Namah Shivaaya, Namah Shivaaya.'

She felt she was collapsing. Spots of colour blossomed and danced inside her tired eyes. She was plunging into the depths ...

And then,

'Paruttyamme!'

Her heart, her limbs, throbbed wildly. A human voice. She could not open her eyes. Her body felt like a limp rag.

'Paruttyamme!'

She opened her eyes with difficulty and got up slowly. Her body trembled like a scrap of palm leaf in a gale. She could not speak. She did not remember where she had left the lamp. She walked towards the door in a daze and opened it with unsteady hands. Someone was standing there. There was darkness outside and in her eyes ...

'Amme!'

'It's me, don't be afraid. Me, Sankaran Nair.'

Her legs were giving way. She crumbled like an uprooted tree. But she did not fall. Two strong hands held her up.

'I've brought a boat. Come on ...'

She wished she could say something. But she could not. There was no strength left in her ...

'I'll hold you up.'

He gathered her in his arms and stepped into the water.

When Parukutty opened her eyes, she thought she was in the middle of the sea. Around her lay a limitless expanse of water. She could hear oars plying. It took her some time to find out where she was. Inside a boat. He was pushing the oars with all the strength he had to battle the force of the water and the eddying whirlpools. Drops of hot perspiration fell on her face and she realized she was lying with her head on his lap. She knew she could raise her head and sit up but she continued to lie there. Keeping her eyes closed, she asked:

'Where are we going?'

'To a spot high enough, where the water will not get to us,' he said, gasping as he plied the oars forcefully to prevent the boat dashing against a tall stump of wood that stood in their way.

6

The old peon Koyamu brought a memo to the classroom. Ramanatha Iyer's history class was in progress. Master read the memo and said: 'V. Appunni, the headmaster wants you.'

All the children stared at Appunni. He found it hard to hide his anxiety. Generally, it was children who had created trouble of some sort who were summoned to the office. The headmaster would then use the cane on both their hands until he had had enough. If the student's offence was a trivial one, he would only receive a long scolding. After which the headmaster would press a pencil with a sharp point against the boy's earlobe. Those who had experienced the latter punishment considered it far more terrible than twelve swipes with a cane.

Why was he being summoned? He did not remember having done anything wrong. Maybe Bhaskaran had made up some story about him.

His legs trembled as he entered the office. The headmaster asked:

'So, are you studying hard?'

'Yes.'

The headmaster then told him that he had been awarded a scholarship. Six rupees a month! He had won it because he had stood first in the half-yearly examination.

So, he did not have to pay fees anymore.

After paying four rupees and thirteen annas, he would have a rupee and three annas left.

A rupee and three annas of his own every month!

'Sign here.'

He signed on a revenue stamp. As he turned to go out, the headmaster handed him a wad of notes.

'They've sent the amount for the last eight months.'

Eight sixes were forty-eight!

He could not believe it. His hands trembled when he took the money. As he left the office with forty-seven rupees and fifteen annas, he felt he had become a great man.

He had been saying his prayers every day. Since coming to the tharavad, he prayed regularly in front of the machu. The Bhagavathi must have blessed him.

They said that the Bhagavathi was the mother of everyone in the tharavad. She resided in the machu. Ammamma often said: 'She's the mother who brought us food.'

An old story.

It had happened a very long time ago. There had been only a woman and her six children living in the tharavad at the time. She used to milk the cow every day and take the milk to the temple. She had to cross a river to get there. She subsisted on the *naivedyam* rice she was given from the temple, the rice that had been offered to the deity.

One year, in the month of Thulam, the river overflowed its banks and no boat could cross. The woman waited on the bank for a long time, milk can in hand. In the end she went home sadly. Her children would have nothing to eat that night. At midnight, someone came to the door and called her. She opened the door and a long arm extended a potful of rice over the threshold.

'Wake up the children and give them this.'

The woman saw a figure enveloped in silk open the door of the machu and disappear inside. She heard the tinkle of ankle bells as well. She never saw the figure again.

That was the Bhagavathi, they said. It was after that incident that the tharavad had prospered.

Appunni felt as if he believed in the Bhagavathi and all the gods that day. He had been filled with anxiety as the date on which he had to pay the fees came nearer. Who would give him four rupees and thirteen annas?

He had become a hero now among the children. He had forty-seven rupees, fifteen annas in his pocket. He had never laid hands on so much money.

When he reached home that evening, he found that the news had preceded him. Bhaskaran must have told them.

Valiamma actually showed him some kindness that day. She called him as well when Bhaskaran and the others sat down to dinner.

He had not realized that a sum of forty-seven rupees and fifteen annas could be so valuable.

Ammamma said to him at night: 'You mustn't waste that money. I'll keep it for you.'

That was how he suddenly acquired two new shirts. Ammamma took a little money for herself to buy sheep heads for soup and medicated oil. He learned later that Kutta Ammaaman asked Ammamma to lend him the rest.

But all this did not upset him. He suddenly felt he was a rich man. Kutta Ammaaman was his debtor! Ammamma had enjoyed his money.

As she sat down to have her soup, Ammamma would say:

'It's he who's a help to me in my old age.'

Meanwhile, the matter of the partition of the property still smouldered. Discussions had been going on for days. But they had reached nowhere.

From the moment she had heard that there was a likelihood of the property being divided, Valiamma had been saying: 'Just give me and my children whatever is due to us.'

Meenakshi Edathi and Cheriachan had no opinion to offer. It was Ammamma who was really distressed.

'That I should have had to see this happen with my own eyes ...'

As soon as the seniors of the village began their discussions on the front veranda, Ammamma would say:

'If only I can stay in this tharavad until I die.'

Valia Ammaaman behaved as if he had completely forgotten that a member of the family named Appunni lived in the naalukettu. He took care not to come face-to-face with Appunni. Appunni tried to keep out of his way as well.

Although the house was full of people, the feeling that he was alone continually haunted Appunni. No one ever called his name loudly. He drank his kanji in the morning, went to school, and came back in the evening. He had his bath in the pond in the compound. Taking a pinch of vibhuti from the wooden basket hanging at the edge of the sunken courtyard in the thekkini, he would make a mark on his forehead, join his palms and pray in front of the machu, and sit down to read by the light of the lamp placed there. No one ever had anything to ask him or say to him.

Valiamma was very upset when she realized that Appunni was never going to return to his own house. She kept saying loudly to herself: 'This place is sure to be ruined. Rubbish swept up from everywhere finds refuge here ...'

Only Malu came and spoke to him and asked him silly questions. She would stand and stare at him sometimes as he studied. He disliked this. Every evening, she told him all that happened that day. Somehow, he detested this thin, dark-skinned girl with the pointed face. He knew she was harmless. But every time she showed him affection, he would feel angry. She would hover around him when she had no work in the kitchen. What are you doing, Appunni Etta? What are you drawing?

Like him, she too was redundant in this household.

She always had a lot of housework to do though, and her clothes were perpetually shabby and dirty.

Thangedathi and Ammini Edathi had clothes made of silk. A fragrance wafted from them as they passed by—compounded of warmed oil, sandalwood, *mattipasha* incense, and screwpine flowers. While Malu gave off an odour of damp cloth that had not dried properly.

Ammini Edathi rarely went to her mother's house and when she did, she always came back in four or five days.

Valia Ammaaman liked one of his children to stay with him all the time. Devaki Edathi, his elder daughter, used to stay with him at first. When she got married and moved to her husband's house, Ammini

Edathi had taken her place. For quite some time, Ammayi had not stayed here for long periods. The last time she had come was for Thiruvathira the previous year and she had stayed a week.

One day Appunni washed his shirt and spread it out to dry. He never wore a shirt inside the house. As he paced up and down the yard in his banian, Ammini Edathi remarked:

'You look good in a banian, Appunni.'

He was always reluctant to talk to her. Whenever she came up to him he felt confused. The form in front of him would fade and he would remember the image of a bare-breasted serpent-girl wearing a narrowly pleated length of cloth below her waist, swaying to and fro in the glow of a lighted brass lamp, a cluster of areca flowers in her hand.

In the evenings, when Valia Ammaaman went out for a walk, Ammini Edathi would stand in the western yard of the pathayappura, teasing out the tangles in her flowing hair. Appunni liked to watch her then without her being aware of it. Her blue silk blouse would glitter with every movement she made. He could glimpse her stomach, the colour of a tender palm spathe, through the unpinned slit at the bottom. She had put on weight since the serpent thullal. Her half-closed eyes would wander over the banana grove that was touched by the evening sun. Her wrists, covered with red glass bangles, always had a moist look. When she ran her fingers through her hair, the bangles would tinkle.

He found it difficult to look straight at her when she stood before him. He would wish that he could look at her vengefully, contemptuously. Valia Ammaaman's darling daughter! The youngest daughter of the man who hated him so much. He wished he could direct all the repulsion he felt for Valia Ammaaman towards her. But when she was actually in front of him, he found he could hardly lift his head. He liked looking at her from a distance. When her hair snaked forward over her shoulder, he would imagine glittering black serpents gliding over her breasts. Her half-closed eyes made him wonder whether she dreamed as she walked around.

The serpents in the shrines were sure to open out their hoods and start to sway, he thought, when she came out to the western yard at dusk. Serpents loved beautiful young girls.

Ammini Edathi was a beautiful serpent. He loved to stand at a distance and watch this serpent with its hood unfurled. He was afraid to go too near ...

One day Ammini Edathi suddenly came up behind him while he was covering his English textbook with a piece of paper he had found on the ledge above the door.

'What are you doing, Appunni?'

Not looking up from what he was doing, he said, 'Nothing.'

'Let me look at your book, Appunni.'

She knelt down beside him and the pleasing fragrance of the jasmines in her hair wafted towards him.

He put down the book he had covered and she picked it up.

She had studied only until the fifth class and could not read English. He felt proud of himself. He could read and write English.

Ammini Edathi turned the pages and asked: 'Can you read all this, Appunni?'

'Yes.'

'Read, let me listen.'

He couldn't do that. Read out for someone else to listen! Was it so enjoyable to listen to someone read? He wanted to show off his knowledge but felt shy.

'Whose picture is this?' she asked, pointing to a page.

'Rani Lakshmibai.'

'Who is Lakshmibai?'

She didn't even know who Lakshmibai was! He knew the whole story of Jhansi's queen. Why relate it to her?

'She's a queen of olden days,' was all he said.

'And this one?'

'This is the story of the flying horse. The prince and princess are riding the horse.'

'Where did they go?'

'To the prince's own country.'

'And then?'

'And then the prince married the princess.'

'And then?'

'And then ... they lived happily ...'

'And then?'

Not knowing what more to say, he suddenly fell silent. Ammini Edathi laughed. And he couldn't help laughing too. But he quickly stopped. She pressed on his shoulder to get up and he caught the fragrance of jasmines again.

'So you know all these stories, Appunni?'

'I have to study them.'

'And you still won't narrate them to me?' She sounded like a small child when she said that. But he did not answer.

'Why don't you say something, Appunni?'

He didn't answer that either.

'Why are you angry with me?'

'I'm not angry.'

She stood there awhile, thinking, then went into the vadikkini.

Quarrels between Valia Ammaaman and Kutta Ammaaman became a common occurrence in the house. Valia Ammaaman was not prepared to let the property be divided. He no longer gave them the paddy they needed. Valiamma's complaints grew steadily louder.

Appunni knew the results of the annual examination before school reopened. He had passed but did not know his marks. He had no chance, he thought, of getting the first rank. But he was sure he would be second. Krishnankutty Variar would be first.

Ammini Edathi asked: 'Did you pass, Appunni?'

'Yes.'

'What rank did you get?'

'I don't know.'

'You'll stand first.'

Would he? He would get a prize then. He had been awarded a proficiency prize at the last anniversary function. He had known only when he saw his name on the notice board.

The hall had been full. He had waited for the prize distribution. He was out of his mind with joy when his name was called out through the microphone. V. Appunni. He felt as though the sound reached out to the whole world. He walked through the crowd and received his prize. An English book with a hard cover and the picture of a bearded man on it.

'You'll be a great person, Appunni.'

Was Ammini Edathi mocking him? No, he felt she was blessing him.

'When you finish your studies and get a good job ...' She stopped. He did not look up but knew that her eyes were fixed on his face.

It was a dark night in the month of Karkaitakam. The wick of the lamp in the thekkini had burned out because there was no oil. He would have to wait until Meenakshi Edathi finished her work in the kitchen to borrow her chimney lamp. After dinner, he went to his favourite spot on the eastern veranda.

Valia Ammaaman was not at home. He had gone to Guruvayoor and would come back only the next day. He worshipped regularly at the Guruvayoor temple once a month. The pathayappura was dark.

Ammamma usually ate at dusk and went to bed. The rainy season aggravated her rheumatic pains. Valiamma and her children had eaten and gone upstairs. Meenakshi Edathi and Malu were in the kitchen finishing their chores.

A wet wind blew in from the fields. Appunni looked into the darkness, thinking of many things.

Ammini Edathi suddenly appeared.

'Are you asleep, Appunni?'

He was startled. He had realized she was next to him only when he heard her voice.

'You didn't get a lamp?'

'No.'

'Father's not here. I'll light the lamp upstairs in the pathayappura for you.'

'No, don't.'

He had never been in the pathayappura; he did not ever want to go there either.

'Why not? Have you finished reading?'

He said curtly, 'Yes.'

'Then why don't you go to sleep?'

'It's not yet time.'

'You said you'd tell me the stories in your book. Why didn't you then?'

'There aren't any stories in that book.'

Ammini Edathi sat down near him.

'Lies. Isn't there the story of the prince and princess who rode the flying horse?'

'Yes, that's the only one there is.'

'What fun it would be to have a flying horse, isn't it, Appunni? We should have had one during the floods.'

Appunni was amused. Ammini Edathi was nearly eighteen but her thoughts were those of a little child.

'That's only a story,' said Appunni, making light of it.

'I know the story of Unni. Do you know it?'

'Which Unni?'

The story of Unni in the Vadakkanpattu, the ballads sung in North Malabar. Ammini Edathi knew them. Unni hid a man inside her hair. She stood in the water, her hair streaming down to her waist (Ammini Edathi had such long hair too, she could hide a person inside it if she wanted to). The man had gone to Unni's room at night, while all her brothers were out. He disguised himself as a *panan* and escaped in the morning.

Appunni liked the story. There was a part of it in verse in his Malayalam book.

When another gust of wet wind blew in from the fields, the cold pierced his body.

'It's so chilly,' said Ammini Edathi. 'Don't you feel cold without a shirt?'

'Um ...'

'How can that Ayyappan sleep on the open veranda outside the cowshed when it's so cold?'

Ammini Edathi's body brushed against his shoulder. Her hand felt warm.

'You're so lucky, Appunni. The room under the stairs is never cold, especially if you close the door and the window.'

He said jokingly, 'Then why don't you sleep in the small room upstairs until the rains are over?'

There was a very small room upstairs without any windows. Broken pots, brooms and mattresses from which the cotton had spilled out were kept in it. Once a year the puja for the ancestors was conducted in it.

Ammini laughed softly.

'I'd be afraid.'

'What's there to be afraid about?'

'All our old ancestors might come in.' Pore Ammaaman, Narayana Ammaaman and the others. They were all dead. There were all kinds of stories about them. Appunni thought of Narayana Ammaaman with dislike and disgust. He had kicked one of his nieces until she died. Long, long ago. When he thought of that niece's ghost ... he was afraid, although he had always told himself he was courageous. One kick, and the blood had poured out of her mouth and nose. A sixteen-year-old girl.

He had never found out what her offence had been. It had happened very long ago. The reason they gave was ... how could he believe it? Would a man kick a girl to death because he found a strand of hair in his rice? It couldn't be that. She must have done something more serious.

'Aren't you afraid to sleep in the room under the stairs?' asked Ammini Edathi.

'Not in the least.'

'You're really brave. Wait till Pore Ammaaman's ghost comes and grips your neck at night.'

Appunni said indifferently: 'Indeed!'

'You've that much courage? I'll scream one night and frighten you.'

He felt uneasy when she slipped her hands around his neck. Her clothes smelled of fine soap.

Pressing her hands lightly against his throat, Ammini Edathi asked, 'Aren't you afraid, aren't you?'

Shivers of delight coursed up and down Appunni's body.

A lamp appeared in the kitchen. Malu.

'Ammini Edathi! Where's Ammini Edathi?'

Meenakashi Edathi was behind her.

Ammini Edathi quickly took her arms away, got up and said:

'Coming. Appunni, close the door of the pathayappura and bolt it.'
Meenakshi caught sight of Appunni. 'You haven't gone to bed?'
Appunni decided he would stop reading.
'I'm just about to.'
'Hurry up. I want to close all the doors and lie down.'
Appunni went to his room under the stairs and groped for his mat.
There was no light there. He was used to spreading his mat out in the
dark. All he had was a mat. He had no sheet to cover himself with.
Ammini Edathi came to the foot of the stairs, a small lamp in her
hand. Malu was with her, she slept in Ammini Edathi's room at night.
'Is there water in the toilet upstairs, Malu?'
'I don't know.'
'Get a pot of water then.'
Malu went away to get the water. Although there was enough space
for her to skirt him, Ammini Edathi stepped over Appunni and stood
by the stairs. Only her face was visible in the glow of the little lamp.
She bent down to see if Appunni was asleep.
He quickly shut his eyes.
'You're pretending to be asleep, aren't you?'
He didn't move.
'I'll come and frighten you at night, alright?'
Malu came with the water and they went upstairs.
They slept in the room right above him. Ammini Edathi slept in
the pathayappura only when Ammayi was there. He heard footsteps
upstairs and the sound of the door to the toilet being opened. Then
the cot creaked. Since the roof was very low, every movement could
be clearly heard.
The cot creaked again. That must be Ammini Edathi. Malu slept on
the floor.
Appunni was not sleepy. A chill wind still blew in through the
window. It must be raining heavily somewhere. Through the window
bars, he could see the cowshed and the branches of the *ayini* tree behind
it like shadows in the darkness. He felt very cold, so he got up and
closed the window.

It was pitch dark inside now. He was not afraid. Ammini Edathi and Malu were in the room directly above him. In the rooms opening out from the corridor opposite it were Valiamma and her children. He could hear someone snoring downstairs, in the room next to the vadikkini.

He lay with his eyes closed. It was enjoyable to sleep when it was dark and cold. He had nothing to cover himself with. His mother used to cover him with a shawl when it rained and when it grew very cold, she used to hold him close to her. But that was in the past.

He thought of them as incidents that had happened many, many years ago.

He could not help thinking of his mother.

His heart grew heavy. He must not think of the past … He closed his eyes tight.

Sleep crept slowly into his eyes.

—When the prince saw the palace that rose from the mass of clouds, he twisted the horse's left ear. He landed on the canopy of the cot. The princess was seated on the silk mattress, playing the veena.

He felt someone touch his chest and woke up with a start. But he did not open his eyes. There was a hand on his chest. His instinct was to scream. Fingers with rings on them moved over his face.

'It's me, Appunni.'

He knew in a second. There was nothing to fear. The tinkle of glass bangles … the palm on his chest felt hot.

His eyes closed again by themselves. But his mind would not plunge into the depths of sleep. Warm breath touched his face. He heard a very soft voice: 'Are you afraid?'

He felt heat coursing through his body that had been numb with cold. Warm, soft hands wandered gently over him. A faint whiff of scented soap … he felt his body exploding.

He wanted to open his eyes.

—The prince and princess were riding on a flying horse through the clouds. What he had thought were clouds were wild jasmine bushes in bloom. He brushed against branches and creepers as they moved.

Flower petals fluttered against his cheeks. They were warm to the touch.

The horse moved rapidly through the wild jasmine bushes. The frightened princess's hands circled the prince's waist tightly. Was he finding it hard to breathe?

Pigeons were seated on his chest, cooing, rubbing their beaks against him. Where was he now? The princess had arrived on the flying horse. The prince with his silk robe and turban—was it not himself? He was twisting and turning now through tall branches. The prince's red silk tunic was slipping down ... thorns were hurting his body ...

The magic horse rose higher and higher, carrying the prince and princess ...

'Appunni Etta, Appunni Etta ...' Malu's voice woke him. 'Do you know what time it is?'

Appunni sprang up, rubbing his eyes. He adjusted his mundu and opened the window. The sunlight flooded in. It was quite late. He suddenly remembered ... he must have been dreaming all night. Everything seemed unclear, like a vision glimpsed in the distance through a film of morning mist. He lifted his mat to roll it and lean it against the wall in the corner. Something fell out.

Shards of broken red bangles. With a yellow line running through them like a golden thread.

The first thing he did was to make sure Malu had left. She had.

He gathered the broken bits and walked into the yard. The pond was full of water. Taking a handful of burnt paddy husk to clean his teeth from the palm spathe tied to the pillar of the bathing shed, he sat down on the square stone used for scrubbing clothes.

He threw the broken bangle bits one by one into the middle of the pond. Watching them dart away like dragonflies and fall with a plop into the water, he thought ...

The shards of red glass could be seen for quite some way down as they sank into the water that the mellow morning sunlight had touched with a tinge of pale yellow.

He felt both sad and disgusted. But beneath it all, he was aware of a secret happiness which he hid inside him like a shining gem.

It was something he could take out and caress when he was all alone and no one was watching.

Many middlemen came to mediate between uncle and nephew. But no decisions had been reached.

Ammamma grew very agitated when she heard them discuss the partition, seated in the front veranda. She had lived in the tharavad for sixty-six years. She wanted to stay there until she died. She said so at least ten times a day.

Whenever she saw Kutta Ammaaman, she would say:

'Can't you wait until I die to divide these pots and pans amongst you?'

Kutta Ammaaman would not say anything. Valiamma wanted the piece of land near the river, the fertile area that yielded three harvests in the year, to be included in her share. She was full of complaints:

'It's I and my children who will suffer. Who will speak for us?'

Not a day passed without Vakil Kumaran Nair and Korukutty Panikker coming to talk things over. Korukutty Panikker said it would not be such a simple matter to divide the property. The lands were scattered over different areas. Each one had to be measured and prices fixed. There were debts against some of them. The various lines of succession in the tharavad had to be sorted out. Before any of this was done, the shares that each person was going to be allotted had to be agreed on.

Valia Ammaaman argued that he was entitled to two shares since he had administered the affairs of the tharavad for many years. It was an old custom to allot two shares of the property to the karanavar, he said. And much of the prosperity the tharavad enjoyed was thanks to him.

When Kumaran Nair brought this to Kutta Ammaaman's notice, the latter cleared his throat noisily and spat.

'Prosperity? The prosperity did not come here to this tharavad, it went to Poonthottam, his wife's place!'

Valia Ammaaman and Kutta Ammaaman no longer talked to each other directly. Kumaran Nair and Panikker acted as their spokesmen. Valia Ammaaman gave them an ultimatum: the partition would take place if he was allotted two shares and if everyone agreed that the field on the north was his private property. If not:

'Let me see how the partition will be carried out!'

It was at this point that the adhikari, Kalathil Nambiar, arrived to mediate.

It was a holiday for Appunni. It was his final year at school. He had to appear for a government examination. He had a great deal to read. He knew a final decision would be taken that day, so he went to the thekkini when Kumaran Nair and Koru Panikker arrived.

The adhikari arrived a little later. Kalathil Nambiar was considered a very important person in the village. As soon as he was seen at the entrance, the easy chair was brought down from the pathayappura. An order was dispatched indoors to send the *chellapetti* filled with betel leaves out for him.

It was the first time Appunni had seen the adhikari. He gazed at him as he came in. The short, stout, dark-skinned man was bald and his body was covered with hair.

'I haven't seen you in a very long time. Do sit down,' said Valia Ammaaman and the adhikari laughed so loudly, it seemed as if the sound would echo through the whole village.

'I'm growing old. My legs can't keep up with the rest of me.'

Vakil Kumaran Nair and Panikker hovered around respectfully. Kutta Ammaaman squatted on the eastern veranda, out of their sight, and doodled on the ground with his nails.

Valiamma and her children found places near the raised wooden platform in the thekkini.

Valia Ammaaman and the adhikari began to speak about rebuilding the kitchen area in the Vazhavil temple. Vakil Kumaran Nair's stance and gait betrayed how upset he was that they had not yet opened the topic of the partition.

It was the adhikari himself who brought it up. 'Well, Kunhikrishnan Nair, your nephew came and told me that he wanted his share of the property. They're talking about it in the village as well.'

Valia Ammaaman went down to the edge of the yard, spat noisily into the banana grove and came back. He said:

'Let him divide the property then.'

The adhikari laughed loudly again. 'You know saying that won't get us anywhere.'

'Why should I care if the property is divided? I'll be glad to get rid of this bundle of rags and tatters. But there's one thing, Adhikari ...'

'Tell me whatever it is, Kunhikrishnan Naire.'

'This tharavad—there's no need for me to tell you, adhikari. In Achumman's time, no other Nair tharavad had such prestige.'

'I know, I know.'

'That's what I mean. You know, adhikari, but the young fellows here don't. There were sixty-four people living here when the tharavad was partitioned. Once it was all divided, much of the prosperity disappeared. Still, it's the place where the Bhagavathi resides. You know that too, don't you, adhikari.'

The adhikari nodded his head emphatically to show that he knew.

'Then do you want to hear something else? All we have now is our reputation and this crumbling and decrepit naalukettu. And yet I carry on exactly as our forefathers used to do. Not that it's been easy. But it's because of me that it's survived. If we start fighting over the handful of pots and pans that are left ...'

Valia Ammaaman stopped. He continued in an even more serious tone, gesturing vigorously, '... it will not be long before the place is completely ruined.'

A soft but firm voice spoke up:

'That would have happened anyway.'

The adhikari turned. Kutta Ammaaman stood before him. Pretending not to see him, Valia Ammaaman went on:

'I would like to see everything go on the way it always has at least until I die. That's why I said what I did ...'

The adhikari looked at both of them. 'There's something in what Kunhikrishnan Nair says. But Kuttan Nair insists he wants his share. In that case, Kuttan Naire ...'

Kutta Ammaaman went down to the yard and stood there with his arms crossed over his chest.

'Let me tell you something Kuttan Nair. There's only you, uncle and nephews, here. Can't you settle things among yourselves?'

'I do not understand what you mean, adhikari,' said Kutta Ammaaman, pacing up and down the courtyard without looking at the adhikari's face.

The adhikari laughed loudly.

'Why not have an agreement that a certain amount of money be paid to you every year, Kuttan Nair? Why divide the property?'

Kutta Ammaaman did not reply to this at once. Vakil Kumaran Nair grinned foolishly and stammered:

'If Kuttan Nair's demands could be met as you suggested ...'

'I know, I know,' the adhikari cut in, not allowing him to finish speaking. 'You sound so eager, one would imagine it's you who are getting a share of the property!'

Kumaran Nair grinned foolishly again.

'What do you say, Kuttan Naire?' asked the adhikari.

'That could have been arranged much earlier.' Kutta Ammaaman came up to the pillar in the veranda. He placed his hand on the easy chair on which the adhikari was seated and said: 'You have to listen to what I have to say, adhikari. I'm quite old now. I'm the father of a fourteen-year-old girl. I've been working for the family since the time I was a small child. And what did I get for it? Four mundus and five paras of paddy a year! Look, adhikari, if I'd worked in someone's kitchen instead I would have earned more, wouldn't I?'

The adhikari chewed on the betel leaves in his mouth and listened to him silently.

Kutta Ammaaman had not finished.

'I heard some talk here about how difficult it is to look after the affairs of the tharavad. But didn't he bring his own family here so they could be well looked after? It's not the partition that will ruin the tharavad ...'

Appunni thought Valia Ammaaman would explode. But he sat very still. Was he going to listen to all this in silence? Appunni was astonished.

Kutta Ammaaman's voice rose.

'Listen to this too, adhikari. Nothing that happens at Vadakkeppat ever upsets the head of this family. All he wants is to be sure everyone in Poonthottam, his wife's place, thrives.'

Valia Ammaaman gave Kutta Ammaaman a terrible look and cried out: '*Eda!*'

'There's no use hiding anything. I'm talking to people who ought to know.'

Valia Ammamman trembled with fury. 'Ungrateful wretch, tell me—was it your old man's property I gave away? Your old man's ...'

The adhikari tried to pacify him. 'Let it go, Kunhikrishnan Naire. Young people say foolish things ...'

'I'm not afraid to speak,' said Kuttan Nair. 'Poonthottam prospers more and more with every day that passes. Do you know, if someone comes from there to visit us, my sisters have to take their food up to the pathayappura. As if our women here are menials who have to serve the Poonthottam folk! People who didn't have a paisa of their own at one time ...'

Ammamma came into the kitchen when she heard them raise their voices. 'Kutta, be careful, people will hear you ...'

'Kuttan Naire!' cried the adhikari. But Kutta Ammaaman went on, infuriated: 'I work like a cheruman and am treated like a mangy dog! If I'd toiled for my own sake I'd have had something to show for it.'

'We'll find a way out.'

Valia Ammaaman clattered up and down the yard in his wooden clogs. His expression said: let him have his say. When it was clear that Kutta Ammaaman had finished, Valia Ammaaman planted himself in front of the adhikari.

'Adhikari, this fellow who's been screaming at me ... he ... he ...' Valia Ammamman seemed to be gasping for breath. 'They were just helpless kids when their old man died. It was I who brought them up. And now they're up in arms against me. Such a thing has never happened here.'

No one spoke for a long time. Then Valia Ammaaman said:

'Adhikari, I will not be able to hold on to this any longer. Let's divide the property. You must do whatever is necessary.'

Inside the house, Ammamma wiped her eyes with the edge of her mundu.

'I got what I deserved for having taken on the burden of this rag-heap. And that's why I say I want two shares of the property. It's not that I want a paisa more than I should get of these wretched people's money. But that's been the custom for ages: that the head of the family gets two shares.'

Kutta Ammaaman's voice rose again: 'That's not possible.'

The adhikari tried to counsel Kutta Ammaaman. 'Don't say that, Kuttan Naire. It's a custom here in the village ...'

'That was in the old days.'

Appunni could not stay longer to listen. Meenakshi Edathi asked him to get her some firewood from the loft. It was one of the tasks he was often called upon to do. Meenakshi Edathi would hold the ladder for him. He would climb up and throw down the sticks of firewood.

What was happening now, he wondered. What were they talking about?

He was not particularly interested. All he felt was the enjoyment of watching a dramatic performance. It was fun to see his uncles attacking each other on the stage!

Adhikari Nambiar left only at dusk. Vakil Kumaran Nair came in looking crestfallen and Valiamma asked:

'Have they come to a settlement?'

'The karanavar is insistent. That the field on the north be declared his private property and that he does get two shares.'

'And what does Kuttan say to that?'

'He has no guts. He should file a case in court, then we could have seen the fun! How many partitions I've seen! But never in my life have I seen one that moves so sluggishly. Makes you fed up.'

Vakil Kumaran Nair was an old friend and welcome even in the women's quarters. When he went to say goodbye to Ammamma, she said:

'Kumara, you have to do something for me.'

'What is it, Kunhikkali Amma?'

'I don't want land or money. All I need now is a mango tree.'

Kumaran Nair had no idea what she meant.

'What do you want me to do, Kunhikkali Amma?'

'I want to die here, in this house. And have the mango tree cut down for my funeral pyre. But it looks as if you people won't allow me even that.'

'What can I say?'

'Don't say anything.'

He stood there for a while, scratching his head. Then he went out.

Nothing was said over the next few days. It seemed as if things had calmed down. And then, most unexpectedly, everything exploded.

Valia Ammaaman received a summons. Kutta Ammaaman was the plaintiff and everyone else was a defendant.

Valia Ammaaman spent the entire day walking up and down the yard until bedtime. He spent all day berating the members of the household. Every now and then, he went upstairs to the pathayappura. When he came down, his face was redder than ever.

'Where's Ammini?' he asked.

Ammini Edathi came down.

'Get ready to go to your house tomorrow. This house no longer belongs to your father.'

Ammini Edathi did not answer.

'You have your own house and your own people, there's no reason why you should go on staying here.'

Ammini Edathi went slowly back to the pathayappura.

Appunni lay awake that night in the room under the stairs. Everyone was asleep. In his heart lay the memory of another night, faint as a dream seen at dawn.

If Ammini Edathi went away, would she never come back? In the beginning, he used to feel confused when he saw her. Now he felt shy. Still, he wanted to see her stand with her hair undone, teasing out the tangles in it. Without her being aware of it, he had often gazed at her through the wooden window bars as she stood in the yard late in the evenings, just before dusk.

Everything was silent. He listened attentively. She was probably asleep. All the same, he wondered—would she come? No, he was just imagining it … still, was that a sound on the staircase? He thought he heard a footstep. His heart throbbed wildly. There was a rustle of cloth. When a hand was laid on his body he gripped it tight.

He sat up and Ammini Edathi sat close to him. She slipped her arm around his neck and held him tight. He did not know how long they sat there like that.

'Appunni,' she said softly. Her fingers ran up and down his back.

'I'm going away tomorrow, Appunni.'

Appunni wished he could see her face. But it was so dark, he could not see anything. He did not ask her when she would come again although the question filled his mind. He played with the glass bangles on the hand that lay over his shoulder.

'Will you come to my house, Appunni?'

'No. How can I?'

'I won't ever come here again.'

Did that mean he would never see her standing in the faint evening light just before dusk, teasing out the tangles in her hair?

'Why don't you say something? Are you angry with me?'

'No.'

'You'll become a great man, Appunni. Don't forget your Ammini Edathi when you become successful.'

No, he would not forget her. He would never be able to forget the beautiful serpent-girl swaying as she sat with a cluster of areca flowers in her hand, her long hair streaming over the bare breasts that shimmered in the radiance of the brass oil lamps.

'No, I won't,' was all he said.

They sat there like that for a long time. His heart still throbbed wildly.

'I'll go and lie down. Go to sleep, Appunni.'

As she got up, she said softly, her lips close to his ear, laughter and tears mingling in her voice: 'Ammini Edathi won't come to your room anymore to frighten you.'

He heard her footstep on the stairs. He lay with his eyes open, troubled and distressed.

Ammini Edathi was ready to leave in the morning. Valia Ammaaman waited for her in the yard, a *veshti* with a thin border on his shoulder and an umbrella in his hand.

Ammini Edathi said goodbye to everyone in the house, one by one. Appunni sat behind a haystack in the western yard until she finished, scribbling on the moss-covered wall with a piece of stone.

He did not see her leave. As he came into the front veranda, a blue silk blouse disappeared into the distance.

Appunni started out for school later than usual. The kanji had been served late that morning. For a few days now, none of the meals had been on time. The paddy seeds meant for the next year had been used up. Valia Ammaaman had sold all the paddy in the granary and the buyers had taken it away in their carts. If anyone in the household asked him for rice, he flung the most obscene words at them.

Valia Ammaaman was seldom at home. He would go to Poonthottam and stay there for eight or ten days at a time. He would leave as soon as the areca nuts and coconuts had been plucked. He behaved as if it was no longer his responsibility to run the affairs of the household.

Kutta Ammaaman did not seem to care either whether the people in the house ate or not. If his own food was not ready on time he would yell at Meenakshi Edathi. Who ran around borrowing rice and paddy from the neighbours. From time to time she would lament: 'It's all my destiny …'

Valia Ammaaman had forbidden the customers who regularly bought paddy from them to give Kutta Ammaaman any money.

Kutta Ammaaman turned elsewhere—he had the huge mango tree near the serpent-shrine cut down and sold it to Kutti Hassan. He bought a sack of rice for the household with the proceeds. When Valiamma asked him to render accounts for the rest of the money, he replied:

'*Oppol*, elder sister, just shut up.'

Men came in through the front yard with axes and ropes, to cut the tree down. Ammamma realized what was happening only when one of them went to the northern veranda to ask for water to drink. She wept the whole morning.

In three months, the outer compound turned into a patch of uncultivated land. Kutty Hassan Haji's carpenters began to saw the trees that had been felled into planks.

Appunni felt increasingly suffocated inside the naalukettu with every minute that passed. What a weird group of people they were, he thought: Ammamma who was always in tears; Valiamma who muttered to herself all the time and walked around clicking her heels; Cheriachan who sat

leaning against the wall, his legs covered with a blanket, holding forth
to whoever cared to listen about the state of humanity; Kutta Ammaaman
who rushed into the house like a hurricane from time to time and
created a racket ...

Hatred—all that filled Appunni's mind was hatred. Only when he
saw Meenakshi Edathi did he feel a twinge of pain. He caught sight of
her once, coming out of Vadakke Veedu with a basket of paddy, creeping
stealthily through the areca-nut grove so that no one would see her,
and his eyes filled with tears.

He had heard that both happiness and sorrow were part of the human
destiny. Then why did God never grant her happiness?

Appunni walked along, thinking of all these things. His companions
had gone ahead. The marks of the bullock-cart wheels still lay on the
clay-covered path.

Bhaskaran had failed the previous year. He was now in the Fifth
Form. No matter what problems they had at home, Bhaskaran and
Krishnankutty faced no difficulties at school. That was how things were
for sons born to the Namboodiri of a wealthy illam ...

Someone was standing by the stone platform on the roadside.
Appunni took no notice of him at first. He glanced at him as he went
nearer and realized it was Sankaran Nair. He felt as if he had trod on
burning coals.

'Appunni!' The man was coming up to him.

Appunni turned his face away and walked on.

'Appunni!'

He did not turn around. He walked quickly, taking long strides.
When he had gone quite a distance, he looked back. No, the man was
not there. He had obviously wanted to exchange small talk and renew
contact. Appunni had heard, he had endured all of it. He had come to
know that Amma had moved to the man's place when the floods
subsided. The things Valiamma had said when she heard! Appunni had
run away, into the yard, it had felt as if his skin was being peeled off. To
have gone off like that with Thengumpotta Sankaran Nair ...

But he had also experienced a great sense of relief the day he had heard the news, as if he had broken a chain that had been wound tightly around him and thrown it away.

And now here was the man, coming to make conversation with him ... Thengumpotta Sankaran Nair is nothing to me, he thought.

The bell had rung ten minutes before he arrived at school. It was Sankaranarayana Iyer Master's class, but he had not come and the Drawing master was there instead. The children were not afraid of him and the class was noisy.

The memo was read out in the second period.

The fee for the government examination had to be paid before the tenth. Fifteen rupees.

The tenth. There were only six days to go.

Where could he get fifteen rupees? Then he suddenly remembered. Ammamma had his money. He could ask for the sum that Kutta Ammaaman had borrowed.

When he got home that evening, he said to Ammamma:

'I have to pay my examination fees. I need fifteen rupees.'

'Ask Kutta Ammaaman, child. I'll speak to him too.'

He decided he would ask Kutta Ammaaman. He had never spoken to him directly. But he was not afraid to. A certain respect for the man lurked in some corner of his mind.

He thought of the day Valia Ammaaman had slapped him. It was Kutta Ammaaman who had come to his rescue that day. He had never spoken to Kutta Ammaaman. But the man who had had the courage to confront that frightful person, Valia Ammaaman, was a hero in his eyes.

Kutta Ammaaman was seldom at home. There were nights when he did not come back to the house at all. He would be with Vakil Kumaran Nair. And there were other rumours about him as well.

When Appunni came back from his bath the next day, Malu said, 'My father is here.'

Kutta Ammaaman was sitting on the wooden ledge in the front veranda smoking a beedi. Appunni was upset by the expression on his face. Kutta Ammaaman had been looking like this for some days now.

Appunni went up to him anyway.

Kutta Ammaaman took no notice of him at first. When he realized that Appunni would not go away, he asked:

'Yes?'

'I have to pay my fees for the government examination on the tenth.'

'And so?'

'Kutta Ammama ...'

'So you've come to ask for your money?'

'What can I do? If I don't pay the fees ...'

'And all this because I took a few rupee-notes of yours? I have no money, no nothing.'

Appunni was on the verge of tears. But he did not cry. He had learned not to cry when he was hurt.

Kutta Ammaaman said as he went in, 'As if people like you are going to study and become Deputy Collectors!'

Appunni swallowed the insult. Malu asked as he walked into the thekkini:

'Did you get it, Appunni Etta?'

Who was she to ask him? He looked at her vengefully and said, 'Go away, girl.'

Ignoring her, he went to the little room under the staircase, sunk in darkness.

Ammamma was upset. 'If only I had some money, child, you wouldn't have been in such trouble.'

No one would have money, he said to himself. Appunni will never have anyone to help him.

He had to pay his fees the next day. There were rich children in the class. Vasudevan Namboodiri—he would have money. His illam was wealthy. His father was insane, so it was he who managed the affairs of the household. He had a gold watch, a ring, and gold ear-studs. It was said that he always had ten-rupee notes in his pocket.

How could Appunni ask him for money? If he borrowed money from him, how would he return it?

But it was a matter of writing an examination. This agony would be over in another three months. After that ...

He had so many hopes.

He finally asked, very hesitantly. Namboodiri said, 'I do have money. But I have to go urgently to Thrissur. I have to buy a harmonium.'

Let him buy his harmonium, thought Appunni. Let him sing with Yashodhara. There were so many stories the students told about them!

Muhammad, who knew all Appunni's problems, took on the responsibility of finding the money. He asked a number of children in the class discreetly but did not get anything from them.

'Appunni, there's something you can do ...'

'What?'

'Can't you get it from Bhaskaran's mother?'

'I won't ask her.'

'Didn't you say she's your mother's elder sister?'

'She is, but I won't ask her.'

'You need the money by tomorrow, don't you? If you have scruples like that ...'

'I can't be so shameless, Muhammad.'

Muhammad did not insist.

Yes, there were people who had money. Valiamma. Valia Ammaaman. But he could not think of asking them.

He lay awake all night. How long he had suffered to reach here, the gateway to freedom. And now everything was falling to pieces ...

He had to hand the money in before four the next day.

With his mother's help, Muhammad promised to make a last effort among the people in his neighbourhood. He told Appunni that if he did not arrive at school before noon, it meant that he had not got the money.

Appunni was quite sure he would pass the examination if he wrote it. And if he passed, he would get a job somewhere. And then ... he would be able to hold his head high, he would no longer need help from anyone.

Everything hung now on the sole obstacle he had to overcome: those fifteen rupees.

He would never get the money. He would never be able to pay the fees. Nothing he wanted would ever happen.

He got up before daybreak. Coming back from the bathing tank after cleaning his teeth, he met Malu by the well. He went past ignoring her, but she stopped him to ask,

'Why are you up so early, Appunni Ettan?'

He did not respond. Everyone was against him. They were all waiting to see him ruined. He hated the naalukettu that stood there enveloped in the faint morning mist and all the people inside it.

He put on the shirt he had worn the previous day. The mundu he had washed was not quite dry but he changed the dirty one he was wearing for it anyway. He picked up the bundle of books held together by a rubber band and stepped out, only to encounter Malu again.

'Where are you off to so early?'

'Who knows where ...'

He stood uncertainly on the veranda, then opened the door of the gatehouse, walked into the fields, and wondered where to go.

He had to pay the fees by four that evening.

Who could he go and see? Who could he ask?

He walked along aimlessly, then climbed onto the road.

The school was on the south but he walked north. The teashop on the road that lay along the river was already noisy and crowded.

He went down again into the fields, then climbed into a lane, walked some way and came upon the slope of the hill. Not stopping to think where he was going, he finally reached the top of Narivalan hill. He suddenly remembered: this was where he had come the morning he had left home. He had met Syedalikutty here.

There was only an expanse of scorched grass on the hillside. The morning sunshine was spreading rapidly over it.

The rock jutting out from the hillside was still there. He sat down on it. Yes, it was here he had sat on that morning that was still so clear in his memory. Two years ago. The hillside had been covered with kannanthali bushes at the time.

Two years had gone by. He felt he had lived a very long time in those two years.

Had the rock that jutted out grown bigger? Maybe it had. The Science master had said in class: 'Growth is of two kinds. Rock and alum deposits grow from the outside. Living beings grow from inside.'

Maybe the rock was growing externally.

While human beings and living creatures grew internally.

How much had he grown in two years? Whenever he looked into the mirror, he felt he had become a grown man. He was no longer the little Appunni who used to walk around in shorts and a shirt. That Appunni had been the son of the woman who pounded paddy at the illam. He was now a person who stood alone in a world filled with people. It did not matter that he had no one of his own. Nor was he afraid of anyone.

As the sun grew hotter, Appunni remembered school. He had to go to school. But when it came to the matter of fifteen rupees ...

That morning he had not prayed at the shrine in the machu when he left the house, something he always did. The spot where the mother goddess who had swum across the river to bring her children food resided.

Why had that mother not listened to his prayer?

His shadow grew longer on the scorched grass behind him.

He got up. He would go to school, he decided. The class teacher would question him.

The Headmaster would send for him. 'Aren't you going to pay your fees?' he would ask. And Appunni would answer:

'No, Sir, I'm not.'

'You know it's the last day today?'

'I know, Sir. I know.'

'A whole year will go to waste.'

'Let it, Sir.'

'Why aren't you paying the fees?'

'I don't have any money.'

'At home ...?'

'I have no home, Sir. I have no one. No one.'

'Poor child!'

That was the one thing they must never say. He did not want anyone to feel sorry for him. The scene would end there.

He was exhausted by the time he arrived at school. He walked through the gate, not looking at either side. He went up to the room at the end of the big building and stood at the door.

The Geography master wore a green coat and had a vertical stripe of sandalwood paste on his forehead. It was his habit while pretending to teach to hold forth on how he had journeyed all over North India and given private classes to the children of some Dewan. He was talking about houseboats now.

Appunni did not dare raise his head to look. It was the second period.

The forty-five pairs of eyes in the class were fixed on him. Master said, 'Well, step in. Has the day broken only just now?'

Appunni was silent. All he did was give him a pleading look. He sat down on the extreme left of the second row. He wanted to check if Muhammad had come. After this period, he decided.

He turned to look when the bell rang and Master folded up the map. Muhammad had not come.

The one-o'clock bell rang. When Appunni went out, Muhammad was standing at the gate, perspiring profusely. He had obviously just arrived. Appunni could not find the words to ask whether he had got the money. The question hovered in his eyes and on his lips.

Muhammad screwed up his eyes and grinned foolishly. He placed his hand on Appunni's shoulder and said, 'I got it, edo.'

Got it? Muhammad pulled out fifteen crumpled, soiled one-rupee notes from his pocket. Appunni wanted to throw his arms around him.

'Where did you get it? Where?'

'Why do you want to know all that? Go and pay your fees.'

'When do I have to give it back?'

'When you have enough money.'

He didn't wait to ask any more questions. He ran to the office. Writer Kurup had not gone for lunch. He paid his fees.

While going home from school that evening, he said to Muhammad, 'I was sure I wouldn't get the money.'

'I asked so many people but there was no use. Then I sent my mother.'

'And where did she get it?'

'Umma went to lots of places and came back home in despair. And then someone who'd heard about your problem came home with the money.'

'Who was it, Muhammad, who?'

'Never mind who.'

'Tell me who ...'

'You won't like it if I do.'

'Unless you do, I ...' Appunni stopped.

'What does it matter who it is?'

'I must know. I must know who helped me.'

'It was your mother who sent the money.'

Amma! Appunni was stunned. No, he hadn't wanted that. Holding Muhammad's shoulder tightly, Appunni said resentfully:

'Couldn't you have told me earlier?'

Muhammad smiled and said gently, 'Why, isn't every rupee of hers worth sixteen annas? Thanks to her money, you were able to pay your fees. Keep quiet now.'

When Appunni was alone at last, he felt weighed down, suffocated.

At night, he had to wait a long time to get a lamp to himself—a chimney lamp filled with reddish kerosene oil that smoked profusely. What was more, it seemed to have a life of its own, it was so capricious. No matter where he placed it, the smoke curled and twisted and blew onto his face.

Malu came and stood behind him. He did not realize she was there until he heard her snapping her knuckles. She asked:

'Did you pay your fees, Appunni Etta?'

'Um,' he grunted.

'Where did you get the money?'

'Never mind where.'

The things the girl wanted to know! He glanced at her as she stood with her cheek pressed on the pillar, her eyes slanted towards him. A disgusting odour wafted to his nostrils from her wet hair. Her eyes gleamed as brightly as the elassu pendant threaded on a black cord around her neck.

He hated it when she came up to talk to him; from a distance, he pitied her. God had given her nothing, not even a pretty face.

His eyes wandered over the lines in the book. He attempted to shift his attention back to them.

Oh, swallow, swallow, if I could follow and light
Upon her lattice, I would pipe and trill
And cheep and twitter twenty million loves ...

He tried to remember how the English master had explained them. The poet was sending a message to a woman who lived in the southern region. He loved her. He confided everything to the bird:

Oh, were I thou that she might take me in
And lay me on her bosom, and her heart
Would rock the snowy cradle till I died.

Had I been you, she would have held me close to her breast and embraced me ...

His attention wandered again. The letters in front of his eyes faded away. A shimmering blue silk blouse. Half-closed eyes lined with kajal. A pleasing fragrance ...

For shame! The things he was thinking about ...

Only three months now for the examination. He dragged himself back to his books.

Why lingereth she to clothe her heart with love
Delaying as the tender ash delays
To clothe herself when all the woods are green

He suddenly thought ... what would Ammini Edathi be doing now?

She would be asleep. Lying on her side on a soft mattress, hugging her pillow in hands covered with red glass bangles.

He thought of a picture he had seen long ago in some textbook, of a princess lying asleep.

A sleeping princess ...

Wasn't it in the Fourth Form that he had learned that story?

A princess who had been sleeping for years. A prince came into her room. He moved the thin curtains, went up to the bed, knelt down and kissed her cheek.

Moist lips against her cheek ...

He felt shy. When he thought of it, it was with shame and a secret delight.

'Give me a kiss now.'

'You won't?'

'Just one. I gave you so many, didn't I?'

He had touched his lips very, very gently to her cheek. And in return? She had kissed him over and over again on his neck and cheeks. When he had lain down with his face pressed against her heaving breasts, a thrill had coursed down his body.

Ammini Edathi had transported him into a world whose existence he had never imagined.

The smoke from the lamp stained his book. Moving the lamp farther away, he began to read again.

Why lingereth she to ...

'Isn't it time yet for you to go to bed?' asked Valiamma, who had come down to get something.

'I have a lot to read.'

'Sounds as if you bought a whole tin of kerosene oil so that you can keep the lamp burning all night ...'

He blew out the lamp at once and groped his way through the darkness into the room under the stairs.

It was a month since Valia Ammaaman had gone to Poonthottam.

He had contracted all the coconuts to the *copra* dealer, Kunhalu, and taken money from him so that Kutta Ammaaman would not be able to sell them. It was Kunhalu who brought this news. They could pluck the coconuts from the tree in the kitchen yard for use in the house. All the rest were Kunhalu's property.

Kunhalu had given them due warning. 'It's property that I paid money for. If any coconuts are taken away before my men arrive, Kunhalu will show his true colours.'

All of them heard what he said.

Kunhalu's family had once subsisted on the meagre quantities of rice his mother had been given from Vadakkeppat. It was the same Kunhalu who was speaking to them now.

It was almost time for the Makaram harvest. They had started to harvest the plot of land near the river without asking Valia Ammaaman for his consent. Stacks of grain were heaped in the southern yard. Everyone in the house felt relieved. There would be enough paddy to satisfy their needs for quite some days.

It was a good crop. The plot near the river was one of the few areas where the soil had not been washed away by the floods. Many farmers had been left with plots full of sand. The cherumans said what they had harvested would be almost fifteenfold. After the workmen had been given their wages, a one-tenth share of the threshed grain, the rest of the new grain, winnowed and cleaned, was stored in the granary outside. Kutta Ammaaman locked the granary and took charge of the key.

The next morning, everyone was stunned when the coolies arrived. The paddy was going to be sold.

Valiamma came to the front veranda and cried out: 'Kutta, you're going to sell this new grain? Don't you want the children here to eat?'

'I've put aside some for them. And there's more to harvest anyway.'

'Kutta, things will be hard for us if you start doing as you please.'

'It's I who am cultivating the land, Kunji Oppol. Did you spend any money to get the grass cut or to get rid of the pests? I know what I'm doing.'

Valiamma was annoyed.

'You can't do as you please unless it's your private property.'

'Then why didn't you say a word when the northern field was harvested and the paddy threshed and sent to Poonthottam? Did your tongue get stuck in your throat?'

Valiamma paced up and down the house, clicking her heels loudly. When Ammamma asked her something, she shouted at her. She raved at Appu and Malu for having come to stay there just to eat all of them out of house and home. She added a comment about Cheriachan having given his title deeds away.

The workmen heaved up the sacks and made their way out.

The day Valiamma heard that the northern field had been harvested, she had sent Bhaskaran to fetch Kunhan Nair, the karyasthan, and complained bitterly to him. Evidently Valia Ammaaman had claimed that the northern field was his private property.

Kutta Ammaaman began to fell the trees in the inner compound and sell them, ostensibly to pay for the expenses of the legal proceedings.

Valiamma lamented constantly: 'This tharavad will be ruined. I and my children will be the victims.'

Ammamma, tired of hearing this, said: 'You have nothing to fear if it's ruined. After all, you have a place of your own and property.'

Valiamma was not pleased. 'That doesn't mean we'll go away. We're not going to leave until we get what is due to us.'

Ammamma said gently: 'Isn't that exactly what I said, Kunjukutty? It's some of us here who'll really suffer.'

Whatever anyone said, it turned into a quarrel. No one trusted anyone else.

Appunni stayed apart from all the squabbles. He did not want to become a subject for discussion. All he longed for was to escape from this blazing fire ...

As soon as he came back from school, he would sit down to read. He would read until dusk had deepened into darkness and the letters on the page were no longer visible. He would go and sit down then in some dark corner where no light fell until it was time for dinner. After dinner, he had to wait until he could get a lamp for himself. And he could not keep it burning too long. Kerosene oil was so expensive.

A grain of rice splashing out of the leaf someone was eating from, a drop of water falling on the ground: all these were enough to start a squabble.

Appunni got up very early every morning. Most days, it was the clatter of the pulley as water was drawn from the well that awoke him. Meenakshi Edathi was always up before the crows began to caw. He would sit down in the mist and cold of the front veranda to read by the faint light of early morning.

The day he had waited for so long arrived at last: the fifteenth of March.

The day the examinations began.

His heart was full of prayers: let me not fail in anything. He felt relieved as he finished each paper. The last examination was over on

Friday. Going back home, he experienced the happiness of being released from a great burden.

His enthusiasm died completely when he arrived home. Kutta Ammaaman and Valia Ammaaman were having a fight.

No one asked him whether the examinations were over, whether he had written them well.

No one cared whether he passed or failed.

Ammamma sometimes gave him a blessing: 'May he find a livelihood for himself.'

The holidays had always been unbearable. And there would be only holidays from now on. At least until the results were out. After that ...? Let whatever was going to happen happen, he thought.

7

ppunni met Ramakrishnan Master unexpectedly at the gate. He was standing on the path in front when Master came that way. He went up to him.

'What is it, Appunni?'

'Nothing, Sir.'

'Is your house nearby?'

'Yes, this is my house, Sir.' He pointed to Vadakkeppat.

'The results will take some more time to come, won't they? What are you doing now?'

'I've nothing to do, Sir. I can't get anything to read around here.'

'Come to my house. Don't stop reading because you can't get books.'

Appunni felt happy.

Ramakrishnan Master's house was a little way beyond the school. Appunni had heard that Master read a great deal and even wrote poetry.

It soon became a habit to walk to Master's house every evening. It was three miles away, near the Post Office. Appunni would first leaf through a newspaper, then Master would give him a book. Master was very talkative and Appunni liked listening to him.

One day, when Appunni came back to the house, Valia Ammaaman's second son, Gopi, was there. Appunni had no right to call him by name, he was expected to call him Gopi Ettan. Appunni had never seen him before. He was talking to Valiamma and Ammamma.

Appunni went in, giving Gopi a dutiful smile.

'I'm glad. May she have a good life. No matter how much gold a girl may have at home, there's nothing like marriage,' said Ammamma.

Valiamma asked: 'Isn't Madhavan Nair going back to Colombo?'

'He says he's not.'

'How much has he earned?'

'I don't know.'

'He worked in a foreign country a good twenty years after all, so he must have made enough,' said Ammamma. 'Your father would not have gone in for this if there was nothing in it.'

'I have to go now. All of you must come well ahead.'

'Still, your father could at least have told us that he was considering this proposal. As he wishes. After all, my children, it only makes me happy to see all of you do well in life.'

Who had done well and how?

Appunni went out to them after Gopi Ettan left.

Ammamma said, 'They've invited everyone. Are you going, Appunni?'

'Where?'

'To Poonthottam. There's going to be a grand wedding on the twenty first.'

'Whose wedding?'

'Ammini's.'

'Umm ...' He did not ask anything more. But Ammamma kept talking. 'The bridegroom is Thekkenkandath Madhavan Nair. Thekkenkandath is an old tharavad. Madhavan ran away to Ceylon years ago. He came back very recently, must have made quite a bit of money.'

'Good for her.'

May all good things come to her, he said silently to himself. May Ammini Edathi have a happy life.

Still, he was aware of an undefinable sense of pain. If he ever had an occasion to meet Ammini Edathi again, it would be as Madhavan Nair's wife. He would never meet her, but if he did ...

The memory of certain dark, cold nights in the room under the stairs came to him. He had been born too late. If he had been born five or six years earlier, he would have been a grown man now. Then ...

He felt distressed.

Once Ammamma knew there was going to be a wedding in the neighbourhood, she could talk of nothing else.

She would count on her fingers as each day dawned: 'It's the fifteenth today.'

'Today, it's the tenth.'

It was time to put up the pandal.

Ammamma would say when she caught sight of Thangedathi: 'I want to see a man come to take my Thangakutty away too. Will I have the good fortune for that, I wonder ...'

Thangedathi would stand before her with her head bent, pretending to look embarrassed.

Valiamma would say: 'You'll live another ten years, Amma. Don't worry on that score.'

Thangedathi was a year older than Appunni. Which meant she was nineteen. Valiamma had had her bridal chamber ready for years.

When Appunni woke up on the twenty-first, his first thought was: it's Ammini Edathi's wedding day today.

Valiamma and the children had left the day before. Malu had gone with them.

Meenakshi Edathi had wanted to go. But Ammamma had said, 'If everyone goes off, what will I eat—air?'

Muttering, 'My fate is to live in this kitchen all my days,' Meenakshi Edathi had decided not to go.

Appunni took one of the books he had brought from Master's house and sat down on the platform to the south of the outhouse. He did not enjoy the story in the book at all. But if he stayed in the house, Ammamma would torture him. All her thoughts were of what was happening in the wedding house at each moment.

When he sat down to dinner that night, Ammamma came and sat at the door.

'Is it late, Appunni?'

'Must be around eight or nine.'

'They must have laid the leaves for the feast.'

She added: 'Couldn't you have gone along too, boy? Wouldn't you have got a grand feast?'

He gathered up handfuls of rice and ate, saying nothing. There was a vegetable curry made with bottle gourd with neither chillies nor tamarind in it. Nothing else. He found it unappetizing.

As he was going to bed, he heard Ammamma say: 'The feast must be over.'

Ammamma's thoughts were fixed on the wedding house. Couldn't she have gone along then, instead of trying to guess what was happening at each moment?

Before he fell asleep, his own thoughts slipped towards that house that he had never seen.

... The pandal would be full of people. The inner rooms would be crowded with women and children. There would be a great deal of noise and confusion.

... People would have started going to bed now. Ammini Edathi would have gone to bed too. Not alone. That man would be with her. That man who had spent twenty years in Ceylon.

... Why had he come back to India after twenty years?

Appunni tried to draw a picture of him in his mind: a bristling moustache with tips that stuck out like the ends of a broom, tattooed arms, and a bony face. Who was he? Whoever he was, Appunni hated him. Not for any specific reason. He just could not visualize that picture without hating him.

... Ammini Edathi would be lying down on the soft, smooth mattress with that black-skinned man. Fair-skinned Ammini Edathi, as beautiful as a fresh banana flower that was opening out.

Why think of all that?

Appunni got up and opened the window fully. There was bright moonlight outside. But it was very hot.

The moonlight lay over the banana plants clustered behind the cowshed. It had a strange radiance. The shadow of the withered ayini tree stood unmoving, looking like a ghost with five heads. This landscape in which the white moonlight lay entangled with shadows had a fearful beauty.

He lay with his eyes open until the moonlight paled. It was only when the cool of the morning wafted in through the window that sleep began to caress his eyelids.

The results had come. Appunni had passed. He had expected the results only in June, so he had not been anxious in the least when the news came. He arrived at Master's house one day, and Master put the newspaper down in front of him and said: 'You can have your tea later, Appunni.'

'What is it, Sir?'

'You've passed. Your number is here.'

An ocean of numbers. But it was not hard to find the number that announced his success. Master had circled it.

He could not have enough of looking at it. When the first wave of excitement died down, he looked for Muhammad's number. No, Muhammad had not passed. And he did not know anyone else's number.

As he walked back over the red clay path lined with screwpine bushes that looked like watchmen holding pointed clubs, he wanted to cry out to the whole world: 'Appunni passed the examinations!' He walked with his head held high.

He entered the gatehouse determined to tell everyone at home the news even if they had no desire to hear it. He heard Valia Ammaaman's voice as he climbed the steps. It had been many days since he had visited the house.

All his excitement ebbed away.

Appunni went into the house as if nothing had happened. He took off his shirt, threw a towel that had turned dark grey and shabby with repeated washing, over his shoulder, and went out again. He would go and have a bath. His most pressing need now was to distance himself from the clamour in the house for a while. His hair felt as dry as coconut husk. It was months since he had oiled it.

There would be plenty of water in the river at the spot just under the bridge. It would be very pleasant there.

He climbed down to the river from the enclosure where sacrificial offerings were made to the goddess. The river was completely dry. It flowed like a thin channel over one edge of the sand that stretched all around as far as the eye could reach. It was amusing to think that this river had once plunged the entire countryside under water. People dug little holes here and there in the sand now to have a bath. People with shabby clothes and dark-skinned bodies. He saw flashes of white and colour some distance away. The girls from the adhikari's house. A little girl in a white frilled dress was playing on the sand, reminding him of the picture of an angel.

He walked over the sand. He had to go four or five furlongs to reach the bridge.

It was at a spot slightly above the bridge that the Bharathapuzha had found another river to keep her company. Which was why there was always plenty of water there, even in summer. The huge railroad bridge was above him and lower down, two women from the potters' huts were having a bath.

Small rocks were scattered over the banks. He sat down for a while on one of them. A passenger train rattled its way over his head and the bridge and the earth around trembled violently. He saw people crowded around its windows and doors. People he didn't know. There would be people of all kinds. Coming from who knew where. Going who knew where.

He thought, this train could be going to Madras, or to Coimbatore.

He had never been in a train. He had seen nothing beyond the village and the high school. He could not even imagine what big cities looked like.

Appuni aimed a stone at one of the huge iron pillars supporting the bridge and it found its mark. There was a resounding clang of metal. The iron pillars were frightening. A man lay dead inside one of them. It was a story often told in the village.

The pillars would not stabilize while the bridge was being built. The white man who was the engineer tried every device he could think of, to no avail. In the end, the contractor conducted a prasnam ritual and the astrologer said that a man would have to be offered in sacrifice.

Pieces of granite were showered on a coolie as he was going down the slope carrying a headload of sand ... He never came up again. And the bridge stood firm. If the story was true, the man must have been suffocated to death. A human soul was imprisoned inside that metal pillar ...

The clear sky above him was a pale blue. The sun had set. Garlands of clouds shot with black and red streaked the west. Pale red rays of sunlight still lay in the water.

Appunni went down to the river to bathe.

He did not get out of the water until it became quite dark. The iron bridge towered above like some frightening creature with rows and rows of legs. The only sound he could hear was the swishing of the water around the legs of the iron pillars. The flash of the railway signal was visible in the distance, like an eye smouldering in the darkness. Appunni felt reluctant to leave the deserted area.

He walked along, cleaving his way through the darkness.

He went to Ramakrishnan Master's house early the next morning. Master was in the front veranda, humming as he scribbled something on a piece of paper. He put it down as Appunni entered.

'Yes, Appunni ...?' Master asked as usual. And Appunni answered as usual, 'Nothing particular, Sir.'

'What are your plans? Aren't you going to do higher studies?'

'No.'

Master knew more or less what Appunni's situation was like, but he asked anyway.

'What are you going to do then?'

'I want a job, Sir.'

'I'll try. But you might not get one right away.'

'If I don't get a job ...' Appunni stopped.

'What is it?'

He turned his face towards the pillar as he spoke. 'It would be better to die then, Sir.' He could not go on.

'I get the English newspaper here. Apply for the jobs you see in it.'

'Yes, I must.'

'Do you know anyone outside Kerala?'

'No, Sir.' Appunni went on as if he could not say enough: 'I have no one, Sir.'

'Let your certificate come. We'll see.'

The certificate arrived within a week. A book with a blue cardboard cover. The marks he had got for the government examination were written in red ink. A total of four hundred and twenty in all the six subjects.

Even Ramakrishnan Master was amazed. 'Seventy-one in English. Ninety-seven in Maths. You should have continued studying, Appunni.'

Appunni smiled sadly.

He walked to Master's house every day to look at the advertisements in the English newspaper. He found something he could apply for only after a month. Clerks were being recruited for the Railways.

Master said: 'Go ahead and apply. Your marks are good, you'll get the job.'

He needed a rupee to buy a form. And another eight annas to send it registered. Where would he find a rupee and a half?

He had time until the fifteenth. Twenty days. But it did not comfort Appunni to know that there was time. He had already been thinking about the one and a half rupees the past two or three days. God, how big a sum it was, one and a half rupees!

He had finished his bath in the river at the spot under the bridge and was walking up to the road, his eyes riveted on the white sand, when a little boy ran up from behind and said,

'He's calling you.'

'Who?'

'Syedalikutty-ka. He's waiting there, near the stone platform.'

Tossing back the hair lying over his forehead, Appunni walked towards the platform. Syedalikutty was waiting there, smoking a beedi, a smile lighting up his bloodshot eyes.

'How big you've grown, Nair-kutty!' he said.

Appunni smiled.

'The food in your tharavad must be very rich.'

Paying no attention to this, Appunni asked: 'When did you come, Syedalikutty?'

'Yesterday evening.'

'Where are you now?'

'Still in Wynaad. Where else would I be? What's all the news, Nair-kutty?'

'Just getting along.'

'Which class are you in now?'

'I've finished school. I passed.'

'You passed your tenth?'

'Yes, I did.'

'What now?'

'Now ... now I have to find a job. Rather than go on staying here ...'

'Are you looking for something?'

'I must. But ...' The problem of the one and a half rupees surfaced in his mind. What if he spoke of it? His pride would not let him.

'Don't worry. You'll find a job for sure.'

'You need someone to recommend you if you want to find a job. And you need to spend money as well. I don't have either. I'm someone nobody wants.'

Syedalikutty listened silently, puffing deeply at his beedi. He seemed to be pondering over something. Changing the subject, he asked: 'How far has the tharavad case progressed?'

Appunni said unhappily: 'It's too shameful to talk about. I'm staying there because I have nowhere else to go.'

'Don't speak of things that God will not forgive you for, child. And don't have such silly thoughts. God must have thought of a way ...'

Appunni grunted.

'Go along now. I'm leaving in a couple of days. I'll try and see you again.'

Appunni wiped his face and neck with his wet towel. As he made to go, Syedalikutty said, 'Once you go through the dark days, you have to wait for the light. God must have thought of a way out ...'

Appunni thought sarcastically—if God had really thought of a way out, he would not be agonizing now over one and a half rupees.

God's ways are really strange, thought Appunni. He did not know anyone who was likely to write him a letter. With great hesitation, he opened the letter on which his address was written in pencil in Malayalam. The letter 'B' was scrawled on top in an ungainly script.

'For very respected Appunni Nair to read'

(Appunni Nair? So Appunni had become Appunni Nair!)

'For very respected Appunni Nair to read, a letter from Syedalikutty.'

'The matter being that I have spoken to the Estate Manager about you. He said he would help. You have to come here as quickly as possible. You must bring all your certificates with you when you come. Take the bus from Kozhikode to Mananthavadi and get down at this place. If you ask in the bazaar, they will show you where my shop is.'

'If you drop me a card to tell me when you are leaving, my boy or I will wait for you at the bus stop. God be with you. Yours sincerely, Syedalikutty.'

Appunni's first thought was that God was Syedalikutty.

It made him very glad to think that he would be able to escape from that dark room under the stairs. Would Syedalikutty's plans materialize?

Just when he had convinced himself that he had no one to help him, people from whom he had never expected help were reaching out to him ...

Forget everything else now, he thought. Go quickly to Wynaad. He needed some money for that. The train fare from Pallippuram to Kozhikode. Then the bus fare from there. And money for food. Who could he ask?

He walked straight to Master's house. Master was in the garden supervising some work. It was a moment of supreme confidence for Appunni. He explained the situation to Master without any hesitation or embarrassment.

'Why should that be any trouble?' Master was only too happy to help.

'Sit down, Appunni. I'll be with you in a minute.'

Master put on his shirt and went out. He took some time to come back. He said, 'Appunni, you're lucky. Here ...' A ten-rupee note!

Appunni felt so grateful, his eyes filled with tears. The words he wanted to say stayed lodged in his throat.

With great difficulty, he said: 'I'll go along then, Sir.'

'Yes, go. Wish you good luck.'

Appunni felt himself melting and flowing into the landscape. He walked rapidly, with the speed of a whirlwind.

Wish you good luck ...

The next day was a Friday. He had to see Muhammad and say goodbye. He would start the day after that. May I never have to come back here, he thought. May I never have to lie down again in the room under the stairs.

He had to say goodbye to Muhammad. Only to Muhammad? No, the rest had faded away. They were only memories now ...

He did not tell anyone his plans that night. No one need know, he thought.

He walked to Muhammad's house in the morning. Only his mother was at home. Muhammad and his younger brother had gone to the village near Ponnani where his sister had moved after she was married.

'Umma, when Muhammad comes, tell him I came looking for him.'

'Who are you?'

'Tell him it was a boy who was in his class at school, Appunni.'

'Paruttyamma's son Appunni Nair. I'll tell him to come and see you.'

'I'm going away tomorrow.'

'Where to, child?'

'I'm leaving this village, to look for a job. Tell Muhammad that.'

'I'll tell him, child.'

She said, as he was going, 'May that mother live long enough to ...'

He did not have many preparations to make. He put aside the shirt and mundu he would wear on the journey and packed the two other shirts and mundus he had in a bag. A shabby towel, the certificate book, and the conduct certificate the Headmaster had written for him were already in the bag. The train from Pallippuram was at nine-thirty in the morning.

He picked up the bag and went to Ammamma's room.

'What is it, Appunni?'

'I'm going, Ammamma.'

'Where?'

'I am going to get a job.'

'Really! May all good things come to you, my child.' Ammamma sat up. 'Where?'

'In Wynaad—that's the name of the place.'

'So the bad times are over,' she said.

He went into the room under the stairs one more time. Had he forgotten anything? There was nothing to forget. Still, he was not sure.

He had reached the front veranda when Valiamma came up behind him to the thekkini and said, 'Appunni, wait. You're going away without telling me?'

Valiamma's tone was full of affection. 'The kanji is ready. Have some before you go.'

He said in a cold voice, 'No, I don't want any.'

'If you need some money for the journey ...'

Her generosity did not surprise him. This was just a beginning ... He went down to the courtyard without turning to look at her and said, 'I don't.'

He glanced back as he reached the gate and saw a dark face at the door. Malu.

He should have told her he was leaving.

He opened the door of the gatehouse and stepped out. Kutta Ammaaman was coming from the opposite side. Appunni moved aside and avoided looking at his face. Then he walked quickly over the high, narrow path that protruded from the field like its spine.

8

The bus was going up a slope. There were steep hills on one side and thickly overgrown valleys on the other. Appunni peered out as the bus creaked over one hairpin bend after another. Forest areas filled with heavy foliage that glittered in the afternoon sun. Rocks with wild banana plants clinging to their surfaces.

Appunni felt that he had changed completely after he had boarded the train at Pallippuram. He was no longer the old Appunni. This was a new, grown up person.

The bus was quite crowded. Next to him was an old man who wore huge earrings and had a woollen muffler wound around his neck despite the heat. There were women and children in both the seats in front and one of the women kept putting her head outside the window and throwing up. When they reached the top of the slope, Appunni peered down through the window. He could see twisting black lines outlining the road that snaked around the body of the mountain. The empty trucks coming from below crept over it, looking like little black ants. Only when looking at the depths below did he realize how high they had climbed. On the right, the ground was covered with thorny bushes, dry leaves, and thickets. Above them were areas that had been cleared. Withered stumps were scattered here and there. Looking at the large expanses of clay-coloured earth outside, the old man with the earrings nudged the red-bearded man seated next to him on the other side and asked him something.

'They're going to plant rubber. Our Koyakutty Haji's children have bought up this entire area.'

A truck loaded with timber had broken down by the roadside. The driver stopped the bus, got down and asked: 'What's the matter?' The man seated on the bonnet with a black turban around his head had obviously lost all hope. He said something in Tamil and the driver started the bus again.

As the sun went down, a pleasant breeze tinged with cold began to blow through the bus. The old man sitting next to Appunni took off the muffler around his neck, covered his ears with it and wrapped it tight again. He murmured an explanation: 'I suffer from wheezing.'

Appunni had told the conductor well in advance where he wanted to alight.

They came to a spot where there was a row of shops and the conductor asked the driver to stop. 'This is the place.'

'We're there?' Appunni wanted to make sure. The conductor nodded and Appunni got out, bag in hand.

A handful of small shops with thatched roofs in the midst of gravel-covered hills. Only two of the shops were tiled. People had actually built a bazaar on this deserted hillside!

Appunni had not written ahead to Syedalikutty. An indefinable sense of fear seized him as the bus roared past him and disappeared.

He entered the first shop he saw and asked; 'Which is Syedalikutty's shop?'

The boy who was handing out things to the customers did not know. Appunni went into another shop. The owner had a greying handlebar moustache and a large iron cross on his breast.

He pointed it out: 'There, just beyond that tiled shop.'

Appunni breathed easily at last.

A shed with a thatched roof. Behind it was a small house with stone walls. There were no customers in the shop.

A boy who might have been nine or ten sat in front of a box. Was this the place? When he saw Appunni hesitate, the boy gave him a stern look as if to say, 'Won't I do?'

'Which is Syedalikutty's shop?'

'This one. What do you want?'

'Isn't Syedalikutty here?'

The boy seemed to be slightly annoyed that he wasn't acceptable.

'Tell me what is that you want.'

'I want to see Syedalikutty.'

The boy called out, without turning his head, 'Bappa, someone's here for you.'

'Who is it?'

Phew! It was Syedalikutty's voice.

'Who is it?'

Syedalikutty lifted the piece of sacking that covered the door at the back of the shop and came out. Placing his hand on his waist, he looked at Appunni in surprise.

'Allah! It's Nair-kutty, isn't it?'

Appunni smiled.

'Come in and sit down. Bring a stool, boy.'

Appunni wiped the perspiration off his forehead and went in.

'What a thing! Why didn't you write a card?'

'I left in a hurry.'

'Good. I hope you had no trouble on the way.'

'No, I didn't.'

'It's the first time you're travelling such a distance, after all ...'

Syedalikutty went in for a moment and came out again.

He described the surroundings to Appunni. A number of Christians had come from Travancore and settled there. All the clearings visible now had once been forest land. Farther interior, there were white men's tea estates. Most of the merchants in the bazaar were Christians. There was just one Nair who had a teashop. And Aythruman Kakka had a shop that sold dried fish.

Appunni wondered whether there were enough customers to buy what was sold on this hillside.

There were about five hundred people living in the vicinity. All their needs had to be met here. Trade had been good until a store was opened on the estate. Now ... 'We just manage somehow.'

Syedalikutty sold provisions. There was another provision shop now and that was Syedalikutty's problem.

It was thirteen years since Syedalikutty had come here, he said. He had been on the estate at first. After that he had sold dried fish. When his customers grew in numbers, he opened a provision shop. His only prayer was that he be able to eke out a living. Neither the house nor the shop were his own. He had to pay a rent of eight rupees. If he could make some money, he could buy both. But he did not think that would happen.

It was Syedalikutty who did all the talking. Appunni listened to everything he said.

There was a sound from behind the curtain of sacking. 'Look ...'

Syedalikutty got up and said, 'Let's have a drink.' He went in. When he saw Appunni stand at the door hesitantly, he said: 'Come on in. There's only my family here.'

Appunni went in reluctantly.

Beyond the door was a room. Two glasses of tea waited for them. Near one of them was a piece of banana leaf with fried bananas and Mysore bananas on it.

'Sit down.' Syedalikutty pointed to the wooden stool. 'With all that travelling in buses and trains, you must be tired. Drink this.'

Appunni sat down, pressed the glass to his lips and took a sip.

A woman wearing a black *kaachi* came and stood at the inner door.

'Pathumma, do you know who this is?'

'Who is it?'

'He's a boy from our village.'

'Really? I don't recognize him.'

'Remember Kondunni Nair? He's Kondunni Nair's son.'

Appunni smiled at Syedalikutty's umma.

'What? When I last saw this child, he was just this high!' Umma lowered her palm to indicate the size of a chicken. Syedalikutty laughed.

'But that was long ago, Pathumma. And you yourself were not such an old woman then!'

The boy came in to take part in the conversation. Syedalikutty said to him:

'Go and sit down in the shop. It's time for customers to start coming.' When the boy went back, he said to Appunni, 'I'm teaching him the trade.'

The boy lighted the lamp in the shop. Through the window, Appunni could see the faint evening light dying out. The bluish smoke that had been clinging to the hillside melted away and clumps of darkness streaked with mist began to descend over it.

Syedalikutty moved his glass towards the wall with his foot and said: 'We usually have a few customers at this time. Sit down. I'll be back soon.' He disappeared into the shop.

Pathumma asked him for news of the village. It had been only two years since she and the children had come away. They had been in debt and had sold the house they lived in to pay off the debt. She had told her husband that she would not go back to the village until they could afford to buy a house and compound of their own.

'You've grown really big. We came that way when we were going to Ayamutti Vaidyar's house, very long ago. You were nursing at your mother's breast then.'

Appunni leaned against the wall and thought, he'd grown. And was still growing.

'I hope Parukutty Amma is not ailing.'

Appunni lowered his eyes and said, 'No.'

'Is she able to manage alright now?'

'Yes.' He prayed she would not ask any more questions.

And then he saw two black eyes darting his way. He made her out clearly only when Umma moved. A thin, fair-skinned girl wearing a white kachi and *kuppayam* and a *thattam* with a border. There was a surprised smile on her face.

'What are you staring at, girl? He's from Kudallur.'

The girl withdrew shyly. Umma said, 'Nabeesa is the older one. She says the village was better.'

Appunni ran his eyes over the interior of the house. The roof was not tiled, it was thatched with grass. The stone walls had not been plastered. There were two doors leading inside. Beyond them was a waist-high platform on which was a lighted chimney lamp. Nabeesa went into the kitchen and came out again. Her necklace gleamed when she moved through the light. He suddenly thought of the half-hidden crescent moon he used to glimpse through clouds when he sat on the rocks below the bridge at home, gazing at a twilight sky that had not yet turned dark.

Pathumma settled down on the doorstep and talked to him until Syedalikutty came back. He felt they had known each other for years.

Syedalikutty said:

'It's not all that convenient here. But we'll manage somehow, won't we, Nair-kutty?'

Appunni smiled. After all, he was not going to stay with them permanently.

'Don't you want to have a bath?'

Appunni hesitated.

'It's no problem. There's a stream some distance away. The water is first class.'

'Yes, I must have a bath.'

'You'll feel much less tired after a bath in cold water. Take off your shirt.'

Appunni took his shirt off, took his towel out of the bag and threw it over his shoulder.

'Pathumma, give him some sesame oil if there's any. I want a drop too.'

Pathumma poured some oil into Appunni's cupped palm and he smeared it over his hair, dry as coconut husk.

'Nabeesa, my pocket lamp.' Nabeesa went from the kitchen to the room next door and came out flashing the torch on her own face. When the light fell suddenly on her, she smiled, showing all her little white teeth. Then she hurried to the door and held the torch out to her father.

Syedalikutty walked in front and Appunni followed. They stepped down from the road on to a gravel path and went quite some way down a steep slope. Appunni heard water flowing over rocks.

The sky above them was grey and the trees in the distance were like stacks of darkness. In the black valley was the astonishing vision of a thousand glow-worms flickering and fading among the thick leaves.

Appunni stood on the edge of the stream and drank in the majesty of a hillside plunged in darkness and silence.

It was very cold. He felt reluctant to get into the water. He sat down on a rock. And Syedalikuty sat down on the ground covered with pebbles and sand. Appunni began to think about his job.

'We'll go and see Menon tomorrow.'

'Which Menon?'

'The Estate Manager. The Sahib has gone to England and Menon is in charge now.'

'Will I get a job?'

'I wouldn't have written to you otherwise, Nair-kutty. I know your problems.' Syedalikutty got up and sat down on a rock near him. Taking out a beedi from his belt, he lighted it and said:

'He'll do it if I ask. He's from near our village.'

Syedalikutty told him about Sankara Menon. His place was around six miles from Kudallur. Syedalikutty had met him while he still lived there. He used to take him gifts of fresh fish at high tide. Syedalikutty had done many things for him.

Appunni was still doubtful. Would people in high positions remember such small favours?

Syedalikutty said, as if reading his thoughts: 'He can't afford to forget Syedalikutty.'

His voice sounded more serious than usual. Appunni did not have to ask him why. Syedalikutty explained—and it was quite a story.

Syedalikutty had just come to Wynaad in search of a job when Sankara Menon was transferred there from an estate in the Anamalais.

Syedalikutty went to see him and Menon gave him five rupees. But it was a job that Syedalikutty needed, not five rupees. Menon no longer remembered the gifts of fish Syedalikutty used to bring him in the village.

'People's memories grow dimmer as their status grows higher,' Syedalikutty said philosophically.

Syedalikutty began to haunt the estate constantly and Menon finally gave him a job there as a coolie. His wages were a rupee a day. Menon was an Assistant Manager at the time. He had a big bungalow on the estate to live in. Syedalikutty slept on the veranda outside the kitchen.

Menon was not married at the time. But there were rumours among the coolies. And a story behind certain favours that had been extended to Maistry Kunhikannan. Syedalikutty paid no attention to all this. But when a new servant woman became part of the household, he changed his opinion. There was Gopalan Nair to do the cooking and estate workers at Menon's beck and call for everything else. And Menon was single.

'A very young girl. I didn't think she was a Nair.'

Although she had come as a servant, the girl had no work to do. All she did was take Menon's food to the table. There was just the one room upstairs and she was there constantly, all afternoon and evening.

The workers ignored her. Gopalan began to protest when she started to wield her authority.

Sometime during this period, Syedalikutty moved to the quarters on the estate.

In time, the servant woman stopped coming downstairs completely.

One night months later, butler Gopalan came to fetch Syedalikutty.

What had happened? Gopalan did not know. It was ten o'clock. Syedalikutty went along with him. Menon was pacing up and down, smoking a cigarette. He told Gopalan to close the front door and go to sleep. When they were alone, Menon took Syedalikutty to the inner room.

'Syedalikutty ...' His voice was not as stern as usual.

'There's something I want you to do.'

'What is it?'

'I'll tell you in a while. Just sit down here.'

Syedalikutty sat down by the fire, basking in its heat. He was surprised and a little scared. Gopalan must have gone to sleep. The room Syedalikutty was in was the reading room. He gazed at the walls, the glass cases filled with books, and the blazing fire in turn.

He had no idea how much time went by.

He got up when he heard Menon's voice again.

All Menon said was, 'Come.' He went upstairs and Syedalikutty followed, full of fear.

Menon raised the wick of the lamp placed in the room upstairs slightly. A faint light illumined the room. The servant maid lay on the bed under a white blanket, her eyes closed. She was moaning softly. And then Syedalikutty noticed—there was blood on the ground and near the bathroom door. Dazed, Syedalikutty muttered, 'God!'

Menon pointed to a white cloth bundle on the bed opposite and said in a low voice, 'Go and bury that.'

Syedalikutty was still dazed.

'Bury it deep at some distant spot. No one must know except you and I.'

Syedalikutty touched the cloth bundle. His hand grew numb. There was something soft and cold inside. He moved the cloth aside. A newborn baby. It did not move.

'There's a shovel in front of the woodshed. Quick!'

Syedalikutty lifted the thing wrapped in cloth.

… A flowering tree grows there now.

'I'll show you when we go to his house. It's only at this moment that a third person knows.'

The water in the stream was as cold as ice. Appunni did not feel like having a bath. When Syedalikutty began to bathe, Appunni plunged half-heartedly under the water.

Wynaad, his job, Syedalikutty: everything faded from his mind for a time as they walked back. Only one image remained:

A flowering tree grows there!

It was the first time he was going to eat in the house of someone who was outside his own family. He had once believed that it was forbidden to drink the water that a mapilla had touched. And now, Syedalikutty sat on one side of him and his son, Mohammedkutty on the other. In front of him was a mound of steaming hot yellow rice and bright red curry. And Pathumma was serving them.

… If you went out, you had to have a bath before you entered the Vadakkeppat naalukettu again. The cheruma folk were not allowed even to walk past the well.

Appunni had no difficulty eating the rice and curry that Pathumma had cooked. He experienced the delight of demolishing many notions he had detested.

They spread a grass mat for Appunni to sleep in the outer room. An old, worn thattam that had been washed clean was spread over the pillow. A faint whiff of attar rose from it.

'Call me if you need anything,' said Syedalikutty. 'Let the pocket lamp be at your head. Call me if you want to go out.'

'Alright.'

'You're not scared, are you?'

'No.'

'You shouldn't be. You're not a child now, you're a man.' Syedalikutty smiled.

Appunni was very tired. It was quite cold. He pressed his face into the pillow and thought: today I'm the guest of the man I hated most!

9

The Junior Accountant, Chandrasekhara Kurup, was going home on vacation. He began to pack his things as soon as he came back from the office. His companion, Abraham Joseph, had not yet returned. Once Joseph finished work, he usually went to the Staff Club to play four rounds of carroms.

Chandrasekhara Kurup kept giving orders to the servant from time to time. Then he would pull out all the things he had arranged inside the big leather suitcase and stuff them in again. He seemed utterly confused.

When Abraham Joseph came back from the club, there was a young, bald man with him.

Joseph said: 'This is Radhakrishnan. The person we heard was being transferred here from the Cochin office.'

Chandrasekhara Kurup stopped packing and held out his hand to Radhakrishnan.

Joseph completed the introduction: 'This is the Junior Accountant, Mr Chandrasekhara Kurup. We've been staying together in these quarters seven or eight years and are good chums. But this man deceived me recently, Mr Radhakrishnan.'

Kurup looked rather surprised.

Turning to Radhakrishnan, who did not know whether to treat this announcement seriously or as a joke, Joseph said: 'He's going to get married. That's the confusion you see now!'

The room was scattered with Kurup's belongings.

'This man had vowed never to get married. He's like that. We have other specimens as well. Have you met V.A. Nair?'

'No.'

'Ah, he's an amusing character. There, those are his quarters. Wait ...'

Moving towards the door, Joseph said, 'Here he comes. I'll call him. Hey, Nair! Just drop in here for a minute.' He clapped his hands.

A tall, thin young man with wavy hair, dressed in a white shirt and khaki trousers, entered.

'This is Mr Appunni Nair. The Field Writer. This is Radhakrishnan. He's been banished from the Cochin office to the mountains.'

Appunni leaned against the table and smiled at his new colleague.

Kurup had started to take his things out of the bag and then stuff them in again.

'When are you leaving?' Appunni asked him.

'Tomorrow. Amma's letter said I should get there today. But I'll reach only tomorrow evening.'

He folded a green blanket and put it into his suitcase. 'Amma had written to me quite some time ago saying she wanted a blanket.'

Radhakrishnan began to talk of office matters. The shortcomings of superior officers, the problems that sycophants created, the severe rules the manager laid down.

Appunni did not say anything. He was more interested in Kurup's activities than in Radhakrishnan's news from the capital city. He glanced at his watch. Six-ten. He got up and said to everyone, 'I'm going.'

'What's the hurry?' asked Joseph.

'I'm on my way back from work.' He moved nearer Kurup and asked, 'Are you leaving early morning?'

'Yes. Seven-thirty. I hope you remember the date.'

'I'll try and come. I'm not certain.'

'You must come. Joseph is coming, so are Kumaran Nair and Ramankutty.'

Appunni's voice was apologetic: 'I may not see you before you leave. Best wishes!'

'Thank you. Thank you.'

Appunni extended his hand to the thirty-five-year-old bridegroom. Saying, 'See you,' to Radhakrishnan, he left.

He walked along the path between the tea bushes, which ended in the road that connected the factory to the office. Bordered on both sides by a steel fence, the road led to Appunni's quarters. There was another person staying with him, Bhaskaran Nambiar. He was ill and had been in hospital all week.

A big table lamp with a dome-shaped shade lighted up the portico. It had not turned dark. The cook, Krishnankutty, always lighted the lamp very early. Bhaskaran Nair had brought him from his village. He was a smart lad, although he was slightly deaf.

Appunni sat down on the easy chair without changing his clothes. It felt good to lie back and stretch his legs out on the stool before him. He was so tired.

He prayed that Bhaskaran Nambiar would be back from the hospital soon. If he were here, he would talk endlessly. Even Abraham Joseph had had to acknowledge defeat before him where talking was concerned.

Kurup's wedding was on the twenty-seventh. Thiruvonam, the harvest festival, was on the same day. It had been Kurup's mother's wish that his wedding should be on Onam day. Kurup had not met the girl he was going to marry. His mother had seen her and fixed the wedding. He was ready to accept whatever his mother decided. His mother was everything to him. He visited his village at least once in six months.

Appunni realized it was five years since he had arrived here. He had never gone anywhere after he came. From the quarters to his place of work, from his place of work to the quarters: five years had gone by in this way.

A three-month period of leave had lapsed. Another one was due.

It was five days to Onam. He suddenly thought of the hillsides in his village, alive with kannanthali bushes.

He felt that it was fifty, not five years since he had left the village. The river, the Karunoor bridge, the fields, the screwpine thickets, the hills: they were all distant memories now. He was trying to forget all of them.

But the room under the stairs to which darkness clung even in the daytime had not faded from his mind at all. Nor the screwpine mat folded up and placed in the corner.

He suddenly wanted to look back over the five years. He had drunk all the bitterness life could hold in that time. Bhaskaran Nambiar, Kurup, Joseph, all of them had many things to say about their childhood. Events that had taken place when they were studying. He always sat silently listening to them. He himself had nothing to say.

He had arrived here with nothing except a bag made of sacking, two sets of clothes, and a towel.

He thought of Syedalikutty, who had done everything for him. Late one evening they had gone to the Estate Manager's house and had not returned until Syedalikutty had obtained a promise from him. Appunni did not have to wait more than a week. He had written out his application only after he was told that he had been appointed Field Writer.

A hundred and forty-five rupees! And free quarters.

The first person he had met was Bhaskaran Nambiar. He was staying by himself since the clerk who had been staying with him had got married and moved. They were bachelors' quarters. Appunni was given accomodation there.

A hundred and forty-five rupees a month! He had never seen a hundred-rupee note his whole life.

Bhaskaran Nambiar said, 'It's not too bad. You get five or six months' salary as a bonus too every year. That's quite something.'

What was a bonus? If you worked a whole year, they would give you an additional five or six months' salary.

Later he met Abraham Joseph. Meeting people was always a painful experience.

Where are you from?

He would tell them the name of the village.

Who do you have at home?

That was a difficult question.

No one in particular.

Father?

He died.

Mother?

'I don't have a mother.' The words tripped off his tongue. He was deceiving himself and the deceit weighed heavily on his heart. It became impossible to correct it later.

'Lucky fellow! Really lucky,' said Bhaskaran Nambiar. 'I have all the appendages possible. And I have to give them all money. Isn't that misery enough?'

Appunni was ill at ease only for a month. Then he became used to the work. When he counted the hundred and forty-five rupees handed to him and realized that the money was his own, he had no idea what to do. His household expenses never came up to more than forty-three rupees.

He gradually got used to his new life.

Krishnankutty came and said: 'The water is hot. Will you have a bath now?'

'Later.'

'Eh ...?'

'Later, I said.'

The boy went away.

Outside, the tea bushes beyond the iron fence had become shadows in the darkness. He had to change, bathe, have dinner. But it was so pleasant to lie on this easy chair and think ...

He had gone to see Syedalikutty the day after he received his first salary. He still remembered clearly that it had been a holiday.

He held out a wad of notes and Syedalikutty said:

'I don't want this, child. Don't waste money. You must put something by for the future.'

To make money: that was his aim from the start. He spent only just what he needed to.

He had no news from his village. He had written a letter to Ramakrishnan Master the day he got the job and received a reply. There had been no reply to the second letter. He had written again. Maybe Master had been transferred.

For quite some days now, he had been thinking of going to the village. Not with any particular objective in mind. Nor because he had a bond with the place. He had never imagined anyone he loved waiting for him there. Still, he had to go back once. He had to go to Vadakkeppat. Let them see, he thought. How the Appunni that no one had wanted had grown. The Appunni no one had wanted could live now without help from anyone.

He did not tell any of his companions that he was going to take leave. They would be surprised if he told them. To them, he was someone who never took time off. They had assumed he had no relatives at all.

He wanted to walk over the path in the centre of the field, holding his head high. Look, Appunni is here!

He had to see Syedalikutty before he left. It was eight or nine months since they had met. In the beginning he used to go often to Syedalikutty's shop, at least once a week. And sometimes Syedalikutty would visit him here.

It was only when he met Syedalikutty that he used to think of the past.

The cook came up again to say: 'The water's growing cold.'

He got up and went in, still thinking.

The estate road curved up to the bus route. At the turning a board showing the name of the estate pointed in its direction. Appunni met the Supervisor, Philip, as he walked along the road. He smiled and was about to walk on when Philip asked, 'Where to?'

'Just for a walk.'

He arrived at the line of shops. There was no one outside Syedalikutty's. He waited for a minute. Mohammedkutty came out.

Appunni asked, 'Isn't your father here?'

'He's in bed. Come in.'

'In bed? What's wrong with him?'

'He's not well.'

Syedalikutty must have heard their voices. He called out: 'Who's that?'

'Appunni Nair.'

'Tell him to come in.'

Appunni moved aside the piece of sacking and went in. Syedalikutty lay on a mat in the room. It was difficult to imagine this was the old

Syedalikutty. He had grown very thin and his bones protruded. He smiled weakly when he saw Appunni. And said:

'I'm not well at all, child.'

'What is it, Syedalikutty?'

'Rheumatism. I can't get up. My right hand and leg have become lifeless.'

Pathumma came up, wiped her eyes and said:

'He's been like this the last three months. The *vaidyar* says it's paralysis.'

'Give him a stool to sit on.'

'No.' Appunni sat down on Syedalikutty's mat. Full of a sense of guilt, he said: 'I didn't know.'

Pathumma dabbed at her eyes. 'It's God's will. For many days now I've been wanting to send word through Mohammedkutty.'

Pathumma's face was empty of the old enthusiasm. Nabeesa came to the door, her eyes too shadowed with sadness. Appunni sat silently, his eyes riveted on the charcoal-smeared floor.

'It's going to be hard to get up again. There's no use saying it, but these children are in trouble.' Syedalikutty's voice was unsteady.

Pathumma told him what had happened bit by bit. Trade was very bad now. They had not paid the rent for the shop for the last five months. She didn't know when they would have to move out. 'Who knows what God has in store for us.'

No one spoke. Appunni continued to sit on Syedalikutty's mat. Nabeesa lit a lamp, put it down on a tin tray and placed it at the head of the mat.

'Pathumma, do you have anything to give him to drink?'

Appunni interrupted quickly: 'I don't want anything.'

Pathumma went inside. Only Syedalikutty and Appunni were in the room now.

'These are all games God plays, child. A punishment for the sins I committed.'

Appunni could not bear to look at Syedalikutty's face.

'At least you can take care of yourself now … that's a good thing.' Silence fell again.

'In his foolishness, Syedalikutty once did something God will never forgive him for ...'

Appunni was distressed, not knowing what to say.

'Your father and I used to eat from the same plate.'

The blood pulsed through Appunni's veins. He rubbed his eyes and said, 'What's the point of talking about it?'

'You don't know, child. If you did ...'

'I've heard. And forgotten.'

Syedalikutty was about to say something but Nabeesa came in at that moment to take a matchbox from the head of the mat, so he did not speak.

'God will not forget. After my eyes close, there'll be this girl, ready for marriage and the boy who's still a little child. God and his games ...'

With great difficulty, Appunni managed to say: 'You mustn't worry, Syedalikutty.'

Pathumma came with a glass of pale, watery tea. Appunni sipped it slowly.

He said, 'I'm going to the village tomorrow.'

A look of astonishment came to Syedalikutty's face. 'Good, do go and return.'

Appunni sat there a little while longer, then got up and went to the inner door. Pathumma was leaning against the wall and Nabeesa stood behind her like a shadow.

'Do whatever you need to make Syedalikutty comfortable. I'll pay the rent arrears tomorrow. Send Mohammedkutty there early tomorrow morning ...'

In the dim light, he saw the tears gleaming in Pathumma's eyes. He said with greater confidence: 'Don't worry. You won't have any more problems.'

He heard a sob behind Pathumma. He went back, stood by Syedalikutty's mat for a moment and said goodbye to him. 'I'll come and see you as soon as I get back from the village.'

Syedalikutty called out as he began to walk away: 'Child ...' He stopped.

'I've been wanting to say this for a very long time ...'

'What?'

'Don't forget your mother. Who does she have but you?'

Perspiration broke out on Appunni's forehead. 'I'll go and see her, Syedalikutty.'

He went out quickly. Lamps flickered on both sides of the road. The evening rush had begun in the bazaar. Not many changes had taken place in the five years that had gone by. He saw the spot where he had alighted from the bus when he first arrived. He had got down feeling bewildered and anxious, the bag made of sacking that contained his old, shabby clothes in his hand ...

... The next evening, he alighted from the train at Pallippuram station as the sun was going down. He hoisted his big leather suitcase and hold-all onto a coolie's head and walked straight on. He would have liked to look around the vicinity of the station for familiar faces. To what purpose? He gave his ticket to the porter and walked along the railway track. He would have to cover three quarters of a mile to reach the Karunoor bridge.

When he came to the bridge, he glanced downward. The huge iron pillars were submerged to more than half their height below the water. The muddy river swirled around them. He walked along the bank of the river and through the nenthran banana grove, where all the fruit had been plucked, and came to the ferry. Three or four people were seated there with empty baskets. They looked at him curiously. Pretending not to notice them, he went down to the river.

The boat was on the other side. He waited near the water. It would take a long time for it to cross. Froth and bubbles swept over the sand. Trails of muddy water crept like red skirt-strings over the sand.

The boat approached, filled with cherumi women carrying bundles of grass and tent-like thatch umbrellas. Ravuthar, the mundu merchant, was there as well with his cloth bundle.

Appunni took off his slippers, pulled his mundu up above his knees, tightened it around his waist, and got into the boat. The boatman gave a single hoot. Two people who were running towards them from the distance quickened their pace.

The coolie unloaded Appunni's suitcase and hold-all and stood to one side in the boat, spitting continuously into the water.

It was not the old boatman, who used to be a tall slim young man with a face scarred by burns. This was a bearded old man.

The boatman's entire attention was on the suitcase, the hold-all, and Appunni, who sat on the plank of the boat, smoking a cigarette and staring into the water. Once the other two passengers arrived, the boatman got down and pushed the boat so that it moved away from the sand. When it was free, he jumped back on the prow and took up the oars.

Appunni realized that the two men seated opposite were observing him keenly. But he did not take his eyes off the river. One of them asked the coolie:

'Where to?'

'Across the river.'

He lowered his voice and asked: 'Who is he?'

'I don't know, he came by this train.'

The other passenger whispered: 'Must be going to the big house.'

Appunni was the first to get out when they reached the other bank. The other two stood aside.

He gave the mapilla boatman eight annas.

'I don't have any change.'

'Keep it.'

The old man's tired eyes gleamed.

The other two exchanged a look full of surprise and respect. Appunni climbed onto the road.

The river and its vicinity looked unchanged. A little higher up, there was a new mosque with brick walls. Appunni walked with his head held high, looking straight ahead.

The fields had just been harvested. He lit another cigarette as he climbed into the big field. An old panan coming from the opposite side wished him long life and moved down to make way for him.

Appunni could see the closed doors of the gatehouse from this distance. He quickened his pace slightly, opened the gatehouse doors

noisily, climbed the front steps and entered the yard. There was no one
outside. He hesitated for a moment. No one in the northern yard either.
He climbed into the veranda and called out:

'Is there no one here?'

No response. Then he saw that the front door was locked.

He went down to the yard again. And discovered a thorn fence dividing
the yard that lay between the pathayappura and the naalukettu.

The coolie carrying the suitcase and hold-all was clearly
growing impatient.

He walked to the western yard and caught sight of the second thorn
fence. Between the pathayappura and the outhouse. A woman was sitting
in front of the outhouse busy with some work, her back to him. A thin,
dark-skinned woman wearing a white rowka.

Appunni cleared his throat. The woman turned. Meenakshi Edathi!

She dropped the winnowing basket in her hand and got up, a look
of astonishment on her face. He realized she was having difficulty
recognizing him.

'Can't you make out who I am, Meenakshi Edathi?'

'Appunni!'

Amazement spread over her withered, sunburnt face. Appunni went
up to the fence.

'Ah, Meenakshi Edathi, so you recognized me.'

'You've grown so tall.'

He pointed to the naalukettu: 'Is there no one there?'

'Don't you know the naalukettu is Valia Ammaaman's? He comes
once in a way.'

'And who lives here?'

'Kuttettan and Malu stayed here for a year after the property was
partitioned. Then they sold it to Raghavan Nair from Singapore. No
one stays here.'

The naalukettu for Valia Ammaaman. The pathayappura for Kutta
Ammaaman. And the outhouse for Meenakshi Edathi.

'Valiamma?'

'She and her children are at their own place.'

Meenakshi Edathi pointed to the outhouse and said: 'This is my house now.'

He had already realized that. He climbed over the pole barrier and walked up to the outhouse. He unloaded his luggage from the coolie's head and placed it on the steps going up. He paid the man and sent him away.

Meenakshi climbed the steps and Appunni followed.

The outhouse was a long thatched shed. It had been used in the old days to stack sheaves of grain in the rainy season and thresh them. Earthen walls had been put up inside to divide the space into three sections.

'Who's there?' A faint, weak voice.

'Who's that?' asked Appunni.

'Ammamma.'

He stepped through the opening in centre of the earthen wall to the other side. Ammamma lay there, under a red woollen blanket.

'Who is it, Meenakshi?'

He knelt down by the mat and said: 'It's me, Ammamma, Appunni.'

Ammamma heaved herself up painfully. Appunni looked at her withered hands, shrivelled like curls of tobacco, and her face lined with wrinkles. Her hair had been cropped very short. She ran her hands over his body and said:

'My child, so you've come at last.'

Appunni said nothing.

'Ammamma can barely see. Now all I want is to be taken away as quickly as possible.'

It was only then that he looked into her eyes. Yellow, like clumps of phlegm.

Ammamma stroked his head and neck again and said: 'You've grown so much, child.'

'It's been four or five years, after all ...'

He could see the kitchen from there. A few soot-stained earthen pots, two bell-metal plates, a chimney lamp standing on wooden pegs.

Appunni got up and went to the outer room. Meenakshi Edathi was looking out of the window, her hand on the wooden bars.

'It's destiny. Even the companion I had at night is gone.' There was a long pause. Then she said in a tone meant to comfort herself: 'At least, those who went ahead don't have to suffer.'

'Where are Kutta Ammaaman and Malu?'

'At Vadakkemuri.'

Appunni's eyes noted the broken walls, the chipped, crumbling floor, the tattered bits of cloth stretched over the window bars.

He looked out through the wooden bars. The Vadakkeppat naalukettu stood closed and locked.

Meenakshi Edathi asked: 'Have you come on leave, Appunni?'

'Yes.'

'There's nothing here even to sit on. Do you want to go to Edathi's place?'

'I'll stay here. I'll be no trouble to you.'

Meenakshi Edathi said without a shred of emotion: 'It's not because you'd have been any trouble to me.'

He took off his shirt and hooked it on the nail on which a grass mat hung. He pushed his suitcase to one side of the room. He undid the hold-all, opened out an edge, sat down on it, and took out a ten-rupee note from his suitcase. He gave it to Meenakshi Edathi and said: 'Buy whatever you need for now.'

At night, there was bright moonlight. The moonlight of the month of Kanni. After dinner, Appunni walked up and down the yard.

The snake shrine was behind the outhouse. The giant tree in the middle of it, shining like the tip of a sword in the moonlight, outlined a fearful form.

He thought of the tales he had heard as a child, of serpents that unfurled their hoods in the moonlight. An ocean of unmoving silence surrounded him. A sudden stream of sorrow flooded his heart, like the strains of an undefinable song.

He felt all the eagerness he had experienced at the beginning of the journey draining out of him.

The news that Appunni had come back after five years spread through the village the very next morning.

It was not the old Appunni who had returned. He was an employee in a tea estate now. He had money. It was ten-rupee notes that Meenakshi Amma sent through the cheruman boy every day to the provision shop, people said. They spoke of the good fortune that had come to Meenakshi Amma.

It was on the morning of the third day. Someone arrived, to see Appunni. An old woman.

'Who is it?' asked Appunni. Meenakshi Edathi said, 'She's a distant relative.'

'I see.'

The woman came up to Appunni. Smiling at him, she tried to start a conversation, but he interrupted quietly:

'What is it?'

'Who is this, now? You've changed completely.'

Appunni did not respond.

'Probably none of you remember. All of you ...'

'I have not forgotten anything.'

'I came as soon as I heard you'd arrived.'

'Why?'

Appunni's voice was very cold.

'I'm no longer all that healthy. I've only all of you to help me. I can't even afford to buy betel leaves to chew. You must give me something.' She smiled as she spoke, the authority in her tone tinged with affection.

'Have you ever seen me as a child?'

'Why are you asking me a question like that?'

'Have you seen me,' I asked. 'Have you ever talked to me? What is the relationship between you and me?'

She stopped smiling.

'We're from the same roots. Can blood relationship be erased?'

'And isn't this a relationship you suddenly remembered? You can go now. You'll get nothing from me.'

She did not say anything more. She hurried out without even taking leave of Meenakshi Edathi and Ammamma. Appunni said: 'The claims of blood relationship, indeed!'

Krishnankutty too came the same day. The Krishnankutty who used to wander around in shorts with red straps had grown into a young man.

'So what's up, Krishnankutty?'

'Oh, nothing ...'

'You're well?'

'Yes.'

The conversation ended there. Krishnankutty stood silently for a while, cracking his knuckles. He went in to see Ammamma and came out in two minutes. Then he came up to Appunni and said shyly:

'Amma asked you to come over, Appunni Ettan.'

'Why, what's the matter?'

'Nothing. She said you could stay there if you find it inconvenient here.'

'I am extremely happy here.'

Krishnankutty looked embarrassed. 'Amma said she wanted to see you.'

Appunni threw a cigarette stub on the ground, stamped on it and said, 'Tell your mother to come here if she's in such a hurry to see me.'

Krishnankutty stood before him perspiring profusely, an awkward smile on his distressed face.

'After all, I've seen a lot of her, haven't I?'

No more visitors came the next two days. Abubacker, who lived by the river, came to see him with some fish. Appunni asked Meenakshi Edathi to pay him for it.

He sat all day in the outhouse, reading. In the evenings, he walked up and down the yard for a long time.

Meenakshi Edathi was the same as always. She spoke only if he asked her something. During the day, time hung heavy.

After dinner, he would walk in the yard again for a long time. There was the stump of a jackfruit tree that had been cut down at the edge of the yard. He would sit down on it and gaze at the snake-shrine below that gave refuge to all the darkness that the moonlight had rejected.

Would serpents be swaying there, their hoods unfurled?

The image of a half-naked girl dancing and swaying in the glow of the oil lamps would surface in his mind. ... He longed for news of her. He could ask. But he did not.

One day, he walked through the lane at the back and climbed up the hill. He had found out from Meenakshi Edathi that the wide slope of land beginning at the channel through which the rainwater drained away and ending at Chathappan's hut had been kept aside for him in the partition.

It was full of gravel and a few isolated bushes. The area stretched before him like a kingdom of emptiness. And its earth was his!

He had more or less figured out the clauses of the partition from the bits and pieces Meenakshi Edathi had told him. The whole of the northern field had been declared Valia Ammaaman's private property. Valiamma and her children had received four shares of the property. The plot of land by the river and a good portion of the fertile area where the summer crop was harvested had gone to them. They had leased out all their land to tenant farmers. Kutta Ammaaman had taken the pathayappura.

The areas that no one wanted had been set aside for those who had no one to argue on their behalf.

The slope covered with gravel and bushes for Appunni. Its blood-red soil had slumbered for centuries. Standing in the middle of it, an image of seed sprouting in it came clearly into his mind.

He stood there a while, gazing at the expanse of horizon beyond the river.

A man wearing a thatched umbrella-hat was coming up the hill. Appunni saw when he came nearer that it was Kutta Ammaaman. The old surly look was not on his face, he was full of smiles. He took off the hat and asked:

'When did you come, Appunni?'

'Four days ago.'

'Meenakshi told me you were on the hillside. Anyway, I can't really talk to you down there.'

So he had come prepared to talk about something, thought Appunni.

'What is it?'

'I wanted to see you.'

He thought of saying, now that you've seen me, you can go. But he controlled himself.

'I'm in a bad situation after the partition.'

'No one's situation has improved.'

'I and Malu live in Vadakkemuri, in a hut in Kuttappu's compound.'

'So I heard.'

'I can't work as hard as I used to. It's the girl's future that worries me.'

Appunni grunted in response.

'As for her, you're her whole life.' Kutta Ammaaman fumbled for words, as if he had more to say.

'What do you want me to do?'

'You're her only refuge.'

A whirlwind of memories blew into Appunni's mind. He said in a cold voice:

'I've not become a Deputy Collector, you know.'

Kutta Ammaaman's face grew pale. 'Why do you say that, Appunni?'

'Well, don't force me to say anything more.'

Appunni experienced a sense of cruel delight when he saw Kutta Ammaaman put on his hat again and walk slowly down the hill.

He sat there a long time, looking at the river in the distance.

It made him sad though, to think of Malu. Poor child! But ...

Somehow the whole affair made him feel disgusted. Most of all with himself, for finding pleasure in taking revenge.

Malu must have grown up. The image he still had was of the thin, dark-skinned little girl with the pointed face who had come and spoken to him as he sat by himself on the eastern veranda the first time he had arrived at the tharavad, many years ago. He felt compassion for her but knew it would be impossible to give her anything more than that.

He went back home only as the crescent moon began to appear amidst shreds of white cloud.

Many faces surfaced in his mind as he lay down to sleep. A girl with half-closed eyes lined with kajal and a heavy mass of shining hair that coiled like black serpents. Eyes full of astonishment and pain in a thin, dark face. Yet another face that reminded him of a half-hidden crescent moon glimpsed behind clouds in the western sky at the hour when evening was turning into night. As they took shape and faded in turn, he closed his eyes.

It was on the morning of the seventh day after he came home that he met Valia Ammaaman. He heard the clatter of wooden clogs in front of the naalukettu as he was pacing the courtyard, smoking a cigarette. He continued to pace up and down in front of the outhouse.

'Appunni.'

This must be the very first time Valia Ammaaman's tongue is struggling with my name, thought Appunni. He twisted in pain as if he had been stabbed.

'Come here for a minute, Appunni.'

'What is it?'

'Come here, to the veranda.' A very gentle invitation. Was this the Valia Ammaaman who always spoke in a voice like thunder?

'I'll stay here.'

They stood on either side of the fence. Appunni was smouldering with anger. He clenched his fingers to hide his impatience.

Valia Ammaaman's face no longer had the old haughty look. A glance was enough to see that he had grown equally weak physically and emotionally. Appunni felt that Ammaaman was finding it difficult to look him in the eyes.

'I've been thinking of coming the last three or four days.'

'Um.'

Looking at Valia Ammaaman's face, now heavily marked by age, Appunni remembered the old image he had of him.

Of the day he had driven him out ... like a mangy dog.

The man who had threatened to break his legs if he set foot in the compound stood quietly before him now.

'I came to tell you something.'

'You can tell me.'

'It was I who took this building when we divided the property. It's the tharavad, after all, the place where the Bhagavathi resides. I thought it should not go to anyone outside the family.'

'Good.'

'There's a debt of five hundred rupees against it. The verdict has been declared.'

Appunni listened attentively, saying nothing. Valia Ammaaman hesitated for a few long minutes, then continued:

'If I don't settle it before the tenth, the court will take possession of the place. It's our tharavad after all, isn't it?'

Appunni grunted.

'There are mapillas who want to buy it. But how can I give a place where the Bhagavathi resides, to mapillas?'

Appunni's impatience had reached its climax. He raised his voice and demanded:

'And what can I do about that?'

'I hear you have money. Just give me five hundred rupees as a loan. We can have papers made out as you wish.'

The image of the old man standing at the fence kept fading from his eyes. All he could see was a fierce, hefty figure vaulting into the veranda with his hand raised and rushing at him.

'I have no desire that this naalukettu should continue to stand.' Appunni held his anger under control.

'What did you say, Appunni?'

'I'll repeat it. I have no desire to see this naalukettu continue to stand. Maybe *you* have forgotten how you drove me out of here. I can never forget it.'

A frozen silence lay between them. Valia Ammaaman said in an unsteady voice:

'Yes, that happened. I grieve for it now. Forget the past, Appunni.'

'That's not so easy.'

'Just when I thought there was no way out, I heard you had come. It's a tharavad that's been here from ancient times.'

'I have the money. But I have no intention at the moment of giving it to you.'

Running his hand over the rounded edge of the fence post, Valia Ammaaman stood still, his head bent. Appunni's eyes were fixed on the ground.

Valia Ammaaman began to walk away slowly. Appunni called out: 'Wait.'

Valia Ammaaman turned.

'It's selling it to mapillas that you object to. What if I buy it?'

Valia Ammaaman looked stunned. He hesitated for a moment, then said,

'I'll think about it.'

'There's no point thinking about it. Let us decide now, this minute. Let me see if I can buy it. What price do you want for the house and compound together?'

Valia Ammaaman fumbled.

'Go ahead and tell me. This is a commercial transaction. If I find the rate acceptable, I'll buy it.'

Appunni was infuriated to see Valia Ammaaman continue to hesitate.

'What is it, doesn't Appunni's money have any value?'

'It's not that ...'

'Then tell me. And remember that you are quoting a price for a dilapidated naalukettu that's falling to pieces.'

'Pookaru Haji offered four thousand ...'

Appunni pondered. 'This thing that lets in no light or air is not fit for human beings to live in. In spite of which I will give you four thousand. If you agree, you can arrange to have the sale deed drafted.'

Valia Ammaaman's head sank farther down.

'What have you decided?'

With a great effort, Valia Ammaaman said: 'Alright.'

'Then you can arrange to have the sale deed made out.'

Appunni waited, listening to the clatter of the wooden clogs die away slowly.

When he went back to the outhouse and lay down, Meenakshi Edathi asked:

'Has he gone?'

'Yes.'

'These are bad times for Ammaaman in every sense.'

Appunni was not pleased to hear the compassion in her voice.

'Why, isn't there wealth at Poonthottam?'

'It's not that. She was a good child. And she's gone.'

'Who?'

'You didn't know, Appunni? It was her first delivery. Poor thing ...'

'What is it Meenakshi Edathi?'

'Amminikutty died last Edavam.'

He said nothing more. Heaving himself up on his elbows, he got up. He went to the door of the outhouse and stood there, holding onto the lintel, his hands trembling and his eyes closed while Meenakshi Edathi murmured to herself:

'Poor child, she was so affectionate.'

Appunni opened the front door of the naalukettu. The thekkini was enveloped in darkness. When he tugged at the bars and opened the window, slivers of light fell in. The air had a wet, musty odour. Even when the doors were opened, darkness lurked in the nooks and corners. Dust lay in heaps on the granite slabs covering the floor of the central courtyard. Termites had eaten their way into the wooden pillars.

He stopped as he entered the northern hall from the vadikkini. The room under the stairs ...

The room where he had spent three years. Would the floor still be wet with tears?

Standing there, he suddenly thought he heard the tinkle of glass bangles in the faint darkness. Did the air still hold a fragrance of jasmine and incense?

There was no pain in his heart, only a great sense of emptiness.

He climbed the stairs. He opened the doors of all the rooms except one.

Rats raced around the room which had been made ready for Thangedathi's future husband.

He had learned that a husband had finally come for Thangedathi. Meenakshi Edathi had told him. He had abandoned her later. The room that had been prepared for him here, in this house, must still be waiting.

Even though it was daytime, he felt afraid, wandering through the naalukettu with its crumbling walls and moist floors. Generations seemed to be crawling through its lairs. The souls of Pora Ammaaman and Narayana Ammaaman must be hovering around, he thought. He remembered the story of the young girl the karanavar had trampled to death.

The naalukettu with its ancient memories belonged to him now. He had spent all the hard-earned money he had accumulated over the last five years on it. But he had a sense of deep satisfaction. It was from here that he had run away once, holding his life in his hands. He had been denied everything that day. For what reason? Because a woman from this house had married someone she loved.

When he arrived at that point, his thoughts began to spin wildly. What kind of life was that woman living now?

She had left this house without anyone's permission. And she had had to grieve for that all her life. No one had stretched out a helping hand to her. The people of the house had performed her funeral rites and purified the place. No doubt they must have experienced the relief of having washed away a blot on their prestige.

That woman's son was now the owner of the naalukettu.

He remembered with pain: that woman was his mother.

He had spent his days deliberately trying to forget her.

She had brought him up after his father died. She had toiled in the pounding shed of the illam to bring him food.

But he had forgotten all that. When she no longer had anyone for company, a man had come to help her and she had not refused his help. She must have reached out for his hand because she had been about to fall down, exhausted. Was that wrong, he asked himself.

Whose fault had it been?

Was it her fault that she had been driven out of this naalukettu? If it was ... he felt as if he could not breathe.

Bathed in perspiration, he came back to the front veranda. The noon sun blazed outside. There was not a breath of wind. The leaves were still.

All these days he had misrepresented things to himself. He had convinced himself that he had no one. He had taken a kind of petty pride in declaring that he was alone in the world. The truth was that there were many people who cared. He had been deceiving himself.

Chains of indebtedness still bound him. His thoughts flew to a small hut in the distant Wynaad valley. He imagined a young Muslim boy sitting in a shop somewhere, counting out coins from a little wooden box on legs. He saw the image of a teacher talking to the children in a classroom somewhere.

Completely shattered, he sank down by the pillars that termites had eaten deeply into.

And tried in vain to pit his gains against his losses ...

10

The young man stopped as he reached the front steps. He said to the woman who followed him:

'Go in, Amma.'

He saw her hesitate and said, 'You can go in fearlessly.'

The slender woman whose hair was just beginning to be touched with grey climbed into the veranda.

The old man continued to stand in the yard, reluctant to follow her. The young man said, 'Come.'

The old man climbed the steps with a look of distress, as if aware that he was following the woman into a place to which he had no right.

The woman said as she entered, 'How dark it is in here, Appunni.'

'It's dark here even in the daytime. The ghosts of all our ancestors must be here even in the day.'

The mother looked at him bewildered.

'Don't worry, Amma. We'll arrange to have this naalukettu demolished. All we need here is a small house that will let in light and air.'

'Demolish it? The place where the Bhagavathi resides?'

The young man laughed aloud. The sound of his laughter dashed against the broken walls, the worn pillars, the dark corners, and flowed back.

The old man still stood confused, his head bowed.

Glossary

adhikari: a man originally appointed by the British to collect taxes in the village. He has local administrative rights

adiyan: word used instead of 'I' when speaking to someone who belongs to a higher social status

avittam: the day after the Onam festival

Bhagavathi: the Mother Goddess

Bhima: the second of the five Pandava brothers, a great warrior

Bhuvaneshwari
puja: a puja conducted in households to the Mother Goddess. Offerings of a fowl and alcohol are made at this puja

Chandramathi: Harischandra's wife, a symbol of suffering and sacrifice

chandu: a red or black paste with which women make a mark on their foreheads

chellapatti: a box that holds all the ingredients for chewing, like lime paste, areca nuts, and betel leaves

cheriambran: young master

cheruma: one of the inferior castes

cherumi: Cheruman woman

chitrakoota stone: a square stone at which the young girls who take part in the serpent ritual consecrate the flower-clusters in their hands

chittus:	gold rings worn in the ears
Dussasanan:	one of the hundred Kaurava brothers. He was killed by Bhima
Embrandiri:	Kerala Brahmins who are originally from Karnataka
gopis:	young girls, playmates of Sri Krishnan
illam:	residence of a Namboodiri
kaachi:	waist-cloth reaching the ankles, worn by Kerala Muslim women
kaikottikkali:	dance performed by women. They stand in a circle, sing, clap their hands and dance in tune to the music
kalam:	a sacred drawing made with coloured powders on the ground. A puja is performed over the kalam drawing
kaliyugam:	the fourth (present) age, a period which will witness the complete breakdown of civilized forms of life and a total loss of moral and spiritual values
karanavar:	the eldest male member of a matrilinear joint family
karyasthan:	person who manages the landed properties
kathakali:	classical dance drama of Kerala, usually based on stories from the epics
kuppayam:	garment worn by Kerala Muslim women
kuruthi:	a mixture of turmeric, lime, and water, used in the kuruthi puja offered to the Mother Goddess
kuruthiparambu:	an enclosure erected in order to perform a special pooja called the kuruthi sacrifice, dedicated to the Mother Goddess
machu:	a small room along the western side of the nalukettu where the household deities reside
mapilla:	a Kerala Muslim
nazhi:	a measure, roughly equal to three litres
Onam:	a ten-day harvest festival. It falls in the months of August–September
pagida:	an outdoor game played with metal dice
panchavadyam:	percussion in which five instruments are used
panikker:	a caste. Usually, Panikkers are astrologers by profession
Parayan:	one of the inferior castes

pathayappura: a building detached from the main house

poothan and thira: dancers who come as heralds of a temple festival. The thira wears a heavy wooden head-dress, semi-circular in shape, and the poothan a mask. They dance and take the paddy kept for them in a winnowing tray.

prashnam: a ritual conducted by an astrologer to find out why a calamity or misfortune might have occurred and to suggest measures to remedy the situation

Pulluva: a caste. They sing and play their instruments at a serpent ritual

puzhukku: a thick preparation of vegetables served with kanji

rowka: a blouse worn by a woman. Instead of fastening it in front with hooks, the ends are taken up and tied together

thalappoli: a procession of young girls who carry platters with lighted wicks, rice, and flowers arranged on them

thangal: a Muslim priest

thattam: head-dress worn by Kerala Muslim women

thekkini: the southern wing of the naalukettu

Thiruvathira
festival: falls in the month of Dhanu (December–January). It is celebrated mainly by women. They sing and dance and pray that they will have good husbands

thulasi: the Indian basil, a sacred plant

uri: container made of rope, suspended from the ceiling, to hold milk or food